Y0-BPT-009

BOOK
SALE

BOOK
SALE

OBSESSIONS

OBSESSIONS

MARSHALL COOK

BLEAK HOUSE BOOKS

MADISON | WISCONSIN

Published by Bleak House Books
a division of Big Earth Publishing
923 Williamson St.
Madison, WI 53703
www.bleakhousebooks.com

Copyright © 2008 by Marshall Cook

All rights reserved. No part of this publication may be reproduced or transmitted in any form or by any means, electronic or mechanical, including photocopy, recording, or any information storage and retrieval system, without permission in writing from the publisher.

This is a work of fiction. Any similarities to people or places, living or dead, is purely coincidental.

ISBN 13: 978-1-932557-79-4 (Trade Cloth)
ISBN 13: 978-1-932557-81-7 (Evidence Collection)

Library of Congress Cataloging-in-Publication Data has been applied for.

Printed in the United States of America

11 10 09 08 07   1 2 3 4 5 6 7 8 9 10

Set in Minion Pro

Interior by Von Bliss Design
www.vonbliss.com

To Harv Thompson

ACKNOWLEDGMENTS

This book wouldn't exist without Benjamin LeRoy, founder and head honcho of Bleak House Books, who backed Mo's play from the get-go. Maybe this will be the Cubs' year, Ben!

The book would exist but wouldn't be nearly as good without my friends Lynn Entine and Sandy Mickelson, who were willing to give the manuscript a perceptive and insightful read and speak their truth to me. Sandy, if you ever want to give up newspapering in Fort Dodge, you could head out to Hollywood and earn good money as a continuity editor.

The novel might exist, but it would have a different killer and a whole lot less fun if not for Alison Janssen, friend, roller derby queen, and editor without peer. Whatever Ben's paying you, it ain't nearly enough.

And finally, I'm not sure I'd exist without Dorothy Ellen Rose Malloy, who has somehow put up with my obsessions all these years.

1

Monona Quinn emerges from the tiny bathroom, a frayed bath towel wrapped around her. She hurries across the small living room and stands shivering in front of the fire, drying her hair with a washcloth.

"Breakfast will be ready in a minute," Doug says from the kitchenette a few feet away, where he works at the stove, scrambling eggs.

"Thank you. For making a fire, too. How was your run?"

"Invigorating. I saw three deer by the side of the road, a mother and two deerlets. They stood still until I was almost on them. I thought they were going to let me pet them. They finally turned and ran into the woods—not ran—bounded!"

Mo walks over, still dripping from the shower, and kisses him. "They're called 'fawns,'" she says, snuggling into his one-armed hug. "I'm so glad we're here."

"Me, too."

"What gave you the idea to give me a writers' conference as a birthday present? How did you even know about the conference?"

"One of my clients—he'd kill me if I told you his name—writes romance novels as a hobby. He comes up here for two weeks every summer. I thought it would be a nice break for you—for us—and you could take a couple of classes."

He turns back to the stove, but she turns him back around and hugs him.

"The best part is your coming along, too. I'm surprised you'd take the time off from work."

"Look who's talking."

"My. You are invigorated."

"What do you expect, when my wife prances up to me, wearing nothing but a dish towel, and throws herself at me?"

"I was not prancing."

"More of a seductive strut, then. But I …"

Her kiss interrupts him. He breaks the kiss and tries to turn back to the stove, but she holds him tightly.

"The eggs will burn."

"We've got more eggs."

"Don't you have to get to school? You don't want to be late for your second day of classes."

"I've got time."

"At least let me …"

She again stills him with a kiss, and he responds, his lips brushing her cheek and caressing her neck.

"An egg is just an egg," he concedes.

He turns and snaps off the stove, deftly removing the pan from the burner.

They walk together into the tiny bedroom, and Mo sheds her towel and throws it at him as she dives under the covers, peeking out over the blanket to watch as Doug pulls off his sweatshirt and sits on the bed to unlace his running shoes.

Mo's heart pounds. It has been a long time since they've made love spontaneously. Before she left for her sister's farm, they'd allowed themselves to become so busy, sex was by appointment only. And when she came back, things were so strained between them, their infrequent lovemaking had been more about negotiation than passion.

He crawls in under the covers. His hands, warm from being near the stove, stroke her bare skin, his touch so thrilling, she forgets to be self-conscious about her goose flesh. When his lips find hers, she gives herself to him.

2

Fletcher Downs opens one eye, finds the view wanting, rolls over, and pulls the covers up over his head. Something nudges him—an arm. He pushes at it vaguely. It nudges again.

He forces both eyes open, vision blurry, expectations bleak, and beholds a terrifying face. All faces, especially unfamiliar ones, provoke terror at such close range and so early in the morning. This one—pale skin topped by spiky blonde hair—belongs to a woman of no less than thirty-five and perhaps as much as forty-five. Her eyes move beneath her puffy eyelids; her lips purse as if preparing to blow.

Myrna? Yes. That was the name, however unlikely. Myrna. She had dotted each 'i' with a heart on the note she'd left on his desk yesterday. First day of class. This one didn't waste any time.

Myrna. Repulsive name. Like some screeching jungle bird. Divorced almost a year, she'd said. Three kids, staying with their father, Marvin or Melvin—who is, of course, a cold, controlling bastard. She came to the conference to "keep a promise I'd made to myself years ago" to be a "real" writer.

Just what the world needs, another "revenge lit" novel from a hausfrau who dumped her husband because the thrill was gone.

This one is no mere naïve suburban divorcee, however. He'd seen cold calculation in her eyes. She believes she's using him, believes he will be her key to getting published. She is, of course, deluded.

He rolls away from her. The clock radio on the nightstand shows 6:28, a desolate time of day fit only for people who deliver things we want and take away things we don't.

He closes his eyes, hoping that sleep will reclaim him. At his age, the agonies of the morning after are beginning to outweigh the pleasures of the night before.

She begins to snore. Loudly. A blunt chain saw biting into sheet metal. Anger stings him fully awake; mocking sleep dances out of reach.

He could nudge her just enough to induce her to shift positions and perhaps cease her incessant braying. Ah, but he might wake her! Aye, there's the rub.

Sleep now impossible, he considers trying to read or even to write a little, but the thought of Myrna waking up and having to be spoken to is more than he wishes to contemplate.

He slips from under the covers and steals to the bathroom, a cold expanse of porcelain efficiency as inviting as a doctor's waiting room. He urinates copiously, passes discreet gas, and runs his hands through his hair, which is still plentiful, Allah be praised, and a distinguished silver rather than gray.

But the face that looks back at him balefully from the mirror shows considerable wear.

Coffee. Surely they have coffee in the "lodge" downstairs. Perhaps they might even have heard of the *New York Times* in this wilderness, but he isn't hopeful.

Something edible, a morning bun or scone perhaps. Perhaps the bookshelves lining the fake fireplace will offer something besides *Reader's Digest* homogenized cream of novel to read while he eats a little something.

It's not as if he'd had much choice. "Heavenly Acres" is the only accommodation remotely resembling a decent hotel in a land blighted by campgrounds and cabins boasting of such amenities as fish-cleaning sheds and outboard motorboat rentals by hour, day or week.

Northern Wisconsin, where "modern resort" means the toilets flush most of the time.

His clothes are folded neatly at the foot of the bed where he left them.

Quietly he pulls on his khaki shorts, sits ungracefully on the floor to slip on his socks, wriggles his feet into his deck shoes, and carefully avoids bumping the bed as he stands and writhes into his polo shirt.

He is being as quiet as—What? "As quiet as a fart in a mitten." Just the sort of thing Lowell Hall, private detective, would say. He pulls a notebook and pen out of his pants pocket and writes down the phrase.

She stirs. He turns quickly to find her breathing deeply, eyes closed, mouth slightly open. Watching her, he wrestles into his windbreaker.

A "Do Not Disturb" sign hangs from the outside door handle. What he needs now is one that says, "Please disturb." Better still: "Please get this whorish strumpet out of my bed and far away from here before I return."

He eases the door shut behind him and limps—an old man when nobody's looking—to the elevator.

3

She hustles into shorts and a T—the conference catalog made it very clear that dress was to be "Northwoods casual." It will be chilly outside until the sun crests the trees, when the day will offer stifling heat. She grabs up her flannel shirt to counter the morning chill and the school's overzealous air conditioning. If she hurries, she'll still have a few minutes to go over her homework before class. She slips into her sandals and stands at the mirror over the rustic chest of drawers, teasing her summer-short blonde hair. She decides to let it finish drying *au naturel*.

"Breakfast is served," Doug announces as she emerges from the bedroom.

She slides onto the bench at the redwood table separating the kitchenette from the living room, and Doug hands her a plate of scrambled eggs and wheat toast, the eggs laced with chopped red peppers, green onions, and tomato.

"Looks great!"

"I hope they're OK. I'm not used to cooking over gas, and everything seems to take longer up here."

She smiles at the "up here." Although they are in the north woods, up on the map, and in the midst of a patchy forest of Norway pines, birch, oak, maple, and cottonwood, the elevation is only slightly higher than back "down" in Mitchell.

He slides in next to her on the bench with his own breakfast, and they sit side by side, eating and looking out at the lake. A thin mist hangs over the water. A crane stands on one spindly leg near the reeds by the shore. Two fishermen hunch over their poles in a dinghy a couple of hundred feet off shore. A small armada of ducks cruises the shoreline.

The fire pops and crackles. She holds her coffee mug in both hands, enjoying its warmth. He puts his arm around her, and they kiss.

"We should get a little cabin up here. Come up on weekends."

"Long walks in the woods. Quiet evenings by the fire. I guess I could stand it."

"How are the eggs?"

"They're good."

"Not too dry?"

"Just right."

For a while the only sounds are the clinkings of fork on plate, the gentle thump of coffee mug on table, and the sparking and fizzing of the fire. Outside, someone calls out from across the lake, the voice echoing in the morning air, and a voice answers from the near shore.

"What's on the agenda in school today?"

"We read our descriptions aloud in creative nonfiction. I'm nervous about it!"

"Really? The renowned page-two columnist for the *Chicago Trib*?"

"Former columnist. And I still have a lot to learn. In research methods, she's going to give us ten questions, and we have to find the answers by Friday."

"Sounds suitably rigorous. What about the mystery writing class?"

"He didn't give us homework."

"Bully for him!"

"I think it's just because he doesn't want to have to read anything we write. His heart doesn't seem to be in his teaching."

"You're just taking this class for a lark anyway, right?"

"Well, yes, but still …"

"This is the great one himself? Fletcher Downs?"

"The same."

"A bit of a prima donna, is he?"

"Honestly, Doug, the way he acted yesterday, you'd think he wrote the Bible."

"He did write a string of bestsellers."

"I believe he mentioned that once or twice. There are rumors about which student—or students—he's bedding."

"Oh, yeah? Should I keep an eye on this guy?"

"I find him rather revolting."

"That wavy silver hair, the authorial goatee, those penetrating blue eyes—"

"How do you know what he looks like?"

"I got his latest book out of the library. The Mitchell branch even had a copy, so you know this guy's famous. Wait a minute. It's here someplace."

Doug pulls a thick hardcover book from the stack on the table and shows it to her.

"*Blood Brothers*," she reads off the cover. "Any good?"

"I guess you'd call it a page-turner. Not my kind of thing, really. I'll finish it, though."

"I'll read it when you're done. But if you don't like it, why keep reading?"

"I dunno. It just seems like you ought to finish a book once you start it."

"Life's too short." She kisses him on the nose.

"We have to work in teams in research methods," she adds, finishing the last of her eggs and mopping the dish with a half piece of toast. "My partner is going to be a bit of a challenge."

"How so?"

"He's a high school kid, supposedly a gifted writer. They send one student to the conference on scholarship every year. He came out with fairly outrageous comments yesterday."

"Sounds full of himself."

"He's really quite remarkable. Seems to remember every word of every book he's ever read. Sci-fi, mostly. And Sherlock Holmes."

"A Baker Street Irregular, huh? Are you coming home for lunch?"

"I should go to the noon forum. I'm going to try to go every day. And if I do that, I won't have time to get home and back before mystery writing."

"What's the noon forum?"

"It's a different speaker every day, one of the teachers from the conference. Today, in fact, it's Fletcher Downs."

"The man himself. Don't get trampled by his groupies."

"I won't. I'd better do the dishes and get going."

"I'll clean up."

"Thanks. Is Fred going to take you out fishing again?"

"I'm on my own this morning. He's taking his grandkids to Hawks' Lake to go miniature golfing. He says I'm ready to solo. In fact, I really think I'll catch one. I've got a good feeling."

"I'm rooting for you."

Doug approached learning how to fish the same way he approaches everything, she reflects as she brushes her teeth. With his typical combination of boyish enthusiasm and a CPA's love of order and systems, he had searched online Web sites with an intensity he usually reserved for the stock market and his fantasy baseball team.

She puts on lipstick and blush. Any more makeup would feel out of place in this rustic setting. When she comes out, Doug is out at the table on the deck, carefully threading line through the eyes of his fishing rod.

"You'd better bring a club, in case you snag one of those monster muskies Fred was talking about."

"For that I'd need a rifle."

He stands, and she takes him by the shoulders and gives him a lingering kiss.

"Thank you so much. I really needed this," she says.

"We both did." His eyes smile at her in a way she hasn't seen in months.

"Hurry home," he says.

"I will," she promises.

And with that she hustles to the car to drive to the campus.

4

Predictably, the "Continental Breakfast" in the hotel lobby is a total loss. Dried out-looking bagels in cellophane and teeny plastic tubs of butter (margarine having apparently been outlawed in "The Dairy State") and cream-cheese-like-substance, to be spread with little plastic knives. Six or seven of the saddest-looking bananas he has ever beheld, adrift in the bottom of a huge plastic bowl. A bleak dispenser of murky cranberry juice. Two industrial-sized coffee urns, one with the black handle for high-test, the other with the red handle for why-bother.

For reading material, something called the *Northwoods Summer Recreation Guide,* put out by *The Shepherdstown Daily Dispatch.* The damn thing doesn't even carry a crossword puzzle. The shelves lining the fireplace hold old VHS tapes of Disney movies and third-rate comedies. Two shelves hold battered boxes of jigsaw puzzles that positively scream "pieces missing." The single shelf of "books" offers bodice-rippers, "historicals," the inevitable *Reader's Digest Pureed Abominations,* and, for his morning dose of humility, a battered paperback copy of one of his thrillers.

He decides to take a walk. Isn't that what one does when confronted with the great outdoors?

He can endure a little deprivation. After all, the price is right. In enticing him to come, Herman Chandler instantly agreed to his ridiculous speaking fee. As Author-in-Residence, he has only to conduct a two-week mystery/thriller writing seminar, deliver a "noon forum" talk on the writing life, which will be a pitch for his books, and give an evening reading/signing. That leaves plenty of time to take his pick among the willing female writer-wannabes.

Perhaps, too, the two weeks away from home will get him going again. He hasn't written anything in over three months, and every time he straps himself in at the computer and attempts to launch another Spirit Sorenson or Lowell Hall, he literally feels like retching. He's sick to bloody death of both of them; his only inspirations involve clever ways to kill them off.

With his agent's approval, he even tried starting a crossover novel starring both of them, one of those "Superman and Batman in one great comic book" gimmicks. It made him doubly sick.

He supposes he's burned out from staying in a succession of same Sheratons and Hiltons, getting up each morning to don "Fletcher Downs, Author" like a bulletproof vest, and making nice-nice with the book-buying masses.

Two weeks in the Northwoods of Wisconsin, along with a hefty paycheck for very little work, might be just what he needs.

He finds himself on a flat, two-lane dirt road, wadding through wisps of thigh-high fog from the slough at the side of the road. He jams his hands deeply into the pockets of his windbreaker, wishing he'd brought something more substantial. How can it be so bloody cold in late July? Reeds and shrubs line the road, with forest starting perhaps fifteen feet back on each side. The trees seem to be of all sorts: firs—or pines, he can never remember which is which—birch, what he assumes are oaks, and some others.

He can't remember if he passed a convenience store on his way in from the campus the day before. They seem to have them everywhere now, and some of them even have drinkable coffee and the nearest metro newspaper. What would it be up here, Milwaukee? Minneapolis? Dare he hope for the *Chicago Trib*?

The slough on his right twists off into the trees. He hears rustlings—Birds? Squirrels? What other creatures do these woods contain?

He shivers. Why in hell doesn't he just go get the keys to the rental car and drive into town? But what if the braying Myrna is awake? He decides not to risk it and walks faster to warm up.

A noise to his left startles him; he whirls to see a flash of white disappear into the trees. A deer? At least the hind end of one. He feels a flush of satisfaction.

Not a bad setting for a thriller. All the Lowell Hall books are set in Chicago (Hall is, of course, a White Sox fan like his progenitor), the Spirit Sorenson series in the Paradise Valley of Montana, where the author maintains a second home. Rustic northern Wisconsin might provide a nice change of pace for Hall.

There's something elemental and dangerous about the woods. The locals have even concocted a forest creature, the Humdrung, a cross between a T-Rex and a Gila monster, with scales, a tail, fangs and crossed eyes. They sell little stuffed Humdrungs in all the stores. Humbug would be more like it.

He rounds a bend only to discover more of the same nothing he's been walking through. He's cold in earnest now, and the prospects of finding a clean, well-lighted place seem dim.

He turns and starts back, crossing over to the other side of the road. A pickup truck rumbles toward him, slowing and swinging to the far side of the road to give him a wide berth. The driver surprises him by waving, and Fletcher belatedly waves back.

They could at least have some sort of mom and pop general store. Everything seems to be "mom and pop" here. "Fuzz and Doris' Bide-a-Wee Lodge." "Red and Ruthie's Humbug Supper Club." "Pete and Brenda's Do-Drop-Inn."

He hears a dog's frantic barking from not far away and freezes, scanning the roadside for something to use as a weapon to defend himself. For a moment, the barking seems to be coming closer, but then it stops suddenly. Fletcher stands another minute before beginning to walk again.

He passes the billboard announcing his "resort" a quarter of a mile up on the right, with "RIDING STABLES AND CAMPGROUND'S" another mile past that. He smiles, remembering a sign he spotted on the highway once he had passed Wausau and entered the forest primeval, an advertisement for "GUNS, AMMO, TOYS, SNACK'S, AND SODA POP." The locals are apparently quite liberal with their apostrophes.

A noise from off to his left startles him. He stops to put a hand to his chest, bends over and takes several deep breaths, the cool air stinging his nostrils. Just another deer, he tells himself. Nothing to be afraid of.

He hears another noise, certainly not a deer, but footsteps rushing toward him. He starts to straighten up and turn. Searing pain rips through his skull for an instant before everything goes black.

5

"There you are! You were out early this morning."

Herman Chandler puffs and stomps into the living room, where Paul Krause has coffee ready.

"Lots to do!" Herman says, a bit breathless. "I needed to get my walk in early. And at this hour, the deer flies aren't out yet."

He unknots his gray sweater from around his waist, wriggles his way into it, and adjusts it at the shoulders to make it fall correctly.

"I think the new logo turned out beautifully," Paul says, "if I do say so myself."

"I agree," Herman says. "It's stunning."

The logo over the left breast on Herman's sweater features the phrase "Writing Without Walls" in discrete blue letters, in the subtle serif Paul created, arching over the school symbol, three birch trees on the shore of a gentle blue lake. "Shepherdstown, Wisconsin" curves like a smiley face underneath to complete the logo, which balances on the word "DIRECTOR" in all caps in a no-nonsense slab sans-serif.

"Sit, sit," Paul says, patting the sofa next to him. "You must be exhausted from all that gerbil activity."

"It was quite stimulating," Herman says, arranging himself on the sofa with a sigh. "The goldfinches are singing up a storm, and the red clover is blooming. You really ought to go out with me tomorrow morning."

"In all the years we've been coming to the cabin, have you ever known me to walk anywhere I didn't have to?"

Herman feigns deep thought. "Not once," he says, and they both laugh.

"Did you encounter any woodland creatures on your adventures?"

"You're my first."

Paul shoots him a look.

"No deer or bear, if that's what you mean."

"How about the touristas at Heavenly Acres? Any of them up and about at this ungodly hour?"

"I didn't get that far. I guess I'm not in good walking shape yet."

"I think your shape is just fine, lover."

Paul spoons honey into the coffee he has just poured and stirs briskly, careful not to rattle the spoon against the sides of the cup. "I'm so glad we brought the Sterling," he says. "I know it's a bit much for the north woods, but it looks so elegant on the oak sofa table."

"Thank you." Herman accepts the cup Paul offers him, takes a tentative sip, nods appreciatively. "Good," he says.

"There's really no substitute for grinding your own beans."

"I'll tell Sonny."

Paul laughs. "Why you continue to put up with that man and his so-called catering I'll never fathom."

"He's a dear man, and besides, I couldn't find another caterer up here that would be any better."

"But those daughters of his!"

"Ruthie and Ronnie try hard."

"A team of musk oxen tries hard. I still wouldn't want them serving me my food."

"You're terrible."

Paul stands, cup in one hand, saucer in the other. He's tall and slender in his powder blue slacks and white cable-knit sweater. His dark brown hair and mustache are neatly trimmed, as always, not a hair out of place. The man manages to look as if he has just stepped out of the salon, even in the Northwoods.

"I'll better see to the morning meal," he says. "We should finish up the scones before they get stale."

"Do you mind if I shower first?"

"I insist, dear. You smell like a wet caribou."

"You just hush," Herman says, but he is smiling.

"Must be all that wonderful exercise." Paul's eyes linger on him. He frowns.

"What?" Herman asks.

"Is anything the matter? I mean, aside from all the usual headaches at the school?"

"Isn't that enough?"

"That generally suffices. But usually by the second day of classes you've started to realize that you'll probably survive the ordeal for yet another year."

"I'm fine," Herman insists. "Just the normal dread of all the students wanting to switch classes, all the teacher complaints about how cold their classrooms are, the late registrants, the non-registrants, you know the drill."

"It isn't easy herding four hundred some students around that so-called campus for two weeks. I just wish I could help."

"You help me more than you can ever know by coming up here with me every year. I'd miss you desperately. I just wished you liked the Northwoods."

"If you've seen one tree, you've seen them all, to paraphrase a former president of fond memory. I'd much rather go out to the school and work with you!"

"Bless you."

Herman sets his cup and saucer on the table and accepts Paul's hand up. They stand side by side, enjoying the view of the placid cove down the hill from the cabin, which keeps them somewhat isolated from the noise of the nearby resort beaches.

"Get your shower," Paul says, breaking the comfortable silence. "You're starting to grow mold. I'd join you," he adds, leaning to kiss Herman on the cheek, "but I'm afraid we wouldn't have time for breakfast."

Herman caresses Paul's cheek. "I love you," he says. "I'm afraid I don't tell you that nearly enough." .

"You're sure I'm not just a bad habit?"

They brush lips.

"Go wash off all that nature," Paul insists. "If you don't get your tush in gear, you'll be late."

"I'm going, I'm going."

"And try not to be so tense!"

"I'm fine, really."

"I know what's worrying you. It's that prima donna guest star you hired—against my objections, as you'll recall. He's already been behaving like a complete ass."

"We call it 'writer-in-residence,' not 'guest star.'"

"Writer? The man's a hack, cranking out those vile horrors he calls novels and then strutting around as if he were Shakespeare incarnate."

"Enrollment's up thirteen percent this summer. The man is a draw."

"The man is a pig. I couldn't stand how upset you were after he tried to renege on his contract yesterday."

"He didn't try to renege. He simply wanted to renegotiate."

"I don't know why you're defending him. He's going to be more trouble than he's worth, mark my words."

"Don't worry about him."

"I'm not. I'm worried about you."

"You don't need to be. Everything's under control where he's concerned."

"Really? You have some sort of containment stratagem you haven't told me about?"

"Nothing as grand as that. I just don't think he's going to give us any further problem."

"I do hope you're right," Paul says after him as Herman heads down the hall to the bathroom, "but I still say that man is nothing but trouble."

6

"So, we have to interview someone from the town?"

The question comes from Joanna Underwood, front row to Mo's right. "I'm sorry," she adds. "That's probably a dumb question."

"Not at all, Joanna. I've probably confused everyone, but you're brave enough to ask." Alanna Taylor steps to the whiteboard, uncaps one of the evil-smelling dry-erase markers, and prints "Interviewing Assignment" in calligraphic lettering.

"I want you to contact a local merchant or craftsperson in Shepherdstown and get permission to interview him or her," she tells the class. "For tomorrow's class, bring in the name of the person and a list the questions you intend to ask."

"That's stupid," Lester Brady pipes up from front row, center, right in front of Mo.

"How so?" the teacher asks calmly.

"Why go to all that trouble if we're not going to write the friggin' article?"

"The point of the class is to learn how to get information," Jim Osterhauser says from the back row. "Like she said yesterday."

Lester turns in his chair, something his large, lumpy body makes difficult.

"What a suck-up," he says in Jim's direction.

In the ensuing silence, the clock on the wall behind Alanna makes a click-thunk as the minute hand advances on the hour, as if that final push to the top of the circle requires extra effort.

"We only have a few more minutes," Alanna says, her eyes on Lester, "and I want to give you your questions for Friday." She picks up a stack of photocopies from the small table to her left and gives a few to the first persons in each row. "The answers to these ten questions will be due at the start of class on Friday."

"Is it a test?" Lester asks.

Alanna takes a breath and rearranges her smile. "More like a worksheet," she says.

"Sounds like a test to me!"

"Why don't you pipe down a minute and let her explain?" Jim says.

Lester starts to twist around in his seat again, but Alanna bends down, puts a hand gently on his shoulder, and says, so softly Mo barely catches it, "Remember what we talked about yesterday?"

Lester nods, avoiding her eyes. "Sorry," he mumbles.

"That's all right."

Straightening up and smoothing her skirt, Alanna addresses the class. "I want you to indicate on your worksheet where you got your information."

"Can we just ask people to tell us the answers?" Lester asks, considerably subdued.

"Sure. But you have to be sure the information they give you is correct."

"How do we do that?" Lester's volume is inching up again.

"To quote our august professor," Jim says, "'if your mother says she loves you, get a second source.'"

"Exactly," Alanna says. "Other questions? Yes, Ms. Underwood."

"Do we have to talk to people? Or can we just find the answers in books?"

"Books. Online. People. Fortune cookies. Just make sure the answers are right and that you can back them up with a reliable source, two if possible. Anyone else?"

None of the eighteen adults crowded into the little classroom has any more questions.

"OK. Let me quickly go over the questions before our time's up."

"Our time is up!"

"We have five minutes, Lester. Maybe you could watch the clock for me and let me know when they're up?"

She reads quickly through the list of questions. Most seem fairly straightforward: How did Allen's Alley, the downtown street devoted to craft shops and art galleries, get its name? Same question for the Triangle Market. When and how did Shepherdstown itself get its name? What was it called before that, and why was the name changed? Who created the town mascot, the Humdrung? What legend does Shepherdstown share with Bemidji, Minnesota? Name the amateur baseball team that once played its games on a field that is now part of the county fairgrounds.

"And finally, what's wrong with Philips Street?"

"What do you mean, what's wrong with it?" Jim asks. "You mean, like, it's got potholes or something?"

"Or something. You'll know it when you find it. Any more questions?"

"That's only nine questions. You said there were ten."

"Right, Lester. I didn't think I could slip that past you. The tenth question is to write your own question for your classmates to answer. Just be sure you know the answer."

"Time's up!" Lester shouts.

"Thank you, Lester. I knew I could count on you. Class, don't forget the noon forum. Our writer-in-residence, Fletcher Downs, will be speaking, and I'm sure he'll have some wonderful insights for us."

The students file out. Jim winks at Mo as he walks by. Bobbie Barnes walks out just behind her and puts a hand on her shoulder.

"I wonder if I might take you to lunch," he says. "Fine dining awaits us in greater downtown Shepherdstown."

He's wrinkled with age but seems quite energetic, and the glint of the sensualist is in his eyes. He's wearing a sweatshirt that announces "HARVARD" and, in smaller letters underneath, "For those who couldn't get into YALE!"

"Why, thank you, Mr. Barnes," Mo says, hoping she looks flattered. "But I'm just going to grab a sandwich here and catch the noon forum."

"Please call me Bobbie. Perhaps dinner, then?"

"My husband will be expecting me."

She almost laughs at his crestfallen expression.

"Ah. You brought your husband along to a writers' retreat. How quaint." He collects the shards of his wounded male ego and attempts a look of dignified disinterest. "In that case, I shall see you on the morrow."

"See you tomorrow, Mr. Barnes."

"Bobbie."

"See you tomorrow, Bobbie."

Still smiling from the encounter, Mo buys a sandwich—turkey and Swiss on a Kaiser roll slathered with mayo—from the concession, finds a spot under a tree on the grounds and settles in to eat and to look over her class notes.

She has scribbled down scraps of information about her fellow students—a habit she picked up covering town council meetings—and runs through the names in the research class she's just had, closing her eyes and visualizing each student.

June Geller, an unfortunately large woman from Dubuque, is writing a historical novel based on her grandmother's experiences as an immigrant. Small, quiet Joanna Underwood is a primary school teacher getting her in-service credits. Jim Osterhauser is writing a book of reminiscences based on his years working on the railroad. Beth Trebeck, young and pretty, in a kind of nerdy way, hopes to write historical romances.

Robert Thyme, an actor and model with the looks to prove it, had a recurring role in one of the soaps in the 1980s. He lives in Chicago and plans to reinvent himself as a screenwriter. Bobbie Barnes, loud and funny and profane, is a retired trial lawyer who wants to write a book about his most famous cases.

That brings her to Lester Brady, her assigned partner for the ten-question project. A gifted-and-talented Shepherdstown High School student, he is enormous, loud, and raucous, with a huge, nearly round head and folds of pasty flesh pockmarked with acne and acne scars. Not an easy personality to deal with, to be sure, but she should have no problems with him.

She looks up to see Herman Chandler, director of the retreat, making his careful way across the lawn toward her.

"Ms. Quinn?" he calls out when he sees that she has spotted him. "Excuse me. I don't mean to intrude on your lunch time."

"That's quite all right." She stands, fighting the impulse to knock off the pine needles she's sure are sticking to her behind. "And please call me Mo."

"Yes. 'Mo,' short for 'Monona,' like the lake in Madison."

"Actually, I'm named for the county in Iowa."

"I'm afraid we have a bit of a problem, and I thought perhaps you could help."

"Of course."

"As you know, Fletcher Downs is to present our noon forum today."

"Yes. They announced it in my classes."

"Good. Good."

Herman Chandler is almost exactly her height, five foot five, and probably fifteen years older than her thirty-seven. He has a rich, well-modulated voice, which he uses to good advantage. Balding and pear-shaped, he certainly doesn't have leading-man looks, but she's read that he's a popular character actor in local theater in Madison in addition to being a full-time arts administrator.

"How can I help?" she prompts.

"I'm afraid our Mr. Downs has yet to make his appearance today, and frankly, I'm getting more than a little nervous."

"I hope he's all right."

"Oh, I'm sure he is. He has a history of being somewhat less than reliable. We knew we were taking a chance when we hired him."

Herman checks his watch. "I was wondering—I know it's short notice."

"Short notice?"

"He still might turn up in time, of course, but—"

She resists the urge to take him by the shoulders and shake the words out of him.

"I was hoping—that you might be willing to pinch hit."

"Pinch hit? You mean, speak at the forum?"

"Yes."

"Mr. Chandler, I'm no public speaker. I'm not even an author!"

"You're being modest. Your column for the *Tribune* received national attention, and rightfully so. And your exploits since you relocated to Wisconsin are quite well known. I'm sure you have some fascinating stories for our students."

"But I—"

"I really am in a bind here."

"Surely one of the other instructors … Perhaps the scheduled speaker for tomorrow could just move up a day?"

Herman flushes with what Mo supposes is embarrassment. "Actually, I couldn't find him. I did ask Ms. Labin, our advanced poetry instructor, who's scheduled to speak on Thursday, but she said she still had a great deal of preparation to do."

She sees the look of desperation in the man's eyes.

"I'll do it, but I—"

"Oh, thank you!" He seems about to hug her. "I'll stop pestering you, so you can prepare your remarks. I'll meet you backstage in the auditorium in—" He again checks his watch. "—exactly twelve minutes."

She fights down a surge of panic as she watches him wade back toward the building. Get a grip, she tells herself. This won't be all that different than speaking to Mrs. Manley's high school journalism class back in Mitchell.

She sits back under the tree, pulls out her notepad, and begins trying to figure out what she can say to an auditorium full of aspiring writers who are expecting a best-selling author and instead will have to settle for a community newspaper editor.

7

Myrna Gillory awakes in a tangle of sheets. The sun hurts her eyelids.

She groans and rolls away from the light. She knows what an empty bed feels like, and this bed feels empty.

Someone raps at the door.

"Maid service?" a timid voice says with a Spanish accent.

"Go away!" She opens her eyes. The clock radio on the nightstand displays 11:27. She's gone back to sleep and slept right through her morning classes.

She fishes the hotel bathrobe off the floor and pulls it on as she pads into the living room. Her manuscript sits on the coffee table in front of the fireplace.

What was it the old bastard said? "Considerable merit." That was it. "Your work has considerable merit, but—" There were a whole lot of buts. Not yet ready to show to an agent. Certainly not his agent. Needs a thorough revision. Perhaps a professional edit. Some of the plot elements don't seem plausible.

He especially had trouble believing the character of the abusive father. She'd made him one-dimensional, completely evil, had failed to "create a compelling humanity."

All this, of course, delivered only after he'd gotten into her pants.

And what a tumble that had been. They'd barely been room in the bed for the three of them, The Great One, his massive ego, and her. Those steamy scenes in his novels must have been fueled by imagination and wishful thinking. The Great One, it turned out, wasn't all that hot in the sack.

She sits on the couch, lights a cigarette, and takes the smoke deep. She started smoking again when she left Daniel, and she isn't even pretending she's going to quit any time soon. Smoking relaxes her and, more importantly, it helps her concentrate when she writes. Besides, who wants those extra ten years to rot in a nursing home?

She has time to go back to her motel and shower and still make it to campus for Fletcher's class. But why shower at her dumpola motel when she can luxuriate in the whirlpool here? She can still change her clothes at the motel.

She stays in the whirlpool until she feels as if her legs have turned to jelly. She feels scummy putting the same underwear back on, but she'll remedy that soon enough. Before leaving she dons dark glasses and a floppy sun hat. She has almost closed the door behind her when she remembers her manuscript and hurries to retrieve it.

Thorough revision. Professional edit. Bullshit. The old bastard just isn't willing to give a young writer a chance. Afraid of the competition, no doubt.

She takes the stairs and exits through the side door, making sure the parking lot is deserted before walking quickly to her old Dodge, sitting between a Lincoln and a Caddy. She drives cautiously down the narrow road toward what passes for a highway in this godforsaken backwoods. She's been warned that a deer might come bounding out at any time and demolish her car.

After a quick change at her motel, she subjects herself to the drive-through at the Mickey D's. It's greasy crap, but it's cheap, and it beats the muck they sell at the school cantina. She drives through town and the two miles west to the campus, which is actually some sort of "experimental forest" where tree huggers conduct seminars on lumbering and conservation and God knows what else. The place includes crude dormitories, but they're closed during the two weeks that Writing Without Walls meets.

There are no parking spaces in the school lot, and she has to walk in from the road. A few students work on manuscripts, read, and eat their lunches at the picnic tables in front of the enormous two-story log classroom building, and others talk in groups of two and three at tables in the large cafeteria inside. Judging from the lack of a crowd, the forum must still be going on.

She walks through the cafeteria and into the darkened auditorium, cringing as the door slams shut behind her. At the podium, a woman who looks familiar is laughing with the rest at something someone has said.

"I was only a summer intern at the magazine," she says when the laughter dies down, "and I never even saw 'Hef.' So I'm afraid I can't tell you what he's really like. Any other questions? We still have a couple of minutes. Yes?"

An old lady in the second row off to the side stands slowly; she seems in danger of toppling back into her seat. "Since you've been involved in so many murders ..." she begins.

"Maybe you could rephrase that," the woman at the podium says.

Laughter again ripples the auditorium. Whoever she is, they're eating her up.

"I mean to say, you've solved so many murders," the lady says, her voice a fragile warble.

"Let's just say I've been in the wrong place at the right time," the speaker suggests.

"I was wondering if you're planning to write any murder mysteries of your own."

"I'll leave that to Mr. Downs and the other experts."

The mystery writing class. That's where Myrna has seen her.

More hands saw the air, but the fat little gnome who runs the school has entered stage right and waddles to the podium.

"I think my time is up," the speaker says. "Here comes Mr. Chandler with the hook. I'll be glad to hang around if anybody has more questions."

Applause swells. The director hugs her and joins in the ovation. Most folks are making for the exits, although many swim against the stream to get down to the stage. Myrna slips out into the cafeteria ahead of the stampede, gets a diet Dew at the cantina, and heads for class, stopping in the ladies' to make quick repairs on her face.

Only two students are in their seats when she gets there, so she ducks out the back door into a small grassy area separating the back of the building from the forest and lights up a cigarette. As she smokes, she considers again what Fletcher said about her manuscript. So he thought the father was "one-dimensional," huh? Without a "compelling humanity." She draws the smoke deep into her lungs, lets it curl out at the corners of her mouth, watches it drift across the brown grass and disperse into the trees.

He should have known the son-of-a-bitch, she thinks bitterly. He should have known him.

8

Myrna Gillory is leaning against the wall in the hallway when Mo gets to the mystery writing seminar. She's short and oddly shapeless, as if her body hasn't quite gelled, and she wears her dyed-blonde hair in spikes. During class introductions the day before, she informed the class that she was newly liberated from her ogre ex-husband back in Crystal Springs, Illinois, and had lost a lot of weight. She somehow manages to look permanently bored and aggravated at the same time.

"I was afraid I was late," Mo says.

Myrna shrugs. "Whatshisface hasn't shown yet."

She reeks of cigarette smoke, and her eyes seem tired under all the makeup. Not a happy lady, for all her new-won freedom.

"Ms. Gillory, right?"

"Yeah. I caught the end of your talk. You killed."

"I was petrified. I didn't have much chance to prepare."

"Didn't show."

"Thanks. Amazing how we can put on our game faces when we have to, isn't it?"

"Is that what you do? Fake it?"

"I wouldn't call it 'faking.'"

Myrna shrugs. "Whatever," she says. "You're married, right?"

"Yes."

"Then you probably know all about faking."

Mo lets that go. "I wonder what's keeping Mr. Downs?"

"Speaking of fakers." Her eyes seem to focus on something just over Mo's shoulder. "I wouldn't be surprised if he didn't even show." Glancing at Mo, she quickly adds, "I'm going to go out and catch another smoke. Come and get me if The Great Pretender actually shows up."

"Sure."

Mo watches Myrna Gillory walk down the hall and slip out the door. She has the distinct feeling that she's just been in a fight but has no idea what they were fighting about, let alone who won.

The other eleven students have formed a circle with their chairs at the front of the classroom. Only one takes note of Mo's arrival.

"Hey, it's you again," Lester says.

"Hi, Lester."

"That Downs guy hasn't shown yet."

"So I see."

"He'd better! I'm working on a mystery novel, and I want to get his feedback."

Lester shoves over so she can slide into the chair between him and a middle-aged man named Jameson, who nods at her. They sit in uncomfortable silence. Lester takes a battered paperback from his pants pocket and starts reading.

"How long are you going to sit there?" Myrna asks from the doorway. "Obviously, he isn't going to show up."

"I think somebody should speak to the director about this," suggests a middle-aged woman named Ruth, who had shared a poem about despondency with several of them over lunch in the cafeteria the day before. "I don't know about the rest of you, but I paid a pretty penny for this class, and I intend to get my fee refunded."

"Good idea," a skinny young man, Stephen something, comments. "This class wasn't worth anything when he was here anyway."

"That's a bit harsh, don't you think?" another woman, upper thirties or early forties, asks. "I thought his stories about becoming established as a writer were quite enlightening."

"You don't have to blow smoke up his ass now, lady," Stephen retorts, slouching even lower in his chair. "He isn't even here."

Stephen has long, dark hair and rumpled but obviously pricey clothes—sports coat, dress shirt, untucked and open at the throat, pre-faded jeans with holes in both knees, and loafers with no socks. Mo's mother would have said he looked as if he slept in the hayloft.

"Why don't we go ahead without him," a pleasant retiree named Harold suggests.

A man named Elsworth Priestly, mid-thirties and nondescript other than the name, stands, stretches, and slings his book bag over his shoulder. "If he does show up," he says to no one in particular as he walks out, "tell him I was here."

The door has barely shut behind him when it opens again, and Herman Chandler takes a cautious step into the classroom.

"No one has seen Mr. Downs on campus today," he tells them. "I called the resort where he's staying, and nobody there remembers seeing him since much earlier this morning. That being the case, I was hoping that one of you could lead the discussion in Mr. Downs' absence." He's looking directly at Mo. "It would just be for today. If Mr. Downs is still unavailable to teach tomorrow, I'll have one of the other fiction instructors take over the class."

Mo glances around the circle. Clearly, none of her classmates seems predisposed to volunteer. "Mr. Chandler, I'm not a teacher," she says, "and I've never even tried to write a mystery, or any other kind of fiction."

"It would just be for today. You wouldn't have to teach. Just—facilitate."

"OK," Mo says. "I'll facilitate. Just for today."

"Oh, thank you." He hands her a sheet of paper. "Here's the class list. I really appreciate this."

Her eleven classmates eye her as Mr. Chandler slips back out the door.

"This is a crock!" Stephen says. "Where's Downs? He obviously doesn't give a shit about any of us."

"Why should he?" Myrna asks. "He's just here to get his ego stroked and make a few bucks."

"If you feel that way about him," Pamela Erickson works up the nerve to ask, "why did you sign up for this class?"

"He's published!" Ruth Bergan says.

"He's successful!" Gretchen Hyman says.

"He sells," Stephen adds.

Mo takes a deep breath. Maybe this won't be so hard after all. They seem to be facilitating themselves just fine.

"I could read something from my novel," Gretchen Hyman says.

"No," Lester says.

"Go ahead," Mo says, grateful for anything that will help kill the hour.

Glaring at Lester, Gretchen arranges herself in her chair, clears her throat, and launches into the first of a thick sheaf of pages. The prose is florid, and she reads like a high school forensics student, over-inflecting and adding frequent gestures.

The piece has the solitary virtue of taking up time, which Mo uses to read over the class roster and match names with faces. She has time to review the list twice while Gretchen drones on. Stephen slouches ever lower. Lester fidgets. The others seem to have sent their minds wherever they go when they're bored. They endure. Time passes.

Ruth favors them with a selection from her own thriller-in-progress. The minute hand on the clock makes its clink-thunks, signaling the imminent end of the hour. Ruth staggers to a stop.

"I guess that's it for today, then," Mo says, hoping her relief isn't too obvious.

"What about tomorrow?" Gretchen asks.

"Yeah?" Myrna says. "What about tomorrow?" She seems to be enjoying Mo's discomfort.

"Any suggestions?" Mo asks the class.

"Let's come dressed as our favorite detective!" Lester says. "And the others have to guess who you are."

"I guess you'll come as Sherlock Holmes," Stephen says. "Do I win?"

Several voice their objections to that plan.

"OK, no costume party. Does anyone else have an idea?"

"Why don't we just read more of our own original material?" Gretchen says.

"Yes!" Ruth agrees.

"Or we could each write a short scene based on the same situation," says soft-spoken Frank Jameson, with the 1950s-style picket fence haircut. "We could compare how everybody handled it."

"That's homework," Lester says.

"Yeah," Myrna adds. "Downs said he wasn't going to give us any assignments."

"Why don't we just let anybody who wants to participate write a scene?" Mo suggests.

"What kind of scene?" Gretchen asks.

"We could each try to reveal why Mr. Downs didn't come to class today."

Frank gives her an approving nod.

"How are we supposed to know what happened?" Lester asks.

"We don't," Stephen says, sounded disgusted. "We're supposed to make something up. It's called *fiction*."

"Bite me!"

"Lester!" Mo says.

To her surprise, he settles back and takes several deep breaths, the redness subsiding from his moon face. "Can we kill him off?" he asks in a subdued voice.

Mo looks around the circle. "Anything goes, right?"

"Great," Lester says.

"OK, then. Class dismissed."

Frank Jameson approaches as she collects her papers and her wits. "Good job, teach," he says, smiling.

"I think I'll stick to editing a newspaper."

"And solving murders. Really, you did a great job of keeping the sharks from tearing each other up."

"They are competitive, aren't they?"

"Perhaps we could have dinner tonight. The Shepherdstown Inn downtown is decent. We could talk about writing. Or we could talk about anything but writing."

He's hitting on me, she thinks with wonder. This nice older man is actually hitting on me! She's beginning to wonder if the real purpose of writing retreats has all that much to do with writing.

"I'll be having dinner with my husband. Thank you, though."

"Gotcha."

She waits for him to leave before gathering her books and following him out. Herman Chandler is waiting for her in the hall.

"Everything go all right?"

"We all survived."

"Splendid," he says, either missing or pretending to miss her sarcasm. "I really appreciate you coming through in an emergency this way. I'm sure Mr. Downs will be here tomorrow, and I'll have another teacher ready to substitute if necessary."

She has planned to stay on campus to work on her homework but decides to go home. She's had enough of the school for one day. She drives through the two-block strip of tourist shops and businesses comprising downtown Shepherdstown and eases onto the two-lane highway heading east out of town. A huge logging truck approaches from the other direction and rumbles past, the airwave slapping the boxy CR-V.

Well before the turnoff for her "resort," she spots the billboard announcing "Heavenly Acres, next left," and finds herself slowing and then stopping to wait while three cars pass from the other direction before she makes the turn.

Just curious, she tells herself. She doesn't expect to find Fletcher Downs, of course. Wherever the renowned author has gone, he'll either return to the school tomorrow to honor the rest of his teaching commitment or he won't, and there's nothing she can do about it. But still, she tells herself, it can't hurt to take a little look around.

9

Feeling more than a little foolish, Douglas Stennett sits alone in a rowboat just off shore. The boat bobs gently as a light breeze riffles the water. White, puffy clouds roll away toward an infinite horizon. The scent of pine mixed with fish intestines pervades.

Kids play on the beach and wade in the water while their mothers sit stationed on towels and plastic chaises, reading books, chatting, sunning.

Several other boats dot the lake. Everybody in these other boats seems to be catching fish. Doug has not had so much as a nibble. His first attempt at becoming an outdoor sportsman is not going well.

He reels in, checks his baits, which appear to be undisturbed, and recasts clumsily. Mastery of casting, like anything else, is simply a matter of repetitions, he reminds himself. He sets the whatchamajiggy that keeps the line from paying out too quickly—would, anyway, if a fish actually took the hook—sits back, and tries to relax.

He's never been good at relaxing, and fishing seems to be nothing more than a pretext for doing nothing. It would be more exciting if he actually caught a fish, he supposes, but the thought of then having to kill it makes him shudder.

Fred Wilkerson has promised to give him a demonstration of cleaning his catch that afternoon, letting him anticipate becoming intimately acquainted with fish guts for the first time. Fred co-owns the Merrynook Buck's Lake Resort with wife Ethel—she joked that Lucy and Desi own the next resort down the road. Fred sold insurance in Tomahawk for thirty-four years, Ethel told them when they checked in Sunday night. Ethel raised the kids, sold Mary Kay Cosmetics, was and is an avid quilter and loves to read mysteries, although she doesn't have much time for quilting or reading during the season. They bought the resort when Fred closed the insurance agency six years before and profess to love running it, although there's "always something that needs doing."

Doug spots Fred, back from miniature golf, patrolling the shoreline in a golf cart, the grandkids with him. Doug reels in. Both hooks are bare. Has a fish actually nibbled off his baits, or have the "fire balls" Fred directed him to buy at the tackle shop in town simply gotten waterlogged and fallen off? Whichever the case, Doug pulls up the anchor and rows for shore. He has managed to get the boat tied up at the pier and is gathering his fishing gear when he hears the whir of the golf cart fast approaching on the dirt path hugging the shore.

"Hey there, young man! Got your limit already?"

Doug walks to the cart, where Fred waits with his two tow-headed grandsons.

"I'm afraid I got skunked."

"Happens to the best of them. I'll take you back out this afternoon, and we'll catch them. Grampa always catches fish. Isn't that right, boys?" He reaches out to tousle the hair of the nearest kid. "You met the rug rats?" he asks, his broad, sun-leathered face beaming.

"Don't believe I have."

"This here's Jonathan. He's eight."

"How do you do, sir?" The young man leans out to shake hands.

"Johnny, this is Mr. Stennett. He's a financal advisor."

"Pleased to meet you."

"Nice to meet you, Jonathan."

"Your grampa could use some help with his finances," Fred says. "Maybe we should hire this nice man, huh?"

Jonathan shrugs. "I guess so."

"Gonna be an NFL quarterback, aren't you, Johnny?"

"Gonna try, Grampa."

"That's the stuff. And this here's his little brother, Timothy. He's six, going on seventy. He's a tad shy, but smart as a whip."

Timothy peers out from behind his grandfather's broad back.

"They look like fine boys. You must be very proud of them."

"You bet I am." He rumples Timothy's hair, causing him to burrow his head deeper into his grandfather's vest jacket. "They've got two little sisters back at the cabin. They're my daughter, Jeannie's, brood. She married a lymnologist. They live down in Madison, but they come up here for two weeks every summer. You've probably seen them out on the beach."

"I might have."

"My son, Robert, isn't married. Don't know what he's waiting for. So—" He looks past Doug toward the boat. "They weren't bitin', huh?"

"Not for me."

"You do like I told you? Row out just beyond the drop off, cast back toward shore, let the bait hit bottom, reel in four turns, and let it sit?"

"I tried."

"They probably just weren't feeding. But say, how about the four of us go out after lunch and see if we can scare up some action? What say, boys? You want to show Mr. Stennett, here, how we catch them?"

"We can't, grampa," Jonathan reminds him. "Mama's taking us to that logger museum."

"Oh, yeah. That's right."

Fred turns his attention back to Doug. "Why don't we all go out tomorrow morning? Real early. You aren't supposed to fish before sun-up, but that doesn't mean you can't be out there, baited up and ready to go. We can see the sun come up over the lake. It's a real pretty sight, isn't it, boys?"

Timothy whispers something to his grandfather.

"I'd better get this show on down the road," Fred announces. "You let me know about tomorrow, huh? We can go out in my boat. She's real comfy."

"Thanks. I'll let you know."

Doug watches the cart scoot off down the twisting path, then lugs his gear up the twenty three steep wooden stairs to their cabin. The sun has cleared the trees, and the air is already warming. He'll bring a book out on the porch, he decides. First he'll make another pot of coffee. But he remembers that he cracked the coffeepot cleaning up after Mo left. He dumps his gear on the porch, goes inside to grab the pot, and heads for the Wilkerson's house, which also serves as office for the resort.

The little white poodle, Juney, runs over to Doug as he approaches. Doug squats and holds out his hand, and Juney nuzzles it, his stubby tail wagging furiously. Doug has never been much for dogs—you had to have one as a kid to appreciate them later, and his parents didn't allow him to have pets—but this friendly little fellow is easy on the nerves.

Juney escorts him across the lawn onto the porch. Doug raps on the screen door, and Ethel emerges from the living room, rubbing her hands on her apron. Behind her, lake, trees and sky fill a picture window running the length of the room.

"Hi, Doug! Hope our fierce guard dog didn't scare you."

She opens the screen, and Juney scoots in and jumps into her arms. "You're my little Juney Bug, aren't you, sweetie?" Ethel coos, and then she rubs noses with the dog.

"He doesn't bark," Doug notes.

"She. Hardly ever. Once in awhile somebody she doesn't care for will come to the door, and she'll raise a stink. She takes a particular disliking to that Lloyd fellow."

"Lloyd?"

"A young man from town. Wanders all over creation. You never know when he might show up. He had a real bad accident when he was a little kid, fell out of a swing and fractured his skull or some such thing. He hasn't been right since, if you know what I mean. He's scared to death of my little June Bug, if you can believe that."

"Hard to imagine."

"Something I can do for you?" She eyes the glass pot in Doug's hand.

"I'm afraid I cracked this. I'll be happy to pay for a new one."

She takes it from him. "These darn things get busted all the time. I've got a spare in the cupboard. You go on in and make yourself to home. I'll fetch it."

Juney jumps up on an overstuffed blue recliner chair and curls up in what is clearly her place. Doug walks to the window, which gives out onto a large deck. The hill slopes sharply down to the lake.

"You have a lovely view," he notes when Ethel comes back.

She hands him a box that evidently holds a new coffeepot. "Isn't it grand? Freddie and I love to sit here after dinner and watch the teal on the lake."

"Teal?"

"Those are the ducks you've been seeing. Won't you sit down? I've got coffee on. And some of those raspberry fig newtons." She laughs. "Except, if they're raspberry, I guess they can't very well be fig newtons, can they?"

"No, thanks. I really should get back."

But she flops down in a padded rocker, and the dog jumps down from the recliner, bounces over, and jumps in her lap. Doug sits on the couch, his back to the window.

"We get loons, too, but for some reason, there haven't been as many this year. You might have heard them last night."

"Is that what that was? I wondered."

"There's no sound quite like it, is there? It can be kind of spooky, especially at sundown. I'll be sitting out on the porch, reading one of my mysteries, and a loon will call. It sends a shiver right up my spine. It really does."

"I can imagine."

"Freddie likes to imitate them. Sometimes he'll sneak up on me when I'm reading and try to scare me." She laughs. "He says I read too many of the darn things."

"My wife's taking a class on mystery writing at the retreat."

"That's what she said, from Fletcher Downs! I don't care for his stories myself. Awfully violent. I like the cozies. Do you read mysteries, Doug?"

"Not really. I picked up Downs's new one, but I haven't really gotten into it."

"I guess you've been involved in enough mysteries yourself, you and that wife of yours. You sure you wouldn't like coffee? Or tea? I can make tea. It's no trouble."

"No, thanks. I'm fine. She told you about that?"

"Didn't have to. We read all about them at the time. I recognized the name when you made the reservation. How awful. The fellow who ran the diner, the parish priest, and a pack of drug dealers in Iowa!"

"So much for peaceful small town life, huh?" Doug notes.

"Oh, every place has its troubles." She strokes Juney, who accepts the loving as her due. "We've had our share. Just last summer, a singer at the country western jamboree turned up dead. Accident, they said. He was out walking by the river late at night, fell in and drowned. He'd been drinking. Some folks think he was pushed."

"Really?"

"Oh, yes. And the summer before that, a rodeo rider got himself hit by a train out on the trestle. He'd had a few toots, too. I don't think drinking does anybody any good. Do you?"

"I suppose in moderation—"

"A sip or a snootful, it's still poison. I guess a lot of entertainers drink and do drugs and all. Not that this one was very famous. The singer who drowned. Kenny Laine, I think his name was."

"Never heard of him, but I'm not a big fan of that genre."

"So, are you and that wife of yours enjoying our little slice of Paradise?"

"It's beautiful. I've never really spent any time in the woods."

"We wouldn't trade it for anything. And for a little out-of-the-way place, we really have some nice nightspots. Have you two discovered Eaton's yet?"

"Eaton's?"

"It's a wonderful supper club. They have a piano player who entertains nightly, and the food is wonderful. I think you'd enjoy it."

"That does sound good," Doug says, warming to the idea of taking Mo someplace nice for dinner. "Is it far?"

"Oh, no. Just another five miles or so up the road. You should call ahead for a reservation, though. I'll get the number for you."

It's several more minutes before Doug is finally able to get away. When he stands, Juney runs over to him, tail wagging.

"Well, look at that! I think she wants to go home with you."

"My wife would like that. She wants a dog."

"Tell her she can come visit this one any time."

"I will. And thanks for the coffeepot. And the tip about Eaton's."

"No trouble at all."

With Juney in her arms, Ethel walks him out onto the front porch. As he crosses the lawn, he looks back and sees her standing there. She waves, then makes Juney wave her paw at him, and he waves back.

He'll definitely make the reservation at Eaton's, he decides. And then maybe he can find someplace with Internet access. Roughing it in the Northwoods is grand, and all, but he really should check the markets.

10

The signs for Heavenly Acres promise "luxury in the Northwoods."
As Mo noses the CR-V off the narrow road into the parking lot, the
compound certainly does create a more imposing impression than
the little mom-and-pop resorts like the Wilkerson's.

Seven rowboats nose up to a long, well-maintained pier to
her left. Ahead, a large wooden A-frame lodge fronts the three-
story hotel and offers a restaurant and "The Inner Circle" lounge,
where "Jenny Stevens and the Northwoods Bearcats" are appear-
ing Friday and Saturday nights. Beyond the lodge, several cabins
stretch out along the shoreline amidst the trees. The grounds also
hold a kids' playground, not in use on a hot, sunny afternoon,
three fenced tennis courts, also idle, and a field with horseshoe
pits and a campfire ring. A sign announces riding stables another
half mile up the road.

It looks like a movie set for a lakeside resort, with all the actors
on break somewhere. But what Heavenly Acres lacks in people it
makes up for in cars. Mo cruises the parking lot in vain and settles
for parking on the shoulder of the road.

As she walks toward the lodge, a mosquito bites her just above
her left elbow, and she swats at it viciously. She swabbed herself
with repellant before leaving the cabin, but apparently, this fellow
didn't notice. Not fellow, she reminds herself. Doug informed her
yesterday that only the female mosquito bites.

"I shall refrain from drawing any parallels to human behavior," he had said with that little boy smirk of his.

She smiles at the memory.

He had thoroughly researched mosquitoes on the Internet before they left Mitchell, along with all other potentially dangerous or harmful aspects of the local flora and fauna. Douglas Stennett was not one to enter into any new situation without arming himself with as much information as he could find.

A maintenance worker appears at the side of a large shed and nods at her as she passes. He wears khaki work clothes, the sleeves of his long-sleeve shirt rolled tightly over his biceps. His face is work-hard and expressionless. She feels his eyes follow her as she passes.

Two middle-aged couples sit on the porch of one of the cabins, playing cards and drinking from tall, sweating glasses. Voices of children at play carry across the water. A solitary jay scolds. The air is still. From far off, a power saw snarls its way through resistant wood.

The lobby has a vaulted ceiling with stairs leading to a loft along the back wall. Under the loft, gas jets feign flames in an enormous fireplace. Large, well-padded chairs surround low tables under floor lamps with shades made of birch bark. The glass ashtrays on the tables are all clean. Deer heads, unblinking and sad, stare down from the walls. Although her father and most of the boys she went through high school with back in Iowa hunted, Mo has never understood the urge to shoot something as gentle and graceful as a deer and stick its head on the wall.

A young woman in a light green suit and powder blue blouse, the "Heavenly Acres" script logotype in darker blue above her left breast, watches her from behind the long reception counter. Behind her, the words "Heavenly Acres," in the same careful blue script, flow across the wall above rows of old-fashioned cubbyholes, some containing keys, letters, messages—most empty. Beneath the cubbies, a long desk holds three phones and three printers, no doubt matched to the three computers on the reception counter. To Mo's right as she faces the desk, a doorway opens onto a back area.

The woman's neutral expression doesn't change until Mo gets about five feet from the desk. Then, as if Mo has stepped on some triggering mechanism, she flashes a smile, her eyebrows arching to indicate interest.

"Good afternoon. Welcome to Heavenly Acres. How may I help you?"

Her name pin identifies her as "Amanda," the "assistant manager."

"Good afternoon. My name is Monona Quinn. I'm attending the writers conference."

"Are you a guest with us, Mrs. Quinn?"

"I'm looking for one of the teachers. Fletcher Downs. I believe he's staying here."

Does the smile flicker just slightly, or does Mo imagine it?

"Are you an instructor at the school?"

"I'm a student. Mr. Downs is one of my instructors."

"Mr. Downs is a guest here." She glances at the cubbyholes behind her. "I don't believe he's in right now."

"Do you know when he's expected?"

"No."

"Perhaps I could leave a message for him?"

"I'd be happy to take a message for you."

The phone rings on the desk. Another green-suited young lady appears from the doorway and answers on the second ring.

"Hello. Heavenly Acres. This is Molly. How may I help you?"

Amanda is waiting.

"May I have paper and pen?"

"Of course."

Amanda produces a half-sized pad of powder blue paper and a ballpoint pen, both bearing the "Heavenly Acres" script. Mo takes them to one of the chairs, which makes a soft "oof" noise when she sinks in.

"Dear Mr. Downs," she writes. "I'm in your mystery writing seminar, and I have a question. Would you please call me?"

She fishes the card Ethel Wilkerson has given her from her purse and copies down the phone number for the Merrynook Resort. She signs the note with first and last name. She tears the sheet from the pad, folds it over once, bends one of the edges up, and prints "Fletcher Downs" in block letters on the outside.

Amanda's smile again snaps on as Mo approaches the desk. Mo hands her the note.

"Thank you," Mo says.

"Of course," Amanda says. When Mo doesn't leave, she adds, "I'll see that Mr. Downs gets your message."

"Thank you."

Amanda tucks the message into a small side pocket in her coat. Mo steps back, scanning the cubbyholes on the wall, then turns and walks across the lobby to the door.

As she steps outside, a loud clang draws her attention to the field to her left, where a white-haired man and a boy of eight or nine, perhaps grandfather and grandson, are pitching horseshoes.

"Nice one, Henry!" the man says. "A ringer!"

The boy starts to take off for the far pole.

"Whoa, now!" the man calls out. "I got to throw mine first!"

Mo drives slowly up the road to the stables, a series of open stalls a few yards off the road giving onto a fenced field that slopes downhill into a ravine. Several horses circle a feeder to one side of the corral. Two donkeys occupy one of the stalls. A broad dirt trail, marked by clumps of fresh horse dung, leads off to the right. Mo parks, gets out, and approaches the stables, picking up the clean smell of horse dung and hay. One of the horses looks up, then resumes his feeding.

"Help you, Miss?"

A short, thin Latino in blue work clothes and black rubber boots trudges up the hill to her right, a pitchfork over his shoulder. Under the brim of a large-brimmed floppy hat, his chin is salted with gray stubble.

"I was supposed to be meeting Mr. Downs here," Mo says. "I'm a little late. Perhaps he's already left."

The man plants the pitchfork at his feet a few steps away from her.

"He's tall. Wavy silver hair. Rather distinguished looking."

"Distinguished." He smiles.

"I was wondering if you might have seen him."

"I have not seen your distinguished Mr. Downs." The man pushes his hat up on his forehead with his index finger. His dark eyes seem kind and alert. "Are you one of those writers from the conference?" he asks.

"I'm attending the conference. Mr. Downs is one of my teachers. *Me llamo* Monona Quinn." She steps forward, hand extended. "*Como se llama?*"

The smile broadens. "Juan Colas," he says. "*Mucho gusto*. But …" He looks down at his hand.

"That's all right. I grew up on a farm."

"In that case—"

His hand is hard and callused. He gives her fingers a gentle squeeze, releases them.

"*Mucho gusto*, Señor Colas."

"Your Señor Downs, he is a very important writer?"

"*Sí. Muy famoso.*"

"If I see this great man, should I tell him you're looking for him? Or maybe it's a surprise, huh?"

She laughs with him. "I probably just misunderstood. I'll see him out at the school."

"You would perhaps like to take a ride?" He nods toward the stables.

"Another time. *Gracias.*"

"*De nada,* Señora Quinn."

As she starts to drive back down the road in the car, she looks back and sees Juan Colas standing with his pitchfork, looking after her. He waves, and she waves back.

She parks in the same space she just vacated on the road in front of the lodge. The sun is still high in the afternoon sky as she hurries to the lodge. When she looks in at the window, Molly is at the desk, talking with a man in an outdoorsy outfit that might have been on a mannequin in an Eddie Bauer store the day before. Amanda is not in sight.

Mo enters and crosses the lobby to the desk. She glances around, as if looking for someone, and retreats to a doorway to the left of the fireplace under the loft and into a hallway lined with numbered doors.

Elevators, stairway, and vending are halfway down the hall. Mo takes the stairs to the second floor. She's fairly certain her message for Fletcher Downs perched in the slot marked 237. It could have been a nine instead of a seven, but she's sure about the two and the three.

What she isn't sure of is how the information might possibly be useful, what she might gain by seeing the door to his room.

A plaque designates Room 237 as "no smoking." The door looks just like the door to Room 239 to its left, just like 238 and 240 across the narrow corridor.

The light is dim, the rug worn.

She taps lightly just below the 237 marker. Getting no response, she taps again, louder. Several doors down on the left, a maid's cart sits outside an open door. Mo approaches cautiously. It seems late in the day for the maid to be cleaning, but perhaps a guest checked out late.

She peeks in at the doorway. The mattress has been stripped, the bedding in a heap at the foot of the bed. Scrubbing sounds come from an inside door to the right, no doubt the bathroom.

"Hello?" Mo calls out.

The scrubbing noises stop.

"Yes?" A head appears in the doorway, Latina, middle aged, frightened or perhaps suspicious.

"I'm sorry to bother you. I'm looking for Señor Downs. Room 237."

"I have not seen anyone."

"I'm supposed to meet him here. He's tall. Wavy silver hair. A very distinguished looking man."

"I have not seen him, Señora."

"I'm a student in his class at the writing school."

"Ah, sí. You are the one."

"I'm sorry?"

"In the future, if you do not want me to clean your room, you can just hang the sign on the door. You do not have to yell at me."

"I *am* sorry," Mo says, catching on. "I wake up cranky."

"Cranky?"

"*De mal humor.*"

"Ah, sí. Peesed off."

Mo laughs. "Sí!" She looks up and down the hall. "*Me llamo* Monona Quinn. *Como se llama?*"

"Maria. Maria Morejon."

"Would it be all right if I left a message in the room for him? I'm afraid if I just slide it under the door, he might not notice it."

Maria Morejon frowns. "You know, he could get another key for you at the front desk," she says.

"I'll be sure to tell him. But I really need to be sure he gets my message."

"We're not supposed to."

"You can watch me. I won't touch a thing."

"Why don't you give me the note? I will make sure that he gets it."

"Thank you," Mo says, trying not to sound disappointed. "That's very nice of you."

She pulls her pad and pencil from her purse, writes, "Call me," and puts down a made-up number.

"*Muchas gracias*," she says, handing the note to Maria.

"OK."

As she goes back down the stairs, Mo wonders if she might have made a big mistake coming. Folks will remember her, and she has even given her real name on the note she left at the desk.

She seems no closer to knowing where Fletcher Downs is, and she has a new question to ponder as well: who was the ill-tempered woman in his room this morning who yelled when the maid knocked on the door?

She urges the boxy CR-V down the bumpy lane to the highway as fast as she dares. In her haste, she misses the turnoff for Merrynook and has to drive another quarter mile up the road to turn around in the driveway at the Buck's Lake Trailer Park. She waits while a semi carrying enormous logs rumbles by, then swings back onto the road and floors it. Doug will be wondering where she's been.

11

"Odoms, you just might be the slowest checker I have ever seen." Jonathan Soggins pauses to make sure his employee get the full impact. "And that's going some, believe you me."

Is "shithead" in the dictionary? Elzie Odoms wonders. If it is, it should have Soggins' picture next to it.

"Do you know what the IPH quota is for this register during this shift on a weekday?"

"I believe you've shared that number with me, sir," he says. "Isn't it somewhere in the neighborhood of three hundred forty?"

"The quota is precisely three hundred and forty items per hour. Some hours you might go over three hundred forty. Some hours you might go under three hundred forty. But you're supposed to average three hundred and forty items per hour over the full length of your shift. Does that number seem unfair to you?"

Rhetorical question. He knows better than to answer.

"I assure you it is not an arbitrary number. The number is based on solid research!"

Soggins is starting to squeak and snort air out his nose, like a bull getting ready to charge, a short, pudgy, snorting bull.

"Yes, sir."

"Just for the sake of comparison, how many items do you suppose Roberta averages per hour?"

From her station two registers down, Roberta's trying to pretend she isn't soaking up every word. Roberta is not good at pretending.

"I'm going to guess it's more than three hundred forty," he says. "Probably somewhere between three hundred forty and a million."

A large man with a shaved head noses his shopping cart into the lane behind Soggins and starts drumming his fingers on the counter.

"He's closed," Soggins says, plucking the "Lane Closed" sign from on top of the display of pocket-sized horoscope and diet books and slapping it on the counter.

Shaved-head scowls but wheels away without saying anything. Soggins turns his attention back to the task at hand, reaming Elzie out.

"Roberta averages four hundred and ten items an hour. Four one zero. Day in and day out. She works the same shift you do."

"That Roberta's really something,"

Not the right thing to say. But then, in the three weeks he's been working at the LottaSav, he's not yet said one single, solitary right thing to his shift manager, or "Sales Associate First Class," or whatever the hell he calls himself.

"Do you know how many items per hour you averaged during your last shift, son?"

"No, sir."

"Would you like to take a guess?"

"I'd guess we're talking somewhere under three hundred forty."

"You averaged two hundred and twenty-seven, son. Two two seven. That's a fair piece short of three hundred and forty, isn't it, son?"

"Precisely one hundred and thirteen items short, sir."

"Kind of pathetic, don't you think?"

"Yes, sir. It's pathetic, all right."

"Why do you think you're so slow?"

"I'm extra careful?"

Soggins leans in so close, Elzie can smell the Altoids on his breath. Soggins pops Altoids by the tinful. "I got another theory, Odoms. Would you like to hear my theory?"

Another rhetorical question.

"My theory is that you just don't give a rat's ass. Not about your quota. Not about your job. Not about LottaSav. Not about anything."

Elzie catches himself fiddling with the tie-string of his official dark blue LottaSav apron. He clasps his hands behind his back, although he'd rather wrap them around Soggins' mushy neck.

"That's not entirely true," he says.

"What's that?"

"I said, 'that's not entirely true.' I do give a rat's ass about my job."

Soggins scowls, not sure whether he's being put on or not. He is among the irony impaired. Irony Deficiency Syndrome. They're no doubt developing a drug for it.

"Listen, here, son. You're flat-out running out of places that'll hire you in this town. I know you got a raw deal with your ma and your brother and all, but you've by God got to suck it up and get with the program here! Am I getting through to you at all?"

"Yes, sir. I read you loud and clear."

Soggins folds his spindly arms over his concave chest. "Just what do you suggest I do, son?"

"Raise Roberta's quota?"

Elzie catches her watching him, and she turns away. When he looks back at Soggins, the manager has turned pale purple, like a three-day-old bruise.

"I'll give you one more day to get your IPH up over three hundred. One day! Or you're out on your ass, brother or no brother!"

"Yes, sir."

"That's still forty below quota."

"Yes, sir."

"I don't think that's too much to ask."

"Yes, sir."

"How's that?"

"No, sir. That's not too much to ask."

"Go take your break."

"Yes, sir."

Elzie takes his apron off, resisting the urge to throw it in his face, folds it and puts it on the counter. Soggins picks it up and refolds it. Elzie walks past Roberta on Register Four and Martin on Register One. Roberta is just finishing checking out shaved-head, who glares, making it clear that Elzie is personally responsible for his shitty life. He's adding at least twenty-five items to Roberta's IPH.

Roberta glances at Elzie, and he mouths the words, "Reamed again."

She frowns. Her eyes fill with pity. "I'm sorry, Elzie," she mouths.

"It ain't nothing," Elzie says aloud. "It ain't nothing at all."

There's nobody in the break room, which suits Elzie fine. Somebody has made a mess of the daily *Distress*. He shoves the paper on the floor, sits in one of the plastic chairs, puts his feet up on the table, and fires up a Camel, drawing the smoke deep.

He used to get on his mother pretty good for smoking, and now, here he is, sucking on a cancer stick himself. He even smokes her brand. When he first started buying, he'd say they were for her, so he had to get her brand, and he stuck with them. When he coughs, he even sounds like her.

He wonders if she's still smoking. If she's still breathing, he figures, she's still smoking. She was never one to let loose of a good bad habit.

He fishes the *Distress* off the floor and gives the front page a sniff. Banner headline: "FLETCHER DOWNS TO SPEAK AT WWW NOON FORUM." In smaller letters, underneath: "PUBLIC INVITED" Big picture of Fletcher Downs, same one they've been running for a month to pimp him. Whenever anybody famous deigns to favor little Sheepdip with a visitation, the *Distress* falls all over itself. Downs looks the part of "famous author." All he needs is the pipe and the hunting dog.

He rips out the photo and sticks it in his pocket.

"Hey, retard."

Martin's standing in the doorway, striking a pose. He always looks like somebody's pointing a camera at him. Elzie gets up real slow, ignoring him, and saunters over to the door, like he's going back to work. Only he grabs Martin by the shirtfront and tries to muscle him up against the wall, like they do in the gangster movies. Muscling is not one of his talents.

Soggins chooses that moment to come barging in.

"Hey! Quit the horseplay! If you don't need a break, you can just go back to work."

He actually said "horseplay." Unbelievable.

When Elzie lets go of Martin's shirt, Martin slaps at Elzie's hand, and Elzie pushes him.

"Now!" Soggins says.

"Call me a retard again," Elzie says, jamming Martin against the wall with his shoulder, "and I'll rearrange your ugly face for you."

"Try it, asshole."

"Just say it."

"I take it all back. Your brother's the retard. You're just the retard's brother."

"I said now!" Soggins shouts.

"If I catch you messing with my brother, I'll lay you out," Elzie says, glaring at Martin.

He gives Martin a final shove and pushes his way past him and out the door.

By the time Mo drives up the narrow, winding lane to Merrynook, the sun has slipped below the treetops. The group renting the large cabin across from the play area has started a fire inside the large circle of rocks outside the cabin, and beer cans line the porch railing. There seem to be three sets of parents, an extra adult, and a dozen children or more staying in the one large cabin. Mo creeps past, waving at one of the children, who has one hand stuck in the lower half of her two-piece swimsuit and is sucking the thumb of her other hand.

Doug's on the porch to meet her. He has showered and put on the good slacks and dress shirt and sports coat he insisted on bringing.

"I'm sorry I'm late. You'll never believe—"

But he bounds down the steps and sweeps her up into a hug, lifting her off the ground. "I missed you," he whispers.

"I can see that! Put me down!"

He does, but only to wrap her in a hug and dip her, going for her lips but kissing her nose instead.

"You must have caught a lot of fish!" Mo says, gasping when he releases her.

"Not a one. I got skunked. Humiliated in front of my brother fishermen. A six-year-old girl outfished me."

"Oh, dear!"

"I wasn't looking forward to having to clean them anyway."

"So, no fish for dinner, huh?"

"You can have anything you want for dinner. We're going out."

"Great!"

"Let's just drive out east on the highway and see what's out that way. There's bound to be a supper club."

"I thought you said you'd never eat at anyplace that calls itself a 'supper club.'"

"I'm in the mood for a little relish tray, with radishes and celery." He kisses her again, this time without the dip. "You can order a Gibson with onions and olives."

"I have to change!"

"Don't you dare change a thing. You look perfect, lady, just the way you are."

The flames from the family bonfire leap up dangerously close to the branches of an overhanging pine as they drive back out.

"So, what did you learn in school today, dear little girl of mine?" he asks as soon as he has maneuvered them onto the two-lane highway, heading away from town.

"Fletcher Downs didn't show up, and the director asked me to fill in."

"Yeah? What did you have to do?"

"I gave the noon forum and taught a class. Not taught. 'Facilitated.'"

"I wish I could have been there. I'll bet you had them rolling in the aisles."

"Or running up them, trying to escape."

"I doubt that. It amazes me, the way you can get up in front of a group and be so relaxed and funny."

"Funny, maybe. I'm sure not relaxed."

"Really? When I've seen you speak, you didn't seem nervous."

"Actually, the talk seemed to go fairly well. How about this place?"

Doug slows for a sign announcing "The Essen Haus," just ahead on the right. A car roars past. The forest on the right opens into a dirt parking lot, nearly empty, and a large stone fortress of a building with drooping awning.

"Naw," Doug says, accelerating back onto the highway. "Looks like a dump. So, this Downs character pulled a disappearing act, huh?"

"He didn't even let anybody know he wasn't coming. Nobody's seen him since yesterday."

"His agent must have gotten him a better offer. Hey—look at that. A drive-in movie. It looks like it's open. The Highway 8 Skyview. How about that?"

"It must have a very short season," Mo says.

"You want to go? After dinner, I mean? I've never been to one."

"Really?"

"I know. Positively un-American, isn't it?"

"That must be a good place up ahead. Lots of cars. Well-lit parking lot.

What's the sign say?"

As they draw closer, Doug laughs. "Dorn Ford Lincoln Mercury. I'll slow down so you can see what the nightly specials are."

"A car dealership, way out here in the middle of nowhere."

"Folks in the Northwoods buy cars, too."

"I thought everybody up here drove a pickup."

Past the car dealership, the forest deepens around them. Darkness is gathering, only a pale glow lingering in the western sky behind them. A star appears low on the horizon.

"Maybe we should turn around," she says. "We seem to have left civilization."

"Oh, ye of little faith."

A car passes in the other direction. The road makes a long, slow bend to the right. When they are again on the straightaway, she sees the sign ahead on the left, neon blinking against the forest.

"EAT," it says, then blinks out. "AT." Blink. "EATON'S."

The cycle repeats as Doug slows and they turn in at a broad parking lot, about half full of vehicles, mostly bulky sedans and coupes.

"Looks like a high class joint," Doug says.

"I'm not dressed for anything too fancy."

"This is the Northwoods, honey. Nothing gets too fancy."

Beneath the blinking neon, a lit marquee announces, "The Musical Stylings of Mr. Francis Fontaine nightly on the 9' Steinway."

Doug parks the car between a block-long Lincoln Continental and a stubby silver Cadillac. She waits for him to circle the car and open the door for her. She takes his arm, and they cross the lot and enter a dimly lit entrance hall with coatroom to the left, restrooms to the right. They approach a lectern, where a short, thin man, perhaps Filipino, in red coat, black slacks, white shirt and black tie waits, smiling.

"And you are—?"

"We are," Doug agrees happily. "And we eat."

"We don't have a reservation," Mo puts in.

"Actually, we do," Doug tells him. "Stennett. Two."

The tables filling the vast room behind the maître d' are only about a third occupied. Each is set with stiff white linen, and each has a candle-lit lantern in the center. The light glints off the silverware and the wine and water goblets.

"Ah. Mr. Stennett." The man scans a large seating chart on the lectern, as if looking for some possible way to squeeze them in. "This way, please." He grabs two large bound menus from the rack on the lectern, turns, and strides into the room.

"Walk this way," Doug says, grinning as he imitates the determined swing of the man's shoulders.

He shows them to a table for four near a small stage holding what must be the nine-foot Steinway grand.

"Your waiter will be Johnny this evening," he says, holding a chair for Mo. "Would you like to look at the wine list?" He scoops up the two extra place settings.

"Yes, please. And the lady would like a Gibson. Olives and onions."

The man produces a wine list from under his arm and sets it, open, before Doug before bustling off.

"We're the youngest people here," Mo notes, scanning the room.

"Pretentious and grossly overpriced," Doug says, looking up from the wine list.

"How did you find this place?"

"Ethel Wilkerson recommended it. Said it was the perfect place for a guy to take his best girl."

"What's the occasion?"

"We're still celebrating your birthday." His dark eyes turn serious. He brushes at a stray lock of hair curling on his forehead. "Long overdue," he says. "You were quite right, what you said when you got back from your sister's."

"I was as much to blame as you. We were both neglecting our marriage."

A man who could be the maitre'd's twin, only with a thin black mustache, materializes at Doug's shoulder.

"I am Johnny," he says, bowing slightly. "I will take care of you this evening."

"Wonderful! I'm Doug, and I'm ready to be taken care of."

A smile splits Johnny's face. "You would like to hear tonight's specials?"

"Nope. The lady would like a Gibson, onions and olives, and I'll have a glass of house red. For dinner, we'll start with tossed salad, honey mustard dressing on the side, chateaubriand for two, medium rare, baked potatoes, no butter or sour cream for me, but give my sour cream to the lady."

"Yes, sir." Johnny bows again. "Very good."

"I'm so glad you're pleased."

Johnny smiles again. "You funny man," he says.

"Oh, he's a riot," Mo assures him.

"I take your order," Johnny says, spinning and hurrying toward the kitchen behind her.

"My goodness," Mo says. "You rarely eat steak. No pun intended."

"Only on very special occasions. I wonder where they got their staff. They certainly don't look local."

A third short, compact Filipino man in red jacket and black pants parts the curtain behind the small, elevated stage to Mo's left and skitters around the piano to a floor mike by the piano stool. Gripping the mike stand as if to prevent it from running away, he blows on the mike, producing a sharp popping.

"Ladies and gentleman, Eaton proud to present to you the musical styling of Mr. Francis Fontaine."

He jumps down and hurries off. The curtain parts, and a large man in a tuxedo emerges. He has to turn sideways to edge around the piano without falling off the stage. Acknowledging a smattering of applause, he bows deeply, his long, white hair cascading over his face. He stays that way for several seconds before straightening and sweeping his hair back with one large hand.

"Thank you so very much, ladies and gentlemen," he says into the microphone. He is already sweating, and the dim light of the dining room glistens on his cheeks. "I am so very pleased to be able to share this evening of song with you.

"I do take requests, ladies and gentlemen. Show tunes a specialty. If I don't know it, I'll make something up. And in fact, this first song is a request."

He brushes back his coattails before settling on the bench, in right profile to the room. As he begins to play, Doug gets up from his chair, comes around the table, and takes the chair next to Mo. He takes her hand in both of his.

"What are you—?"

"Listen."

The musical stylings of Mr. Francis Fontaine seem to favor a great deal of extra flourishes, and it's a moment before Mo recognizes the song.

"That's that Carole King song. Did you request it?"

"I did. Yes, ma'am."

"You had this whole thing planned."

He ducks his head, a little boy caught in a good deed.

When the song is over, they both applaud loudly.

"And now, ladies and gentlemen, it's show time!" Francis Fontaine roars, not using and not needing the microphone. He launches into an extravagant medley from *The Music Man*, ranging up and down the keyboard, throwing his hands back over his shoulders, pushing his wavy hair back with a forearm, all without missing a flourish.

Doug leans over and whispers, "Rumors of Liberace's death were apparently greatly exaggerated."

Paying no attention to the musical marathon a few feet away, Johnny brings their drinks and moves Doug's place setting over for him. The long-stemmed Gibson glass is frosted, and a wooden skewer holding three onions and three olives sticks from the top. Francis Fontaine keeps up a steady stream of oldies, broken only by occasional patter, as Doug and Mo enjoy their drinks and salad and dig into the chateaubriand. They are contemplating the dessert menu when the pianist finally stands.

"You're most kind, ladies and gentlemen," he says, the sweat pouring off him. "Thank you so very, very much. I always conclude the set with the same number. It has become my signature."

"'My Way,'" Doug hisses. "Wanna bet?"

She shushes him.

"This was written by a very talented songwriter named Mr. Paul Anka—"

Mo jumps when Doug elbows her.

"—especially for his dear friend, Mr. Francis Albert Sinatra. You may have heard Mr. Elvis Presley perform this song. Here's my rendition of—'My Way.'"

"Don't you dare laugh," Mo hisses. "Or sing along."

Francis Fontaine struggles a bit lowering the mircophone on its pole. When he gets it adjusted to his satisfaction, he again fluffs out his coattails, sits, and remains motionless for several moments.

"Worst song ever written," Doug whispers as the pianist plays the introduction. "With the possible exception of 'Bright Elusive Butterfly of Love' or 'MacArthur Park.'"

"Hush!"

In a serviceable baritone, Mr. Fontaine renders words to accompany his piano stylings. When he finishes, Doug stands and leads the applause.

Johnny brings Mo her dessert, a small wedge of key lime pie, and she's actually able to coax Doug into taking a taste.

"I'd like to ride into town with you tomorrow morning," Doug announces when they are back on the road. "If it's all right."

"Of course it's all right! But what about fishing?"

"The fish will never miss me."

"Do you want to sit in on a class?"

"Actually, there's a fellow in town I want to chat with. Runs a little baseball memorabilia shop on Philips Street. Fred Wilkerson told me about him. He says he used to play ball professionally. Fanning, I think he said. Fred Fanning."

"He probably has stories to tell. Maybe I should use him for my interview for class."

"I want to look around and see if there's anyplace with access in town, too."

"I thought you weren't going to work while we were up here."

"I just want to look up a few things."

"Things like stock prices?"

"Other things, too."

"There's a computer lab at the school. They have Internet access. I'm sure they'd let you use it."

"Great. I'll meet you after your afternoon class. We can go out for dinner afterwards."

"Eaton's again?"

He laughs. "As wonderful as it was, maybe we can try another place tomorrow." He glances over at her. "If you want to go in early, there's a daily Mass in town, too."

"Is there?"

"Yeah. Fred and Ethel are good Lutherans, but they have a list of all the area churches. St. Joe's lists a daily Mass at six-thirty. It's about a mile west of town. You just take the highway all the way through town."

"Are you saying you'll go to Mass with me?"

"Unless you think the roof might cave in on us."

"Isn't that our turn?"

"We pass a trailer park on the left first."

"Doug, I don't know what to say. You've never—"

"Don't read too much into this. It won't kill me to go to a Mass with you once in awhile. Unless you mind."

"Of course I don't mind! How about this one? This looks familiar."

"Not yet. There's a big sign, remember?"

An occasional light shows through the trees, perhaps indicating the presence of one of the isolated cabins that dot the area, but otherwise, the black of the forest merges with the black of the sky. It's as if they're driving in a long tunnel. They pass the car dealership and then the Essen Haus.

"Did Mrs. Wilkerson tell you anything else interesting?" Mo asks to break the silence.

"Yeah. In fact she did! She said that last summer a country western singer got drunk and took a little late-night dip in the river. He never came up."

"That's terrible!"

"I guess Mitchell isn't the only little town where people turn up dead now and again."

"He wasn't murdered, though, was he?"

"She attributes it to demon rum. She also said that a rodeo cowboy died here the year before. Got hit by a train. He'd been drinking, too."

"Good heavens."

"There's the sign, see? Our turn's right up ahead."

Two men sit drinking beer by the embers of the evening's bonfire as Doug pilots the CR-V past them. When he parks and snaps off the lights, the darkness rushes in on them. A light from across the lake glimmers on the inky waters. The silence is absolute.

She leans into his kiss. "It's been a lovely evening," she says. "Thank you."

"I don't think we'll soon forget the musical stylings of Mr. Francis Fontaine."

She laughs with him. Silence reclaims them.

"Would you care to come in for a nightcap? I'll show you my collection of stuffed owls."

"You sure do know how to sweet talk a gal."

They bump hips walking up the three steps to their porch with their arms around each other's waists, and he laughs.

"Shhh. We'll scandalize Mrs. Wilkerson."

"She's probably got the binoculars on us right now."

She tries to share his laugh, but the mention of death has sobered her, making her think again of the tragic murders of two of the people she had come to call friend in their adopted hometown. But when Doug actually scoops her up and carries her into the cabin, she allows herself to be swept away by his rare bubbly mood. Their lovemaking drives death right out of her mind, at least for the night.

13

Roberta's standing out by the curb, acting like she's waiting for somebody.

"Hot date tonight?" Elzie says.

She blushes. "I'm sorry Soggins got so mad at you," she says.

The parking lot's almost empty, and there's only one lane lit up inside. Martin doesn't get off for another hour. Then he and Soggins will close up. Somebody comes out of the pizza joint at the end of the mall, a girl and a guy. Date night in Sheepdip.

"He just likes to have somebody to chew on," Elzie says.

"I could help. Show you how to scan faster."

"That's right. You're Roberta the IPH queen."

"I don't mean it like that. I've just been doing it longer."

"How long have you been working for dear old LottaSav?"

"I started working after school when I was a sophomore."

"Stick with it. When you die, they'll toss a seventy-five-year service pin into the box with you."

He starts to walk across the parking lot.

"I know why you're being so mean," she says to his back.

"Who says I'm being mean?"

"It's because this is when it happened, isn't it?"

She catches up to him, her hands jammed in her sweater pockets. She's hunched over like she's freezing cold.

"When what happened?"

He crowds her, smelling her sweat. She starts blinking and looks away.

"You know," she says.

"What do you know about it?"

She shrugs. She still can't look at him. "Just what everybody else knows."

"They don't know anything."

"Don't you get lonely sometimes?"

The doors hiss open behind them, and a woman dangling a plastic LottaSav sack from each paw shuffles out. She sees them and veers off, almost falling off the curb.

They're almost to the DQ when Elzie stops to fire up a Camel. A breeze cools the sweat on his face. Roberta's really puffing from trying to keep up.

"Do you want an ice cream?" she says. "I'll treat."

"They don't have any ice cream."

She frowns, confused. "At the Dairy Queen?"

"It isn't ice cream. It's chemical slop."

She goes inside. He finishes his cigarette, and then he goes in. There's nobody else in there, just the skinny skank behind the counter. She's got the Goth look, black hair, black lipstick, white skin, nobody home behind the eyes.

Roberta orders a cone, and Elzie gets a large Reese's Pieces Blizzard. She pays. Three stools and a counter line the window. She plops her big rump on one of the stools, and he climbs up on the third one, leaving one between them. He starts working on his Blizzard, but when he comes up for air, she's just sitting there, staring at him. Her vanilla slop is starting to run down the sides of the cone.

"You'd better start licking."

She takes a lick, getting white glop on the tip of her nose.

"I told Dr. Fleeger about you," she says.

"Who's Dr. Fleeger?"

"My therapist."

"You're kidding me. You are kidding me! You were talking about me with a therapist?"

"I share everything with Dr. Fleeger. That's the only way she can help me."

"Help you do what?"

The slop is starting to run down onto her hand, but she doesn't seem to notice.

"I've told you," she says in her tiny voice.

The skank has gone in back someplace, so they've got the place to themselves.

"Tell me again."

"I have self-esteem issues."

"Hard to believe," he says, jabbing the little red plastic spoon into his Blizzard. "A stunner like you."

"You enjoy hurting me," she says.

"Aw, come on, Roberta. I'm just kidding a pal. We're pals, aren't we?"

She looks right at him then. Her eyes are some kind of green, but in this light, they look almost red.

"Are we, Elzie? Are we pals?"

He reaches out, takes the cone from her, and tosses it into the wastebasket under the counter. She looks down at her hand.

He hands her a couple of napkins from the little dispenser on the counter, and she tries to pat the goop off.

"What did you say about me to Dr. Feelgood? You tell her I'm being mean to you?"

"I told her about your mother!"

He scrapes out the last of his Blizzard and dumps the cup and spoon in the can. "Did you decide I have low self-esteem, too?"

"She says you have abandonment issues and that you feel guilty."

Her wrist is sticky from the cone. Pain registers on her face. She's not scared, though. She's got a spine after all.

"You're hurting me."

"You got no right," he says, releasing her. "Talking about me with your shrink."

"I wish you'd talk to her. She could help you."

"I don't need help!"

The Goth skank's back behind the counter, and she's looking at him as if he's sprouted fur and fangs. He winks at her, and she gets busy counting peanuts or something.

"I don't need help," he says again, real quiet, like Clint Eastwood in the Dirty Harry movies. "I just need people to keep their noses out of my business."

"You might lose your job, Elzie."

"Big whoop."

He snatches another napkin out of the dispenser and dabs the goop off her nose. "The jails are full of people with high self-esteem," he says.

And then, because that's such a damn good exit line, he gets up and leaves.

14

The side door to the church is locked, so Doug and Mo walk around to the front, where a glassed-in sign announces, "St. Joseph's Catholic Church. Masses 9:00 and 11:00 Sunday. Daily Mass 6:30 AM MWF and 12:00 noon TTh. Eucharistic adoration T 12:30-3:30. Confessions by appointment. Monsignor Bernard Callahan, pastor."

A car drives by slowly, a middle-aged woman driving.

"Attendance doesn't seem to be brisk for the early Mass," Doug says.

Mo tries the door handle, but the door's locked.

"This is Wednesday, right?"

They walk back to the sign. Doug checks his watch. "I guess you have to know the secret password or something," he says.

"You're limping again."

"My heel's bothering me a little."

"But you ran this morning anyway."

He kisses his fingertip and touches it to the tip of her nose. "It's not bad," he says.

They wait a few more minutes, but when it's clear that nobody is coming, they drive back through neighborhoods of small, ramshackle houses, most of them showing signs of having been indifferently cared for. They have no trouble finding a parking place on Philips, Shepherdstown's version of Main Street.

"That's one of the questions on my quiz for research methods," Mo says as they get out of the car on opposite sides. "'What's wrong with Philips Street?'"

"I'll tell you one thing that's wrong with it. Look at this. Parking meters on the buildings instead of out by the curbs! I'll bet a lot of folks don't even see them."

He digs around in his pockets for change.

"You wouldn't think a town this size would have parking meters at all," Mo says.

"I don't know why they bother. It's only ten cents for an hour."

Doug inserts a dime in the meter and twists the dial, and the little needle lurches up to the one hour marker halfway across the dial. They are the only ones on the sidewalk at this hour. Music pours from a speaker on the signal pole at the corner, the singer proclaiming himself to be "like a rubber ball" that bounces back to "you—oo—oo—oo—oo!"

The sign in the window of "Vic Paul Clothier" says, "We'll pay your parking ticket for purchases over $50."

They wait at the corner of Philips and North for the town's sole traffic light to change. The walk sign lights, but a few seconds later, it starts to blink its warning as they hurry across.

"The Humdrung Café. What do you think?" Mo asks.

He peers in at the window. "Looks clean enough, I guess."

"Come on. Let's give it a try."

The seven old-timers occupying the stools along the counter glance up as Mo and Doug enter.

"I don't think we have to wait for the maître d' to seat us," Doug says.

He fishes an abandoned copy of the morning *Milwaukee Journal-Sentinel* from the counter as they pass. They take the second of four booths, all empty, along the wall to their left. The middle-aged waitress comes to take their order and fill their coffee mugs. Doug orders apple wheat pancakes, no butter, no syrup, and Mo tries the "Humdrung omelet." They swap sections of the paper while they wait for their food.

"So, tell me how you plan to spend your day in greater downtown Shepherdstown," Mo prompts while they dig into their meals.

"I'll definitely check out the baseball card shop and browse the bookstore. Maybe hit the library, see if they have any local histories."

"My last class doesn't get done until two-thirty."

"Don't worry about me. I'll find plenty to do."

"I just hope you don't get bored."

"Couldn't be worse than fishing."

The town is waking up as they get back out on the sidewalk. Doug has to wait for three cars and two pickups to pass before he's able to back out from the curb. The morning rush, Shepherdstown style. He drives Mo the two miles west of town to the campus and pulls up in front of the main building to drop her off.

"You be a good girl in school today," he says as she leans over for a goodbye kiss. "Do what teacher tells you."

"I will. Don't let the humdrung get you."

She closes the door behind her, and Doug reflexively locks it. She taps on the window, and he lets it down with the automatic switch.

"Could you get me some sunscreen? I want to get out to the lake this afternoon."

"Sure."

"We passed something called the LottaSav on the way in. They'll have it."

"Probably a couple hundred brands. I hate those places!"

"I know you do. Maybe there's a little pharmacy downtown."

"I'll check."

"Thanks."

Driving back into town, which is 2.4 miles from campus by the odometer, Doug feels sudden elation, a heady sense of adventure. Really should do this sort of thing more often, he decides. Funny how hard it is to pull yourself away from the daily routine, but once you're exploring someplace new, home seems so far away, almost another life.

Their space in front of the café has been filled, so Doug parks across the street. The card shop isn't open yet; Doug walks to the barbershop next door, where a thickset man in white apron, rumpled tan slacks, and cheap plastic sandals with white socks sits in the only barber chair, reading the morning newspaper from Duluth. Two men occupy chairs flanking the floor ashtray under a mirror that runs almost the length of the wall across from the barber chair. One man is smoking a cigar, his face shrouded in smoke. The other chews a toothpick. Both look as if they might have been in those chairs for decades.

The barber glances up from his paper. The two men in the chairs give no acknowledgment of his presence, but Doug feels sure they've checked him out.

"Haircut?"

"I guess I could use some tidying up."

The barber extracts himself from the chair with a grunt. "I guess I'm up to a little tidying this morning."

He takes out a whiskbroom from his apron pocket and makes an elaborate show of cleaning off the chair where he's been sitting.

"Hop aboard."

The barber's license on the wall behind the chair bears the name John Burkess and carries the likeness of a much younger version of the man who ties a white bib around Doug's neck. The license was issued in 1953.

"Nice head of hair," he notes.

He flourishes a long scissors, making it clack like a musical instrument. He combs Doug's hair straight back and begins snipping rapidly.

"You're out early," he comments.

"I took my wife to the early Mass at St. Joseph's, but it was locked up. The sign said they're supposed to have Mass Wednesday at six-thirty."

"Monsignor lost his associate last year. He's had to cut back."

Locks of Doug's black hair flutter to the floor.

"You here for that writers deal?"

"My wife is. I'm just along for the ride."

"Your wife's a writer, is she?"

"Edits a weekly newspaper. She used to have a column in the *Chicago Tribune*."

"The *Trib*, huh? You folks from the Windy City?"

"I was born and raised there. She grew up on a farm in Iowa. We moved to Mitchell thirty-two months ago."

"Cubs or Sox?"

"Cubs."

"Too bad."

The man with the toothpick laughs. The man with the cigar might be asleep with his eyes open except for the occasional puff of smoke.

"Where you folks staying?"

"Out at Merrynook."

"The Wilkersons. Nice folks."

"Yes, they are."

"Doing any fishing?"

"I got out after them yesterday."

"Doing any catching?"

"I'm afraid not. The fish must be too smart for me."

"Mister, there's very few things on this earth dumber than a fish. You're looking at two of 'em right now."

Toothpick gives Burkess the upraised middle digit. The other man just grins around his cigar and sends up a smoke signal.

The bell over the door jingles as a short, fat man wearing a tattered white T-shirt and low-slung khaki shorts with suspenders barges in.

"Hey, John, Gerry's got candy bars five for a dollar, he's got Snickers and Hershey bars, you want me to get you some, I can get you some candy bars."

"Just coffee, Lloyd. Thanks. You get yourself some candy bars, though, OK?"

Burkess stops his snipping long enough to pull three one-dollar bills out of his pocket and place them in Lloyd's upturned palm.

"Thanks, John, I'll bring back some candy bars, maybe these fellas would like some, I'll get all kinds, he's got all kinds of candy bars, five for a dollar."

Lloyd's still talking as the door closes behind him.

"Gerry's got candy bars," the barber says, resuming his snipping. "Five for a dollar."

"So I gathered. Who *was* that?" Doug asks.

"What was that, you mean," Toothpick says.

"That's Lloyd. He hasn't been right since he got clonked with a metal swing when he was just a tad. He's harmless."

"I ain't so sure of that," Cigar rouses himself long enough to say. "Little bastard's got a temper on him."

The barber scoffs. "He just gets impatient, is all. Must be frustrating, being simple like that."

In a few minutes the barber swings the chair around and gives Doug a hand mirror.

"You want any more off?"

"No. You took off plenty."

The barber gives him a dusting with the talc brush and sweeps the bib off, snapping it in the air to shake out the hair. The sign next to the license on the wall lists "Haircut $8.00." Doug gives him a ten and tells him to keep the change.

"Do you know when that card shop opens?"

"When Fred Fanning feels like opening it. The bastard hasn't been in here for a haircut in fifteen years."

Toothpick laughs again.

Doug rubs his neck as he walks up the block. He'll have to take another shower before going to bed, or his neck will itch and keep him awake. He sees his reflection in the window of a furniture store, and it strikes him that he is a man at leisure. He likes the thought. It's been a long time since he's felt leisurely.

Lloyd reminds him of Mo's slow friend, Dilly, back in Mitchell. In the city, folks like that end up panhandling on downtown streets and sleeping in doorways—or in jail. But small towns have a way of assimilating them. They have their place, such as it is.

The sign in the window of the card shop offers "Sports Collectibles," but the window display includes comic books, graphic novels, old lunch boxes with images of TV cowboys and space cadets, and lots of other non-sports-related treasures.

Finding the door open, Doug goes inside and browses the packed shelves. He takes down a battered volume of the Rover Boys and sees that it's marked fifteen dollars in pencil on the inside flyleaf. He's tempted to buy it and notes its location when he puts it back on the shelf. Since Mo inherited Father O'Bannon's collection of signed first editions, Doug has started taking an interest in old books as an investment.

A man in his thirties, with dark, oily skin and curly black hair down over his shoulders, emerges from a side doorway and approaches, rubbing the palms of his hands on his denim pants.

"Help you find something?"

"I'm just enjoying looking, if that's all right. You've got some great stuff."

"Thanks. Lots more in back. Any particular team you're interested in?"

"Cubs."

"Got lots of Cubs. Got lots of everything." The man sizes him up. "You grew up with Ernie, Ronnie, and Sweet Billy Williams, I bet. Fergie Jenkins. Kenny Holtzman."

"You got it," Doug says, grinning. "I'm interested in the old timers, too."

"I got the whole 1944 Cubbies team. Nicholson, Cavarretta. Nicholson led the league in home runs and ribbies that year."

"Strikeouts, too."

"You got it. Freddie Fanning." The man reaches across the counter to shake hands.

"Doug Stennett."

"I'm a Milwaukee Braves man myself. I've got the complete team from 1957, the year they beat the Yankees in the World Series."

"Spahn, Burdette, Aaron. A great team."

"Schoendiest made the difference. Once they got the redhead, you knew they could win it all. Just a minute. I'll get them." Fred goes into the back room and comes back four minutes later, bearing a metal box. He sets it carefully on the counter, opens it, and lovingly extracts a thin plastic holder.

"What's wrong with this picture?" he asks, handing the holder over.

"The backward Henry Aaron! In mint condition. Must be worth a lot."

"Couple hundred, tops. They didn't catch the mistake and ran the whole series this way. There's still a lot of them floating around."

"Too bad."

"I wouldn't sell it anyway."

He hands Doug the other holders, one at a time, Warren Spahn, Joe Adcock, Johnny Logan—

"Frank Torre! Joe's big brother. That's right—he played behind Adcock at first and did some pinch hitting."

"Remember this guy?"

"'Hurricane' Bob Hazel. He tore up the league after they called him up from the bushes."

"Who'd he replace?"

"Billy Bruton."

"Hey, you're good."

"Whatever happened to Hazel?"

"Hurt his arm or shoulder or something in spring training the next year, got sent down, and never made it back to the bigs."

"A one-season wonder."

"That's one season more than most people get."

"That's true."

Doug talks a lot more baseball with Fred Fanning—it's one of the few things that can slow him down—before finally buying a set of contemporary Cubs cards for his son, Lawrence, although it's been years since he's shown any interest in collecting them.

"Been real nice chatting with you," Fanning tells him as he hands the paper sack across the counter. "You gonna be in town for awhile?"

"This week and next. I might be back in. There's a lot to see."

"Any time."

Now that he's bought something for his son, he decides to get a gift for his daughter, Cynthia, too. He heads two doors down to the Philips Street Bookstore. The sign on the door announces, "Finbar O'Brien, Primary Print Purveyor."

A poster on a table just inside the door bears a large color photo of a smiling man with wavy silver hair. "Author Signing, Wednesday Night, 7:30," the thick black type under the photo proclaims. "Fletcher Downs, author of *Blood Brothers*." A pyramid of the novels covers most of the rest of the table.

"You must be expecting quite a crowd tonight," Doug says to the redheaded man sitting on a stool behind the counter. The man looks up from the book he's reading, snaps the book shut, and stands.

"If he shows. He haven't shown up at the school since Monday."

"He isn't there today either?"

"Not that anybody's seen. He's supposed to teach a class at one o'clock."

"I know. My wife's taking that class."

"Is she now?" The man walks out from behind the counter, hand extended. "Finbar O'Brien," he says, grinning. "Folks call me

Finny. I'm the owner, proprietor, and janitor, except that blessed little cleaning gets done."

Doug takes the shake and returns the grin. "A pleasure."

"Likewise, I'm sure. And you'd be—"

"Douglas Stennett. Doug."

"And what county would your people be from, Douglas Stennett?"

Doug laughs. "It's my wife you'd be wanting to talk to. Monona Quinn, of the Iowa Quinn's, and as Irish as Paddy's pig."

"You don't tell me now? And a writer to boot!"

"Journalist. She runs the paper down in Mitchell."

O'Brien's pale, shaggy eyebrows arch. "Of course—the one who catches the bad guys. I've read about her."

"That's the one."

"My gosh! She's famous, man! She should go on Oprah!"

"That's all we need."

"So, what can I do for you this fine day, Douglas Stennett? I've got books for all interests and ages."

"I'm looking for something for my daughter. She plans to be a professional photographer. At least this week."

"Right this way. I've got a beautiful book of photos by Wisconsin's own Zane Williams that will take your breath away. I've even got a signed copy."

Doug tucks the book under his arm and browses the whole store, paying special attention to the small business/finance section. At four minutes before noon, he goes to the counter to pay for the photography book.

"I hope Downs shows up tonight," he says, nodding toward the poster as he hands two twenty-dollar bills across the counter.

"You and me both, brother. I'll have an angry mob on my hands if he doesn't."

Finbar counts out the change into Doug's palm. "You thinking about getting lunch? The little coffee shop next door has wonderful sandwiches and homemade soups and pies."

"I spotted a Subway up the street. I think I'll just head there."

"Suit yourself. You always know what you're getting at a chain, huh?"

Doug finds himself a little shaky with hunger as he waits his turn to place his order at the Subway. Meeting new people exhausts him, and he's done more socializing in one morning than he might do in a typical week.

Seven people are ahead of him, and the line moves slowly.

"Six inch, honey oat, turkey and pepperjack cheese with spicy mustard, tomatoes and red onions," he tells the young lady when it's his turn.

"Hi, Jeannie, you got my sandwich ready yet, I'll eat first and then sweep up and take out the garbage."

The fat little man with suspenders from the barbershop. Lloyd.

"You'll have to wait a couple of minutes, honey," the girl at the register, Jeannie, says. "We're real busy."

"I'm hungry NOW!"

"Shhhh. You have to use your inside voice in here, Lloyd. Remember?"

"I know but—"

"It's OK," says the other worker, who, like Jeannie, looks to be high school age. "I'll make it for him."

"He always orders the same thing," Jeannie tells Doug. "Chicken breast on wheat bread, no mayo, no mustard, no nothing. It's not hard to make. Anything to drink?"

"Just a cup for water, please," Doug says.

"You want chips? A cookie?"

"No. Thank you."

She rings him up and bags his sandwich. "Enjoy," she says.

"I'm sure I will. Thanks."

Doug finds a bench in the shade in a little park at the end of the block, where a small war memorial lists the names of the folks from Shepherdstown who have died in battle. Considering the size of the town, it seems like a long list, 112 names, including seven Heinsons and four Zauphs.

Doug chews each bite carefully a dozen times. He still has almost two hours before Mo will be done with her mystery writing class, and he remembers seeing the newspaper office down the street, so he decides to walk down and see if the afternoon paper is out.

The words painted on the window say "*Shepherdstown Daily Dispatch*," but the bullpen style office could be for a real estate or insurance agency. Each of the three desks holds a computer with large-screen monitor and a modern phone console with headset. Two of the desks are occupied, the one in front by a large woman with thick black-rimmed glasses, who is talking on the phone and typing at the same time, the one to the rear of the room by a young, slender woman with shoulder-length brunette hair. Her fingers are flying over the computer keys the way Mo's do when she's writing.

A stack of thin newspapers sits on the counter separating Doug from the rest of the room. He picks off the top one, notes that it bears the day's date, and scans the centered, all-caps headline: "AUTHOR A NO-SHOW FOR NOON FORUM." The same publicity shot of Fletcher Downs smiles out at him.

"Help you?"

The stocky woman, whose black hair looks as if it could have been sprayed on, has finished her phone call and is addressing him.

"I'd like to buy a copy of today's paper."

"Thirty-five cents. You can just leave it on the counter." The woman turns her attention back to her computer screen.

Doug digs in his pocket for change. "Are you the editor?" he asks.

Without taking her eyes from the screen, the woman nods toward the back of the room. "Becky," she calls. "Somebody to see you."

"Oh, that's OK—"

But the young woman pops up and walks across the room toward him.

"Becky Hafner," she says. "What can I do for you?"

She doesn't look old enough to be the editor of a high school newspaper.

"Douglas Stennett. I was just picking up a copy of the paper."

"You in town for the writer's conference?"

"My wife is. She edits the weekly down in Mitchell."

"Where's that?"

"Southeast of Madison. It's very small, only a couple of thousand."

"Did you say Mitchell?"

"Yes."

"Holy cats! Those murders, the priest and, what was it, a storeowner?"

"The diner."

"Sure. We picked up her stuff off the wire. She's famous."

"So I'm told."

"Wow. She's here? I'm almost embarrassed to have her read my stuff."

"Oh, I'm sure—"

"Tell her not to hold the layout against me. That's all done at the central plant in Wausau. I don't even know what the thing's going to look like until we get the papers."

"I'll tell her."

"If she has any comments on the writing—we run a lot of wire copy and stuff from the syndicates, but I write all the local stuff myself. Millie Van Beuzen is the advertising department." She nods toward the woman at the front desk, who is again typing and talking on the phone. "It's just the two of us."

"Sounds like a lot of work."

Becky shrugs. "Yeah, but the pay's lousy."

Doug laughs. "I wonder if you could help me with a question about the town," he asks.

"Will if I can."

"My wife's taking a research methods class, and the instructor gave them a worksheet. One of the questions is, 'What's wrong with Philips Street?' Do you have any idea what that means?"

She frowns. "There's a lot of things wrong with Philips Street. Maybe it means those stupid parking meters."

"I don't know. It just says—" Doug groans. "I don't think I plugged my meter when I came back from dropping Mo off at campus."

"You'll have a ticket, sure. They finance half the city government with parking violations from tourists. Hey, Millie? What's the matter with Philips Street?"

"What isn't?" Millie shouts back.

"Nothing else specific comes to mind," Becky tells him. "If your wife has a minute and wants to stop by, I'd sure love to meet her."

"I'm sure she'd like that."

"Thanks. And remember to tell her we don't have anything to do with the layout. That's all done in Wausau."

"Right."

He sees the papers tucked under the wiper blade of the CR-V from halfway down the block. Not one but two parking tickets flutter in the early afternoon breeze. Each comes with a small brown envelope, already addressed to the local police department, to hold the twenty-five dollar fine "in lieu of court appearance."

Fifty bucks for a half-day's parking—he might as well be in Chicago. He tucks the tickets in the bills' compartment of his wallet to deal with later.

He's almost back to the campus when he remembers the sunscreen. Cursing himself, he pulls to the side of the road, waits for a lumber truck to rattle by, makes a Y-turn, and speeds back to the LottaSav.

The large, sloped parking lot is only a quarter full. Doug parks and sprints inside.

"Where's the sunscreen?" he asks the plump girl checking out a customer at the nearest register.

"Aisle five," she says without pausing, the items flying over the scanner with a steady beep-beep-beep.

"Thanks."

He hurries to aisle five, limping again on his sore heel, and grabs up the first likely looking tube.

She's handing change to her customer when Doug gets back. There's only one other checker on duty, a skinny kid at register four. His face is covered with acne blossoms.

"Find everything OK?" the girl asks, taking the tube from him. Her nametag identifies her as "Roberta."

"Yes, thanks."

"Didn't you want sunscreen?"

He takes the tube from her and reads the label. "I grabbed the wrong thing. I'm sorry. I do want sunscreen. I'll—"

"That's OK. Hey, Elzie! Take this back to aisle five and get some sunscreen? What strength?" This last is directed at Doug.

"I don't know. Strong, I guess."

The boy, Elzie, shuffles toward aisle five, clearly in no hurry. When he reemerges, he tosses a tube at her, and she fumbles and drops it.

"Thanks a lot," she says.

He says nothing, but the look he throws her is pure malevolence.

Doug pays for the sunscreen with exact change, and Roberta drops the tube into a small plastic LottaSav bag for him, tucking in the receipt.

"You have a real nice day, now," she says, already taking a basket from an older woman next in line and starting to feed her purchases to the scanner.

"Thanks. You, too."

Doug glances back at the store as he walks down the slope. He can't be sure, with the sun glinting off the glass, but he thinks he sees the other checker, Elzie, watching him from the window.

15

The dark blue CR-V turns onto the horseshoe road of the forestry center. Mo walks over to the car as Doug guides it into one of the few vacant spaces in the parking lot in the middle of the curving drive.

"You got a haircut!"

"Yep. Got 'em all cut."

"My goodness! What else did you do?"

"Oh, I had many adventures, my dear."

They walk to the classroom building with arms around each other's waists. Only a few students are seated at the tables in the cafeteria.

"The computer lab is back this way," she says, leading him down a long hallway past the bookstore and several classrooms.

"Did Downs show?"

"Nope. We had a substitute."

"What did the sub do?"

"Nothing, really. Gave us a canned lecture on the elements of fiction. We had each made up a scenario to explain Downs' absence. 'The Case of the Missing Murder Maven.' She said we should be ready to read them in class tomorrow."

"Does the one who gets it right get a prize?"

"I think the prize should be for making up the best story. The truth is probably pretty tame."

"You think?"

"My best guess, he's shacking up with one of the students. Mr. Chandler got a call from Downs's wife this morning, wondering why she hasn't heard from him."

"The guy's got a wife?"

"Yes, the poor thing."

"What did Chandler tell her?"

"I don't know. I imagine the conversation was a bit awkward. Here's the lab."

They enter a small room lined on three walls with computer stations. Two of the stations are in use. Alanna Taylor looks up from the computer at her desk in the center of the room, gets up and approaches them. She is about Mo's size and shape and perhaps ten years older. She's wearing a tailored tan suit, in sharp contrast to the Northwoods casual attire of most of the other teachers and students at the school.

"You must be Doug," she says, extending a hand.

"I guess somebody had to be."

"Doug, this is Alanna Taylor. She runs the computer lab and teaches the research methods class I've been telling you about. Alanna, this is Douglas Stennett."

"I'm so happy to meet you, Mr. Stennett."

"Call me Doug."

"Outside of class, I go by 'Lang.'"

"Have you seen Lester?" Mo asks Alanna. "He was supposed to meet me here."

"No, I haven't seen him all day."

"I hope he's not sick."

"I can assign you a new partner if you want."

"How about if Doug helps me?"

"Works for me."

"Is it OK if he uses one of the computers now?"

"Absolutely! I'm happy to have them in use. As you can see, not many students are taking advantage of the open lab hours."

"Thanks," Doug says, all but rubbing his hands together in his eagerness.

"Just give a holler if you need any help."

"Doug is a techie," Mo tells her. "The computer program hasn't been made he can't figure out."

"Oh, I don't know about that," Doug says, obviously pleased that she said it.

They take stations seven and eight along the back wall, and Mo pulls out her quiz questions. When she glances over at Doug's screen, she sees that he's already accessed his business email account. When she gets her Internet connection, she types in the site address for Google.

She decides to pursue something that's been bothering her since Fletcher Downs' autobiographical ramble in class Monday, a comparison he drew between writing novels and driving at night. It sounded familiar to her, and she decides to check it out. She types "night driving novel writing" on the search line and clicks "Search."

She gets 2,900,000 matches. The second source listed takes her to "The Web's Most Humongous Collection of Writing Quotes," where she finds "Writing a novel is like driving a car at night. You can see only as far as your headlights, but you can make the whole trip that way," attributed to E.L. Doctorow.

"Whatever else he is, Downs is a plagiarist," she says, pointing to the screen.

Doug reads the quote. "What's the old joke around academia? Steal from one source, it's 'plagiarism.' Steal from many sources, it's 'research.'"

Doug goes back to his stock market quotations, and Mo searches the database for the history of Shepherdstown. She's easily able to find the town's original name, "Buck's Lake," and the reason for the change to "Shepherdstown." A man named Phillip Shepherd owned the railroad that was putting in a line through northern Wisconsin to serve the fast-developing logging industry. The city fathers of Buck's Lake persuaded him to run the line through their town by offering to rename the town after him.

She's also able to find the answers to three of the other questions. A man named Jerome Thompson created a grotesque little monster he called the "Humdrung" for the northern Wisconsin State Fair in 1896. When he exhibited it, he stood behind a screen and made his creation appear to move by pulling on wires. The Humdrung was a big hit, and someone—probably Thompson himself—started spreading rumors that a real live Humdrung had been spotted in the woods outside of town. The trickster—again presumed to be Thompson—even created huge Humdrung footprints to support the story. Thompson began telling people he'd seen the Humdrung and invented a whole mythology about it: it could only see at night; it only ate long-haired cats and rotten fish; it liked to rub its scaly back against trees. Despite the absurdity of the monster and the stories, many townsfolk apparently believed in the Humdrung.

Some may have also believed in the giant woodsman known as Paul Bunyan, who was said to have visited the woods near Buck's Lake, thus tying the area to Bemidji, Minnesota, which Bunyan and the great blue ox, Babe, were alleged to call home.

Bunyan would have been a welcome addition to the lineup of the Buck's Lake Loggers, who played town baseball at Harvey

Pinyon Stadium on Sundays at the turn of the century, the site of what is now the county fairgrounds.

That took care of questions three through seven and question nine. For number ten, she has to invent her own question. But that still left one, two, and eight: how did Allen's Alley and the Triangle Market get their names, and what is wrong with Philips Avenue?

"I'm going to have to do some legwork downtown," she tells Doug. "I need to find somebody to interview anyway."

"You should interview the characters I met at the barbershop."

She gathers up her purse and notebooks, and they head back down the hall.

"I had a thought about your missing mystery teacher," Doug says.

"What's that?"

"Remember how you said he was probably shacking up with a student? Well, wouldn't that mean that one of his female students would be AWOL, too?"

"It might. Everybody was there in the mystery writing class this afternoon. All the women, anyway."

"How about the males? Maybe Downs swings from the other side of the plate."

"Lester wasn't there, but I really can't see the two of them together."

"Anybody else?"

"Yes, actually. Elsworth Priestly hasn't been back since he walked out of class yesterday."

"Interesting."

"I don't know, Doug. Downs struck me as being aggressively hetero."

"It wouldn't have to be a student from that class, would it?"

"I guess not. Let's check at the office."

They find Gen Beringer sitting at the desk in the office commandeered for the writers' conference. Herman Chandler had introduced her at the first noon forum as "The heart and soul of WWW." President of the local chapter of the Regional Arts Council, she had been volunteering at the conference for as long as anybody could remember.

She looks up, squinting behind her thick glasses as if trying to bring Mo and Doug into focus.

"Yes? May I help you?"

"I was wondering if any of the writing students missed class the last two days."

"Now why would you want to know a thing like that?" She folds her hands and places them in front of her on the desk.

"I was just—wondering."

"I see. Well. I have no way of knowing that information. We don't process the attendance until the end of the summer when we issue the continuing education units." She turns her gaze on Doug. "And you would be—?"

"I'm sorry. This is my husband, Douglas. I'm Monona Quinn. I'm taking three classes."

"Yes. I know who you are."

"Doug, this is Gen Beringer. She's the—"

"Onsite Administrator. We process the attendance reports at the end of the summer, when we issue the CEUs. The State requires that we be able to certify that those students granted CEUs have actually earned them through their attendance in classes."

"And a CEU would be—?" Doug asks.

"Continuing Education Unit."

"Ah. Continuing Education Unit. Is that like college credit?"

"No, Mr. Quinn. It is not like college credit."

"It's Stennett, actually. Douglas Stennett."

"Doug, maybe we should—"

"What are CEUs good for, then?"

The woman takes a deep breath, huffing the air out through her nose. "Many teachers use them for in-service certification," she says slowly, as if explaining for a very slow child or a non-native speaker. "Some receive merit pay increases based on their attendance at conferences such as these."

"Doug? We'd better get going. Thanks so much. Sorry to have troubled you."

"No trouble at all. That's what I'm here for."

"Who *is* she?" Doug asks as they walk out into the cafeteria, now nearly deserted.

"Shhh. She'll hear you."

They walk out into brilliant sunshine, but dark clouds are massing in the west. The air, which was hot and heavy with humidity when they went in, has cooled considerably, and the breeze has stiffened.

"T-storm coming," Mo says. "Feel it?"

"Yes. The air's electric."

"Want me to drive?"

"Sure, if you want to."

They buckle up, and she drives slowly around the long horseshoe drive and out onto the county road.

"I wonder what happened to Lester."

"I'd say your gifted and talent partner took a powder. Who wants to go to more school in the summer at that age?"

"Maybe. He seemed pretty excited about working on his mystery novel, though."

"So, what's the matter with my haircut?"

"Who said anything was wrong with your haircut?"

"You looked at it funny when you asked me where I got it."

"No, I didn't. Did I?"

"Yeah. You did. And you keep glancing at it, maybe to see if any of the hair has grown back yet."

"It's fine, Doug. I'm just surprised you got one here, from somebody you don't know."

"Just feeling adventuresome, I guess."

"What else did you do?"

"I met the newspaper editor, for one. She looks as if she's about twelve years old. She says she really wants to meet you."

"Why? What did you tell her?"

"I didn't tell her anything. She knew all about you. I keep telling you you're famous."

She groans.

"Come on. You love it. Admit it."

"I do *not* love it! Maybe this editor would be a good person to interview."

"Don't bother asking her about Philips Street. I already tried. Oh, yeah. I almost forgot." He rummages around in the glove box and pulls out the two violation notices. "Not one, but two parking tickets! I need to stop at the police station."

"You're going to contest them?"

"Wouldn't do any good. I just want to face my accusers. Twenty-five bucks a pop! Now we know why they hide the parking meters."

The police station on the western end of Philips Street has its own parking lot—with no meters.

"Are you sure you don't want to just pay the fine without a fuss?" Mo asks as they get out of the car. "There's a drop box by the door."

"I'm not going to make a fuss. I just want to see if they wear masks and point guns at you when they rob you."

Doug holds the door for her but then takes the lead as they approach the receptionist's desk. The nameplate on the desk says, "Marjorie Lafferty," but the burly man in the rumpled tan suit sitting at the desk with his hand jammed into a bag of Sun Chips is decidedly not the Marjorie type.

"Lafferty," he says around a mouthful of chips. "Help you?

Doug glances at the nameplate.

"*Harry* Lafferty. I'm just minding my wife's desk while she's on break."

Doug leans over the counter and holds out the two envelopes. "I got tagged twice this afternoon."

"Welcome to Shepherdstown," Lafferty says, grinning. He gets up with a grunt, wiping his hands on his pant legs, and reaches for the tickets.

"Hell of a way to treat a visitor," Doug says.

"Ain't it, though?" He frowns at the envelopes. "You gonna pay, or would you like to stick around and see the judge in a week or two?"

"I'll pay," Doug says, fishing his wallet from his slacks pocket. "I just wanted to see if you could keep a straight face when I give you the money."

"Did you now?"

Doug hands two twenties and a ten across the counter.

"Would you like a receipt for that?"

"You bet."

Lafferty, whose suit looks to be two sizes too small, returns to the desk, sits with another grunt, and rummages around in the top drawer. "Where in the sam hill does she keep the—? Ah. Here we go."

He flips open a receipt book and applies a stubby pencil to it with great concentration. While he works, he fishes another handful of chips from the bag and crams them into his mouth. He looks up and catches Mo watching him.

"Want some? Thirty percent less fat. The wife's got me watching my weight."

"No, thank you."

"You here for the writers dealie, are you, Mr. Stennett?" he asks Doug when he returns to the counter with the receipt.

"Not me. My wife is the writer."

"That a fact?" He turns his attention to her. "Do you write romance novels? My wife loves them."

"No. I'm a journalist."

"Nothing but the facts, right?" He laughs. "You don't know anything about that Downs guy, do you? His wife has called three times, wondering where the hell he is."

"She taught his class for him Tuesday," Doug volunteers, nodding at Mo.

"Really? You a friend of his?"

"I never met him before this week. Herman Chandler, the director of the school, asked me to pinch hit."

"Chandler." Lafferty shakes his head. "There's a piece of work." He hands Doug the receipt. "Well, if this Downs character shows up, tell him to call his wife, willya? And do enjoy the rest of your stay in our fair city. Oh, and how'd I do, Mr. Stennett?"

"Do?"

"At keeping a straight face."

Mo takes Doug's arm and steers him toward the door but then stops and turns back. Lafferty has resettled at the desk, his hand again in the chip bag, apparently trying to dredge up the last shards.

"Mr. Lafferty?"

"Yes, ma'am."

"I'm having a hard time with one of the questions from my research methods class. I was wondering if you could help me."

"This a law-enforcement question, is it?"

"I don't think so. The question is, 'What's the matter with Philips Street?'"

"How's that?"

She repeats the question.

"What in hell does that mean?"

"I was hoping you could tell me."

"Haven't a clue."

"I'll say he hasn't a clue," Doug says as soon as they're again outside. "That guy could use about thirty percent less fat between his ears!"

"You're just mad about having to pay your debt to society, you scofflaw." Mo takes him by the arm. "Let's go get a good dinner and not let anything ruin our evening."

They select the Shepherdstown Inn, which has a strong German motif, a huge variety of beers on tap, mediocre food, and slow service.

"That's what's wrong with Philips Street," Doug says when they reemerge. "It doesn't have a decent restaurant."

"I'll see if Alanna Taylor will accept that answer on the quiz."

Mo spots the paper under the windshield before Doug does and braces herself.

"Oh, for the luvva—I fed the damn meter!" He snatches the paper. "Don't tell me it took us longer than an hour to—Damn! It is a ticket! Another one!"

"You hit the trifecta!"

"It isn't funny."

"Not even a little bit? I'd better drive. You might run somebody over."

"Only if that Lafferty clown happens to be out taking a stroll."

Seeing the LottaSav as they leave town reminds her, and she pulls into the lot.

"What are you doing?"

"I'm going to buy a prize. 'The Mystery of the Missing Murder Maven.'"

"Why should you buy the prize? And from this place?"

"I'm sure they'll have something."

"They have everything, if it's cheap junk."

The LottaSav is doing a brisk business, with lines at all four open registers. Mo and Doug walk up and down the aisles, which display an incongruous mix of items, a full shelf of store-brand snack items next to a display of auto tires next to a freezer case full of frozen chickens.

In the toy section, items have been pulled off the shelves and left on the floor, and the packages have been pawed over.

"Look at this." Doug picks up a small cube-shaped box. "A Slinky! I didn't know they still made these things. Did you have one of these when you were a kid?"

"Of course! What is this?" She's frowning at the clear plastic package in her hand, out of which stares a little blue robot with a clock in its belly.

Doug takes it from her and examines it, front and back. "It's an alarm clock!" he decides. He takes another one, this one red, down off the shelf. "You should get this," he says. "It would make a great prize."

"What's the second one for?"

"Me! This thing is really cool! Let's get batteries. It takes four double A's."

"You're serious."

"This is even better than a Slinky."

"All right, then. A robot alarm clock it is."

Five registers are open when they get back to the front, each with two or three people waiting, most with heaping carts. There doesn't seem to be an express line, so they pick what they hope will be the lesser of five waits. Mo takes one of the tabloids from the rack by the register and starts to leaf through.

"That's Roberta," Doug says.

"How can you tell if the robot's a boy or a girl?"

"Not the robot. Our checker. Her name's Roberta. She kept me from buying insect repellent instead of sunscreen."

Mo goes back to a page full of grainy photos of the latest starlet caught "packing on the pounds."

"I told you to stop coming in here!"

A skinny male checker two registers down seems about ready to hit a dumpy little man in shorts and suspenders.

"I've got a right to be here!" the man shouts back. "Same as everybody else!"

"That's Lloyd," Doug says. "The checker's name is Elzie."

"It looks like Lloyd and Elzie aren't the best of friends."

Roberta has left her post at their register and hurries over to the confrontation. "It's OK, Lloyd," she says.

"It's not OK!" Elzie says. "He might shoplift something!"

"You know better than that." Roberta turns back to Lloyd. "Why don't you come back in a little while?" she says. "We're awfully busy right now."

"I got a right!" Lloyd says to Elzie.

"Get the hell out of here!"

A milk-bottle shaped man in black pants and white dress shirt closes in on the argument. "Odoms!" he shouts. "That's it! You're fired!"

His pimply face clouded with fury, the skinny young man tears at his blue LottaSav apron, ripping it as he struggles to get it off.

"You can take this job and shove it up your flabby ass, Soggins!" He throws the apron at his antagonist.

Lloyd, wide-eyed and gaping, looks from Soggins to Roberta to Elzie, then turns and stumbles out into the parking lot.

"Just get the hell out of here," Soggins says. "I'll see that you get your time."

Elzie turns on Roberta. "Thanks a lot for sticking up for him!" he says.

She's crying too hard to respond.

Elzie turns and stomps toward the pneumatic doors.

"I can help you on aisle three," a thin, blond young lady calls to them from the next register.

Through the window, Mo sees Lloyd stumbling down the slope toward the road. Elzie stands at the top of the slope and then runs after Lloyd.

"Help you folks here?"

"Come on." Doug nudges her. "Let's buy our robots and get out of here."

"I hope that poor man will be all right!"

"That poor man," Doug says, guiding her by the elbow to the next register, "is never going to be all right."

16

Elzie got fired. Fired means you can't work there any more. Elzie is being very bad. Elzie is yelling at Lloyd. Sometimes Elzie is mean to Lloyd.

"Hey! Stop, you!"

Elzie is following Lloyd. Elzie shouldn't follow Lloyd. If Lloyd has to, he can hit Elzie. Hitting is bad. You shouldn't hit. But sometimes you have to hit. Elzie is being very bad.

"I want to talk to you!"

Elzie's hand hurts Lloyd's shoulder. If Lloyd has to hit Elzie, he can.

"I don't want to talk to you!" Lloyd says.

"What? I can't even understand you, you freaking nincompoop."

"I amn't a nincompoop"

"You don't even know what that word means."

Elzie hits Lloyd's shoulder with his hand. It isn't a punch, because he doesn't make a fist. He hits Lloyd with his flat hand. If he makes a fist, Lloyd can punch him.

"It means—"

"It means dumb! D-U-M-B dumb! You're a dummy."

"I am not."

Elzie is wearing his old cloth cap. His face is red. He has little holes all over his face. Lloyd wishes he had a cloth cap like Elzie has.

"Are you crying? You're pathetic. You know that, don't you? Do you know what 'pathetic' means?"

Lloyd shakes his head. His eyes sting. Elzie should go away now. If he makes a fist, Lloyd will hit him.

"Look it up in the dictionary. You'll find your picture right next to the word."

Elzie hits Lloyd's shoulder again. It's more like a push. If he makes a fist, Lloyd will hit him.

"You know what you did back there? Do you?"

Elzie is getting madder. Lloyd doesn't want him to be mad. He does very bad things when he's mad.

"You got me fired. That's what you did. Because of you, I don't have a job any more."

Elzie is making a fist. Lloyd's fist hits Elzie. Elzie's head turns sideways. Blood spills out of his mouth. Lloyd's fist hits him again. Elzie starts to fall. Elzie falls down on the pavement. Elzie's head hits on the pavement. Elzie doesn't move. Lloyd is running into the street. The car has to stop.

Elzie made a fist, and so Lloyd hit him. Elzie was going to hit Lloyd, and Lloyd hit Elzie. Elzie's head hit the pavement. The man in the car is mad at Lloyd because Lloyd got in the way of his car. That's why he's honking and shouting. He shouldn't shout. He's a bad man. Elzie made a fist. Lloyd hit him and he made a fist. He made a hit on the pavement. His head hit the pavement. Lloyd's side hurts. Elzie made a fist and the pavement hit him. Sometimes Elzie gets very mad at Lloyd.

Elzie is Lloyd's brother.

17

"Oh, God! You're bleeding!"

Elzie tries to sit up. Blood streams from the side of his head and pools on the pavement. His dirty cloth cap is on the pavement next to him.

"Thanks for telling me." He hits his elbow as he falls back. "I thought my brain was leaking."

"Help is coming. Mr. Soggins called 911."

Elzie curses and closes his eyes.

"You shouldn't curse."

Roberta tries to hold her LottaSav apron on the wound, but he slaps at her hand. A middle-aged couple speeds up as they walk by.

"I'm bleeding to death, and you tell me not to cuss. Beautiful. Perfect."

Mr. Soggins leans over them. "Stay still, son," he says. "We've got an ambulance coming. You're going to be all right."

As if in confirmation, the siren wails from downtown. A moment later, a black and white Shepherdstown police car pulls into the parking lot, lights flashing. The siren trails off.

Elzie tries to sit up, but Mr. Soggins puts a hand on his shoulder, holding him down.

"Easy, son," he says.

Sergeant Lafferty gets out of the car and walks over slowly, frowning.

"Odoms," he says. "I mighta known."

He grunts when he bends down to take a closer look. Elzie glares up at him. "What happened?" the sergeant asks.

"He got into it with Lloyd," Mr. Soggins says. "I saw the whole thing from the store."

"He didn't mean anything by it. He was just scared. He gets crazy when he's scared," Elzie says.

"They had words in the store. I had to fire Elzie. It was the last straw. It's one thing to be insubordinate with me, but when you start accosting the customers—"

"He's not a customer," Elzie says. "He's Lloyd."

"What happened out *here*?" Sergeant Lafferty asks Mr. Soggins. "How did Lloyd wind up slugging Elzie here?"

"Lloyd ran outside, and Elzie followed him," Roberta says.

"I just wanted to get him calmed down so he wouldn't go run into a truck or something."

"Elzie pushed him, and Lloyd hit him," Mr. Soggins says.

"That little bastard can hit hard!" Elzie's eyes close, his head resting on Roberta's LottaSav apron.

Another siren is coming closer.

"You saw it, too?" Sergeant Lafferty asks Roberta.

"Yes. Shouldn't you be doing something—?" She gestures toward Elzie.

"Head wounds always bleed a lot. It looks worse than it is."

"Thanks, Lafferty," Elzie says without opening his eyes. "I feel better already."

The ambulance crawls slowly up the hill, its engine making a throaty growl.

"You go on home," Mr. Soggins tells Roberta.

"My shift doesn't end until eight."

"That's all right. I'll take your register if we get busy."

"But I—"

"Go on. Get some rest."

Her father's old Dodge turns over on the third try, and she drives slowly out the highway past the turnoff for the fancy resort, pulling in at the Buck's Lake Trailer Park. Her mother's car isn't in its space by their trailer. Roberta has the key in the lock before she realizes that her mother has again neglected to lock the door. The trailer is a mess, ashtrays overflowing, beer glasses sitting on the counter, empties all over the place.

Roberta throws the bottles in the recycle bin, washes the glasses and the rest of the dishes in the sink, and finishes off a container of sour no-fat cottage cheese. She pours herself a glass of no-fat milk and settles in on the couch with her book. It's about a fifteen-year-old girl who's a lifeguard at the pool at the Dunes hotel in Las Vegas, who's having sex with her boyfriend, and who's being hustled by a guy who says he's a talent scout but who's obviously a sleaze.

Roberta thinks about calling the hospital to check on Elzie, but Carney jumps in her lap and starts purring, and she doesn't want to disturb him. She hasn't noticed it getting dark outside. A mother screams at her kids. The jerk next door revs his engine and roars off, and she smells the gas fumes for fifteen minutes.

She wakes up when Carney digs his claws into her leg jumping down. Somebody's pounding on the door. Her book has fallen on the floor, face down and open, and she stoops to pick it up so the spine won't get broken. She gets on tiptoes to look out the small window in the front door at the same time that Lloyd yells, "Berta! Open the door! It's meeeeeeeeeeeee!"

She opens the door and steps back as Lloyd bursts past her and stands in the center of the room, his fists clenched. He starts jumping up and down, and the whole trailer shakes.

"Lloyd! Honey! It's all right."

She rushes over, then darts back and slams the door just as Carney dashes out from under the kitchen counter and streaks across the room. Carney veers off, bounds on the couch and climbs the curtains, turning to stare down at Lloyd from the valance.

"Elzie's not home!" Lloyd says. He chants the three words again and again as Roberta puts her arm around him and tries to get him to settle down. She finally gets him to sit down on the couch next to her.

"I know, honey. He had to go to the hospital to get his big owie fixed. Remember? At the store?"

Lloyd nods but says, "NoooooooOOOOOOO!"

"Shhhh. Shh. It's all right. Just take a big breath. That's right."

Lloyd moans, hugging himself and rocking back and forth violently. Roberta gets a half-empty bag of Chips Ahoy cookies from the kitchen and the Richard Scarry alphabet book from the hall closet. Carney glares down at her as she sits back down next to Lloyd, who clutches himself as if his stomach aches.

"You want a nice cookie, honey?"

"Yes, please. Do you have Chips?"

"You bet."

She holds out one of the cookies from the bag. With his arms still wrapped around his stomach, he leans forward, and she holds the cookie to his mouth so he can take a bite. Crumbs tumble down his chin while she feeds him the rest. He makes soft moaning noises as he chews and swallows.

"Can I have another one?"

"If you take it with your hand."

Roberta hands him another cookie and digs out one for herself. She opens the Scarry book, and he lets her rest it half in his lap and half in hers.

"Look at all the boats!" she says, pointing. "What's this one doing?"

Lloyd frowns, studying the picture. "Squirting. That's the fireboat."

"That's right! And who's that?"

She's pointing to a seagull, but Lloyd is looking elsewhere on the page.

"Doggie! Bad doggie!"

"That's the doggie in the police boat. I think he's a good doggie."

"No! Bad dog!"

"Why is he a bad dog, honey?"

"Dogs bite you!"

"See the car? Sticking out the back? And another car in the front? The boat is taking the cars across the water. It's the—"

"Bad dog!" Lloyd points at the dog in the window of the boat.

"It's another doggie! And what's that?"

"Seagull. Dogs bite you!"

"Let's look at the trains now."

They eat cookies until the bag is empty. She shows him the trains and planes, cars and rockets. Lloyd especially likes the logging truck, which is like the trucks he sees out on the highway, and the hook and ladder, which is so long it needs two drivers, one to steer the front and one to steer the back.

Lloyd lies back on the couch, closes his eyes, and begins to snore softly, sounding like she imagines a little bear cub might sound, hibernating in its den. He has a streak of blood on his face, probably from when he was fighting in the parking lot with Elzie. She gets a cloth from the bathroom, wets it with warm water, and carefully rubs away the blood without waking him. She gets the extra blanket from the closet and covers him and tries to move his head into a more natural position.

She gets her book from the stand next to the door where she left it and settles in next to Lloyd on the couch. After a few minutes, she hears Carney plop down behind her and pad across the bare floor. He jumps up and settles in her lap again.

She reads only a few pages before she, too, falls asleep.

18

Doug sleeps fitfully, awakening disoriented and sluggish. He remembers waking up when Mo came in to kiss him good-bye before going to school, but he doesn't remember going back to sleep. He lies on his back, waiting for a wave of panic to pass, and tries to figure out rationally why he would oversleep like this, for the first time in memory.

The moment his foot hits the cold wood floor, pain flames from his heel up into his groin. He yelps and sits down quickly. Swinging his leg back up on the bed makes the pain flare, and he lies as still as possible, aware of his throbbing pulse, of his rapidly beating heart, of the sweat welling on his forehead.

He becomes aware of the light outside, of the bird song, of voices from the pier below, the rhythmic dipping of oars in water. He gets up on his elbows and drags his body into a sitting position, his back against the flimsy headboard of the bed.

"Son of a bitch!" he says, and then he laughs.

He goes through his mental list, all the things he must remember before he gets up. Then he begins to plan. He's due for a seven-miler, maybe eight. He's late, so there will already be logging trucks out on the highway. He'll go directly to the Heavenly Acres access road, which only requires a little over a quarter mile of running on the shoulder of the highway.

He starts sweating again when he pulls his athletic sock on over his heel. He needs new jogging shoes. The old ones may be making the heel worse. Maybe he should start wrapping the heel when he runs. Ice after, for sure.

He steps gingerly into the kitchen area. The sunlight is brilliant on the lake. Last night's rainsquall has washed the world clean. There will be mud. He lays the towel out by the door for when he gets back.

He takes two Advil with his orange juice and stretches out slowly in front of the picture window in the living area. He'll have to start running very slowly and let the heel work itself out.

When he steps out onto the porch, the cool morning air pricks his bare arms and legs. He has not missed a day running now in two thousand, one hundred and ninety-eight days, eight days into the seventh year. If not for the broken ribs that interrupted his running for almost a week, the streak would stretch intact for almost twelve years.

He walks carefully down the three porch steps, holding onto the railing, and allows himself to walk up the gentle incline past the empty slab where the CR-V would be parked. The thought of her enjoying herself in class makes him smile.

He checks his running watch. 7:42. He should be done and showered long ago.

He starts the stopwatch and begins shuffling along the narrow, winding road. The Wilkersons' little white dog, Juney, sits on the lawn, watching him silently. The wreckage of last night's bonfire smolders; beer bottles line the porch railing. As he runs up the gentle incline leading out to the dirt county road, the pain is manageable. He'll just have to go a little slower for awhile.

He catches himself counting his steps and counts randomly to make himself lose track. He focuses on his breath, and the breathing becomes his mantra as he begins to lengthen his strides, his body seeking its rhythm. The pain is steady but only spikes if he missteps on the uneven roadway. His feet haven't learned this road yet, and he must watch his steps to avoid rocks, potholes, and erosion gullies.

Quickening the pace makes the pain flame up again, so he drops into his survival shuffle, a pace at which he feels confident he could run all day.

Maybe not this day, though.

He checks his watch. He's already been running for eight minutes and thirty-four seconds, and he isn't yet to the highway. Got to pick up the pace.

His feet lick the road and disappear, lick and disappear. If he made a movie of his life, he'd start with this image—feet, legs and road—and the steady, rhythmic breathing. A second camera would pan back to reveal a man running, elbows flaring slightly at his sides, posture erect, head up.

At the highway he jogs in place while a lumber truck rumbles by. He crosses the highway to run on the left shoulder, facing traffic, which is light coming from town. The watch shows 14:32 at the turn at the Heavenly Acres road. When he ran the route Monday, he ran the same distance in 11:58. Must pick up the pace on the level road.

The dog barks from its pen next to a sprawling ranch home, the huge, manicured lawn an oasis of order amidst the scraggily scrub brush and trees. Lab mix, good dog, just doing its job, protecting his people and his territory.

He feels tightness in both inner thighs. A cramp is developing in his right calf and a side stitch on the same side. He must be favoring the bad heel, throwing off his stride.

He catches himself counting his steps again, in sets of four. He tries to stop counting but gives in to it. At last the entrance to Heavenly Acres slides into view as he plods into a long bend to the right in the road. Another quarter mile to the stables. He checks his watch. 33:18. At this pace, it will take him over seventy-two minutes to finish the route.

Got to pick up the pace after the turn.

The sky has darkened, a blanket of angry black clouds spilling over the western horizon.

Ahead on the right, the slender Mexican he has seen two days ago at the stables is walking in the same direction Doug is running. The Mexican has his head down and carries some sort of long-handled tool over his shoulder. Although the man appears to be walking slowly, it seems to take much too long for Doug to reach him and pull ahead.

The horses line the fence, watching him as he approaches. Perhaps they're waiting for the Mexican to feed them. One huffs air through its broad nostrils as if in disappointment.

"Sorry. I'm not the guy who brings breakfast," Doug tells them, and one raises her head, seeming to listen.

He touches the stable gate and turns in a wide circle to head back. Before he crosses to the left side of the road to face traffic, he studies his footprints coming the other way, and for a moment he gets the heady sensation that he will soon meet himself on the road. He sees from the prints that he is dragging his right foot, favoring the heel. That's what's throwing off his stride.

The Mexican approaches, head down, arm wrapped over the handle of whatever it is he's carrying.

"Good morning," Doug tries as they pass each other.

He gets a mumbled "Morning" in reply.

He tries to smooth out his stride, but the pain in the heel intensifies. He doesn't realize how hard he has been sweating until the first cold raindrop strikes his cheek. He looks up, letting the rain hit him full in the face. The pain is worse with each step now.

The rain stays soft and steady for perhaps a minute, quickens, and erupts in hard sheets, making it impossible to see more than a step ahead. Gooseflesh prickles his arms and legs. His shirt and shorts become sodden and heavy, and his shoes and socks feel like wet towels wrapping his feet.

The rain pounds him. Pain rises in waves from his heel into the pit of his stomach. The heel feels as if it will at any moment blow itself apart. He stops. Bends over. Puts his hands on his knees. Gulps down air. Rain pelts his back. He flexes his knees slightly, spiking the pain.

The world does not come crashing down on him. In truth, it seems not to have noticed that he is no longer running. On some level, well below rational thought, this surprises him. In the midst of his pain, it seems a revelation: *I can stop any time.* He takes a tentative step. Another. The pain, while severe, isn't as bad as when he runs. He will walk, then. He wonders how he should record his distance in his log. It occurs to him that it might not matter. The rain drums the road.

He neither sees nor hears the little man until he is upon him, the short, fat man in short pants and suspenders, Lloyd, his bowl-cut hair plastered to his scalp. He stands in the reeds and brush off to the side of the road, watching Doug. His face breaks open, revealing jagged teeth, manic eyes.

Doug is running before he realizes he has started again. The rain drums the road, his chest, the top of his head. The pain in his heel is relentless. He risks a glance back; Lloyd still watches him. The madman's face breaks open again, and Doug realizes that he is grinning back.

It occurs to him that the poor little man might need help. He turns and walks back slowly. Lloyd's expression doesn't change as he watches Doug approach.

"Are you OK?"

"Dead!"

"You're not dead."

"Dead!"

Lloyd turns and scuttles off. Doug watches after him, the rain drumming off his scalp and running down his face. As he turns to resume his walk back to the cabin, he glimpses something off the road. Reeds have been flattened in a narrow path from the road where Lloyd was standing into the boggy forest. Perhaps a deer has nested there for the night.

Doug steps carefully off the road, mud sucking at his running shoes, and follows the trail of bent reeds off into the trees. He feels like an idiot for doing it, but he couldn't feel right walking away without investigating.

He reaches the line of trees fifteen or so feet off the road and takes a step into the forest. The growth is dense enough to keep most of the rain off him, and he begins to see more clearly. He scans the forest slowly, not really expecting to see anything. He is ready to turn back to the road when he catches sight of something white at the base of the trunk of a bifurcated birch. It could be peeled birch bark, but it seems too bright, almost silvery.

Doug takes a step toward the tree, another, struggling to pull his feet out of the sucking mud. The image on the poster in Finbar O'Brien's bookstore flashes through his mind, and he knows, even before he reaches the tree, his stomach twisting, his skin prickling, exactly what he is about to find.

19

"Who wants to go first?"

Irene Crowley's eyes scan the circle. The gruff fellow with the picket-fence haircut grins at her and thrusts his hand in the air.

"I'll put you all out of your misery," he says, looking around at the others. "You might as well give me the prize right now.

"Go ahead. And you are … ?"

"Jameson's the name, and thrillers are my game." He flips open his notebook and finds the page he wants. "I wrote this in about twenty minutes," he says.

As Mr. Jameson begins to read in his loud, confident voice, Mo scans the circle. Lester Brady is absent again, as is Gretchen Hyman, but Elsworth Priestly has reappeared. Everyone else seems to be accounted for, everyone, that is, except, of course, for Fletcher Downs. He has been kidnapped by a band of survivalists holed up in a cabin in the woods north of town, according to Mr. Jameson.

"They think he'll be a big help to them," he concludes, "when the final confrontation comes. But they find out he's a real candy ass, nothing like the guys in his books. So now they have to figure out how to get rid of him." Mr. Jameson leans back with a satisfied grin. "Dramatic irony. Pretty good, huh?"

"Does anyone have any feedback for Mr. Jameson?" Irene Crowley asks.

"It isn't finished," Stephen Stieve says.

"Yes, it is," Mr. Jameson says. "It's one of those, what do you call it, indiscriminate endings."

"Indeterminate," Irene Crowley corrects. "Indeterminate endings."

"I think it's lame," Mr. Stieve says.

"I suppose yours is better?" Mr. Jameson says.

"Why don't we just go in order around the circle," Irene Crowley suggests. "Ms. Bergan, isn't it? I remember you from fiction basics. What did you come up with?"

Ms. Bergan's story has Fletcher Downs going undercover to track down a terrorist cell in Shepherdstown.

"That guy couldn't track down his own toenail clippings," Mr. Stieve notes, drawing a glare from Ms. Bergan.

"Mr. … I'm sorry. I don't know your name."

"Dorland," the school principal says.

"Have you written a scenario for us, Mr. Dorland?"

"If that's what you call it."

He reads in a flat monotone, running out of breath before he runs out of sentence. His convoluted fantasy involves an underground labyrinth, a time warp, and a quest for something, Mo isn't quite sure what.

Pamela Erickson, the mousy librarian, reads next, in tiny, breathless phrases, spinning a lurid tale of sexual bondage that leaves even Mr. Stieve speechless.

"Thank you, Ms. Erickson. That was very, uh, interesting," Ms. Crowley manages. "You're next, Mr.—"

"Turvald. The Humdrung ate him."

"That's it?"

"That's it."

"Admirably concise, Mr. Turvald."

"Thank you."

"That brings us to you, Ms.—"

"Mrs. Yates. I didn't do one. I was going to, but I—"

"Don't apologize!" Mr. Stieve says. "It's not like she's our real teacher."

Irene Crowley glares at her antagonist, who slouches down in his chair, smirking as he examines a fingernail.

"Does this mean you didn't invent a scenario for us, Mr.—?"

"Stieve. I don't 'invent scenarios.' I write fiction."

"My apologies, Mr. Stieve. Did you write a fiction?"

"He was murdered."

"You sound pretty sure of yourself," Mr. Jameson notes. "Did you kill him?"

Mr. Stieve huffs his contempt. "No, I didn't kill him. A psychopath did."

"Why would he do that?" Mr. Jameson presses.

Mr. Stieve shrugs, no easy feat from so low in the chair. "He's a psycho. That's what psychos do. Maybe he sacrificed the body to the Humdrung." He glances at Mr. Turvald, who has been staring at him but now looks away.

"Why would he pick Mr. Downs?" Ms. Bergan challenges.

"Why not?"

A sharp rapping draws their attention to the door, which opens to reveal a clearly agitated Herman Chandler in the doorway. Harry Lafferty looms behind him.

"I'm sorry to interrupt," Mr. Chandler says.

Lafferty shoulders him aside and steps forward. "Folks, I'm Detective Sergeant Lafferty, Shepherdstown PD. I'm afraid I've got some real bad news." He hooks his thumbs in his belt loops and tips his head back as he looks at their faces around the circle. "Fletcher Downs is dead."

"No shit?" Mr. Stieve murmurs.

"Oh, my God!" from Mrs. Yates.

"You can't be serious!" Mr. Dorland says.

Mr. Bergan giggles, then blushes and presses her fist to her mouth.

"I'm afraid I'm dead serious," Lafferty assures them, striding up to the circle of chairs. "I'm going to need you all to stick around for awhile, so I can talk to you." He seems to be studying their faces. "One at a time." His eyes cast around the circle. "You first."

"Me?" Mr. Stieve sits up.

"You."

"The rest can wait in the library," Mr. Chandler offers. "Nobody's using it."

He herds them into the hall, through the cafeteria and past the auditorium into the open area that serves as the library, with chest-high bookshelves forming natural partitions but leaving an open space in the middle for six tables, four chairs to a table.

Mr. Chandler starts to walk away.

"Whoa up," Mr. Jameson says. "Aren't you going to tell us what happened?"

Mr. Chandler would clearly rather not. His face clouds, and he has even more trouble than usual getting the words started.

"They found his body, Mr. Downs' body, by a slough west of town, near the resort."

"Heavenly Acres?" Mo asks.

"Yes."

"Who found him?" Mr. Jameson presses.

Mr. Chandler glances at Mo, flushes deeply, and looks away. "Actually, it was the husband of one of our ... One of you. Mr. Stennett."

The floor opens up and swallows Mo, and she tumbles down an endless tunnel. She forces herself to take a deep, slow breath.

"How awful," Mrs. Yates says.

"Do they think he was murdered?" Mr. Jameson asks.

"My God in heaven," Ms. Erickson murmurs.

Mr. Chandler escapes back down the hall.

"Who would do something like that?" Mr. Dorland asks no one in particular.

"Maybe Ms. Gillory, here, knows." Ms. Bergan nods toward Myrna Gillory, who is trying to slip unnoticed into the open area. "She didn't read us her story yet."

"Where you been, Myrna? Out hiding the evidence?" It's the first time Elsworth Priestly has spoken, his first contribution to the class, in fact, since he walked out two days before. He sits alone at the farthest table.

"I was out copping a smoke, if it's any of your business."

"Bad habit," Priestly says, smirking.

"Where have you been?" she counters. "I thought you'd dropped out."

"They said I could substitute another class, but I couldn't have a refund. So I figured I might as well come back."

"You got an alibi?" Gillory smiles as she says it.

Priestly laughs. "You think I did it? Funny. My dough's on that mental defective, Lester. That guy is a hole in search of its donut."

Nobody laughs.

"He did disappear after the first class," Jameson notes.

"Why would anyone want to kill Fletcher Downs?" Erickson asks.

"What about that other one?" Bergan asks at the same time.

"What other one?" Jameson asks her.

"That woman who talked so much the second day. You know. The one—"

"The one with the huge jugs," Gillory says.

"Well, there you have it," Priestly says, spreading his arms, palms up. "The woman with the huge jugs did it. Maybe she bludgeoned him to death with her—"

"That's enough, young man," Dorland says, sounding every bit the principal.

"Assault with a friendly weapon, would you call that?" Turvald says, looking extremely pleased with himself.

He draws a snort from Priestly.

"Stop it, all of you!" Yates says with surprising heat. "A man, someone we know, has been—You know."

That brings the conversation to a temporary cease-fire.

"I wonder if we're in any danger," Erickson says.

"Why would we be?" Jameson's voice rises above the others.

"I don't know. Why would anyone want to kill Mr. Downs?"

"Maybe Sherlock, here, has it figured out."

Priestly leans back in his chair, his head resting against one of the bookshelves. "How about it?" he adds, looking at Mo. "Can you shed any light on our little mystery? Everywhere you go, people seem to wind up dead, and you seem to have a real knack for catching the killers. Isn't that right?"

They're all looking at her now.

"Looks like I'm just in time for the lynching."

They all turn toward Stieve, who stands in the opening between bookshelves.

"I hate to break up the party, but Lafferty's done working me over with the rubber hose. Quinn, he wants you next."

Mo gathers up her purse and notebook and hurries down the hallway. She certainly has no reason to fear an interrogation from the police detective. But still, anxiety roils up in her as she walks the empty hallway, murmurings drifting from the classrooms on both sides of her. She recites the end of the 19th Psalm silently to steady herself.

How awful for Doug to have found the body. She feels somehow to blame. Of course it isn't her fault, either that Fletcher Downs was killed or that poor Doug discovered the body, but something Priestly said about her is certainly true: everywhere she goes lately, somebody winds up dead.

20

Gen Beringer is waiting for him in the hallway when Herman Chandler gets to his office.

"You have company," she says, nodding toward the closed door. "Irate parent."

"Is it about—?"

"No. Word hasn't gotten out yet."

"Who, then?"

"A Mrs. Gloria Gruszlonick. The woman weighs three hundred fifty pounds if she weighs an ounce."

"Gruszlonick—?"

"Lester Brady's mother. The 'gifted' high school kid, remember?"

"What does she want?"

"Your head on a platter, from the looks of her."

"Marvelous."

"You want me to tell her you're busy?"

"No." He takes a deep breath. "Once more into the breach, dear friends, once more."

"What?"

"Shakespeare. *Henry V.* I believe it's Act 3, Scene 1."

"Well, of course. Why didn't I know that?"

Why, he wonders as he pushes the door open, do extremely large women make such extremely unfortunate wardrobe choices?

The woman in question overlaps one of the three high-backed chairs arranged around a circular conference table. She wears orange and white striped coolats and a sleeveless top that comes close enough to matching to look like a mistake. A tattooed serpent snakes up her enormous upper arm and curls behind her ear.

"Chandler?" Her fleshy face ripples with the force when she spits out the name.

"I'm Herman Chandler."

"You owe my son an apology. And you owe me money!"

"Would you care for some coffee, Mrs.—?"

"No."

Herman takes the chair opposite his adversary. Paul insists they bring the table and chairs up from Madison each summer, so that the little makeshift office can have something besides the dreadful institutional school-district furniture. The line has been discontinued; he has no idea where—if at all—he'd be able to get a replacement for the chair straining mightly to hold Mrs. Gruszlonick.

"Let's cut right to the chase. My boy was assaulted. You're in charge. I hold you personally responsible."

"Assaulted?"

"That's what I said." She leans forward, letting her arms drop on the table like fleshy pipes. He tries not to stare at the snake.

"Your son was—?"

"Assaulted! By one of your instructors!"

"One of the teachers physically assaulted—?"

"*Verbally.* He was *verbally* assaulted. He suffered great mental distress." She snuffles, and for a horrible moment, Herman thinks she means to cry. Instead, she rubs at the sweat on her massive upper arm and wipes her hand on her coolats. "I might sue."

"Perhaps if you could tell me the particulars, Mrs. – "

"Gruszlonick. Gloria Gruszlonick. Lester Brady is my son."

"Yes, of course. I remember discussing Lester's situation with you over the—"

"Lester is not a 'situation.' He's a human being. He's got feelings."

"Of course he—"

"You told me on the phone that he'd have no trouble being accepted here. 'A warm and receptive learning environment,' you said. Ha!"

The last explosion almost lifts Herman out of his chair. He considers the possibility that he might have a heart attack and die. It seems not an altogether unpleasant proposition at the moment.

"Perhaps if you could give me some idea of what actually transpired, I could—"

"One of your so-called instructors called my boy a moron! *That's* what actually *transpired!* And that wasn't all. He told me son to shut up! He's been taught not to use that kind of language. He's been raised better than that. And to have his teacher say that kind of thing to him. Why, it's just—"

Herman braces himself while Mrs. Gloria Gruszlonick searches for the exact word to express what it just is.

"—malignant!"

He wonders if she means something else, 'malfeasance,' perhaps. Sheridan might have appreciated the moment.

"You find this funny, Chandler? Your instructor calls my boy a moron, and you sit there grinning like a, like a—"

"I assure you I do not find this funny in the least, Mrs. Gruszlonick. I take—"

"You do not assure me one itty bitty bit, Chandler. You do *not* inspire confidence."

Her face has bunched up like a huge fist, her eyes barely visible in the folds of flesh.

"The incident took place in the classroom?"

"No. The 'incident' did not take place in the classroom. It was after class, in that dump you call a cafeteria. There were plenty of people around who heard him say it."

"How exactly—?"

"I demand a full refund of Lester's tuition! I also demand that his so-called instructor be fired! Right now! Or else!"

Herman's fairly sure Lester was a full-scholarship student, but it doesn't seem prudent to mention it at the moment. He knows he should be taking thorough notes of the conversation, but he doesn't dare get up to get a pad and pencil.

"May I ask which of our faculty allegedly called—?"

" 'Allegedly!' Did you say 'allegedly'?"

"I—"

"Don't you *dare* question my boy's word, you little toad! If he says the instructor called him a moron, that instructor called him a moron!"

"I didn't mean—"

"Are you going to fire him?"

"I will certainly take appropriate—"

"Appropriate! You'll can his ass! That's appropriate!"

"Who is the teacher in question, Mrs. Gruszlonick?"

"That pompous ass you call a writer-in-residue."

"Fletcher Downs?"

"How many pompous ass writers-in-residue you got here, Chandler? I want him canned immediately. He should not be allowed to set foot in a classroom again. And he has to apologize to my son! In front of everybody!"

Herman swallows bile. "Mrs. Gruszlonick," he manages, "I can assure—I give you my word that Fletcher Downs will never set foot in a classroom here again."

The part about the apology, he thinks, would be considerably harder to arrange.

He finally manages to cajole Mrs. Gruszlonick and her snake out of his office with the promise of an abject public apology to young Lester, not from a mere instructor but from the director himself. She would have preferred the head of the 'writer-in-residue' on a pole, not knowing that the head had already been battered beyond feeling any further atrocities.

He sits at the table, shell-shocked, until Gen Beringer pokes her head in at the door.

"How'd it go, there, Henry the Eighth? You survive?"

Herman stands and strikes a pose. "'The game's afoot. Follow your spirit, and upon this charge cry "God for Harry, England, and Saint George!"' It's *Henry V*."

With that, he exits, stage right, to use the private phone in the school office to call Paul with the horrible news.

21

Mo knocks on the door jamb and steps into the classroom. Lafferty perches on one of the too-small desk chairs still drawn up in a circle. He's turning the robot alarm clock over in his large, meaty hands.

"That's Lloyd," Mo tells him, taking a chair across the circle from the sergeant. "At least that's what my husband calls him. He has another one he calls Floyd."

"'Lloyd,' huh?" Lafferty examines the bot in his hands as carefully as if it were a live grenade. "Same name as the kid who was out there when your husband found the body."

He sets the robot on the desk next to him and turns his full attention to Mo. "I suppose Chandler filled you in?"

"He said that Doug found Fletcher Downs."

"What was left of him. He'd managed to get his head staved in."

"How awful. Do you think he was murdered?"

"Looks like it. I hear you're an amateur homicide detective."

"Just in the wrong place at the wrong time."

He flips open the same sort of narrow notepad Mo uses. As he pages through, Mo glimpses sketches but can't make out what they are.

"You write mysteries?"

"No. I haven't written any fiction."

"What were you doing in a mystery writing class?"

"I was just curious. It seemed like too good an opportunity to miss."

"How's that?"

"Oh, I don't know. Famous best-selling author and all."

"You a Fletcher Downs fan, are you?"

"No. I've never even read any of his books."

Lafferty chews on the eraser end of the pencil, which makes Mo's mouth want to pucker. "Me, neither," he says. "Marjorie started one and said it was full of bad grammar. So. Was it?"

"Was—?"

"The class. A good opportunity."

"He was only there for the first class."

"Right. Monday. Did anything unusual happen in class that day?"

"Unusual?"

"Disagreements? Tensions?"

"Did any of the students seem like they wanted to kill him? No. I think we were all a little disappointed that he wasn't better prepared. He mostly just talked about himself and plugged his books."

"Is that why this Presley guy—? Wait a minute." He thumbs back several pages in his notepad. "Priestly. Elsworth Priestly. What in hell kind of a name is that?" He looks up. "Is that why this Elsworth Priestly wanted his money back?"

"I guess so. I really don't know."

"What about this Brady character?"

"Lester?"

"Yeah. He dropped out, didn't he?"

"Yes. He was supposed to be my research partner in another class. He stopped coming to that class, too."

"A pretty strange duck. We had a complaint from his mother last year. One of his teachers at the high school apparently wasn't duly impressed with the young man's genius. I think she wanted us to arrest the poor guy. He and Downs have any problems?"

"Not that I saw."

"You took over the class when Downs didn't show Tuesday. Is that right?"

"Mr. Chandler asked me to facilitate the discussion. One of the other instructors in the school took over the class Wednesday and today."

"And you'd never met Downs before?"

"No."

"Any idea why someone might have done this to him?"

"No."

"No theories?"

"I'd heard he sometimes got involved with his students. Just stories."

"'Involved.' You mean he slept with them?"

"Yes."

"I heard that, too." Lafferty studies his notes. "Can you think of anything else that might help?"

"Not really."

"Nothing unusual?"

"I've never been to a writers conference before. It all seems unusual to me."

Lafferty flips his notepad shut and sticks his pencil in the wire coils. "If you think of anything else—" He pulls a card holder from his shirt pocket, thumbs a card partway out, and holds it out for her.

"I will."

Mo takes the card and stands. Lafferty remains seated.

"I do hope you catch whoever did this," she says from the doorway.

"We'll give it our best shot. In a small town like this, somebody sure as hell knows what happened. Would you ask—uh—?" He flips open his notepad. "Ask Myrna Gillory to come in here, please?"

"Yes."

She's almost out the door when his voice at her back stops her.

"Ms. Quinn?"

She turns. "Yes?"

"You will let me catch the bad guys, won't you?"

"Of course."

"Good. I wouldn't want you getting hurt."

She hurries down the hallway. Rustling sounds come from the classrooms, teachers' voices rising to give last minute instructions before their students disperse. Soon, everyone in the school will know what happened.

As she approaches the library, she hears voices. Stephen Stieve sounds agitated. Myrna Gillory is standing, her back to Mo, facing Stieve.

"I was just asking a question, damn it!" he's saying. "You didn't have to—"

Catching sight of Mo, he stops and turns away, thrusting his hands deep into his pockets. Gillory turns and sees her.

"I—We were just discussing—"

Mo waits, but Gillory doesn't finish the sentence.

"Sergeant Lafferty would like to talk with you next," Mo says.

"Me?" She looks startled. "My turn on the hot seat, huh?"

She scoops up her purse from one of the chairs and, avoiding eye contact, pushes her way out through the bookshelves. Her sandals make a staccato clicking as she walks quickly away.

22

The county mountie is writing something on his notepad when Myrna Gillory comes in. He lets her stand while he finishes. He holds the pencil as if he isn't used to having a thumb and isn't sure how to operate it.

"Myrna Gillory?"

"That's right."

"I'm Detective Sergeant Lafferty. Have a seat, Ms. Gillory."

"I'd rather stand."

"You in a hurry, are you?"

"Sure. Aren't you?"

Lafferty nods toward the chair facing him. "Sit down, Ms. Gillory. Relax. I'll try not to take too much of your time."

She sits. When she glances up, he's looking at her. Small town cop—red-faced and jowly, with heavy eyelids and eyes that reveal no more intelligence than that of a cow chewing a cud. She folds her hands on the desk and fights down the urge to start talking.

"OK." He smiles, as if something has been resolved in the dim reaches of his mind. "When was the last time you saw Fletcher Downs alive?"

"Monday in class. Just like everybody else."

"Monday afternoon."

"That's right."

"Class got out at, what, two-thirty?"

"Sure."

He slashes at the paper with his blunt pencil. "Did you have any contact with him outside of class?"

"I saw him in the cafeteria."

"When was that?"

"Before class on Monday."

"Did you talk with him?"

"No. Why would I?"

"You didn't see him after class on Monday?"

She shakes her head. Her nose itches, and she rubs it with the back of her hand.

"Not at all?"

"No."

He makes more scratches with his club-pencil. He gets about five words on one narrow sheet of paper. He wets his thumb to flip to the next page.

"What kind of teacher was Downs?"

"How many kinds are there?"

He doesn't respond.

"I only had him in class that one day, and all he did was talk about himself."

When Lafferty again makes no response, she goes on.

"I guess that makes him no kind of teacher at all. Just a bullshitter."

"What did he tell you about himself?"

"What a big deal he is. All the famous writers he's met."

"What did you want him to talk about?"

"I wanted him to teach us something! That's what we were there for."

"Were you pretty upset?"

"Upset about what?"

"That he didn't teach you anything."

"Not especially. I don't really expect much."

"Why'd you sign up for his course?"

"Because he's a famous writer." When he remains silent, she adds, "I was hoping he'd refer me to his agent."

"Writers have agents?"

"The ones who get published do."

"Is that right? It's not what you know, it's who you know, huh?"

"Something like that."

"Did you ask him?"

"Ask him what?"

"To refer you to his agent?"

"You can't just ask like that. You have to get them to read some of your stuff."

"Did you get him to read some of your stuff?"

"No. I never got a chance." She swipes at her nose with the back of her hand.

"What do you write, Ms. Gillory?"

"I've written a novel."

He nods, making a note. "Must be a hell of a lot of work," he says. "I have a hard enough time just trying to read one."

"I'll bet."

He looks up at her. A smile works itself onto his face. "Is it?" he asks.

"Is it what?"

"A hell of a lot of work to write a novel."

"I suppose."

"And you do all that without knowing if anybody's going to publish it?"

"Yeah. A bitch, huh?"

He shakes his head; his jowls jiggle. "You must like to write," he says.

"Not really."

He raises an eyebrow.

"It's more like I don't feel right until I've written."

"Sounds like drug addiction. You don't feel good until you've had your fix."

"It's not like that."

"After awhile, it stops feeling good when you do it, but it feels rotten if you don't."

"It's not an addiction."

"More like the fella who keeps hitting his head with the hammer, then, maybe?"

She feels his eyes on her. Loud voices, laughter, and the shuffling of feet roll in from the hall.

"You know about the fella who kept hitting his head with a hammer, don't you? His friend walks up to him and says, 'Doesn't that hurt?' and the guys says, 'Yeah, it hurts! It hurts like hell!' So the friend says, 'Then why are you doing it?' and the first guy says, 'Because it feels so good when I stop.'"

She forces a smile.

"You didn't think that was funny?"

"I mighta heard that one before."

"But writing's like that? Feels so good when you stop?"

"If you say so."

He seems to write down every word she says. He's filled about fifteen little pages.

"Did he make anybody else mad? Maybe somebody expecting him to help them get an agent?"

She shakes her head, then, realizing that he isn't looking, says, "Not that I know of."

"Anybody else upset because he didn't teach you anything the first day?"

"One guy tried to get his money back when Fletcher didn't show up the next day.

"Who might that be?"

"His name's Presley or something."

Lafferty picks up a rumpled sheet of photocopy paper. "Elsworth Priestly?"

"Sure."

"Is it or isn't it?"

"I think so."

Lafferty gives her the little jowl shake. "'Elsworth!' Wonder what his parents were smoking, huh? Did Priestly come to class today?"

"Yeah. He's here. He said they wouldn't give him a refund."

Lafferty makes a note, then puts the pencil down and closes the notebook. She hadn't been aware that she was tensing her shoulders, but she feels them relax now.

"Is that it?"

"That's it. Unless you can think of anybody else who might have had a run-in with Downs."

"Well, there was one thing, but it probably doesn't have anything to do with anything."

"You never know, Ms. Gillory. Why don't you tell me about it, just in case?"

"It was when I saw Fletcher in the cafeteria on Monday."

"This was before class."

"Right. Just before class. He was talking to Chandler. They both seemed upset."

"Chandler?"

"The guy who runs the program."

"You have any idea what they were talking about?"

"It might have had something to do with how much Fletcher was getting paid."

"What makes you think that?"

"I heard Chandler say something about how Fletcher had signed a contract and that he ought to honor it."

"What did Fletcher say to that?"

"I don't know. They stopped talking when I walked past."

The notepad stays closed on the table, the pencil stuck through the spirals.

"Anything else?"

"I can't think of anything right now."

"If you do—" He stuffs two sausage fingers into his shirt pocket and drags out one of those little holders for business cards. He peels a card off and puts it on the table, snapping the edge like a Las Vegas blackjack dealer. "You'll give me a call, won't you?"

"Sure."

She bumps her leg on the table when she gets up.

"Will you send this Elvis Priestly fellow in next, please?"

"Sure."

Hurrying down the empty hallway, she catches a whiff of something foul. She feels at her armpit, and her fingers come away damp.

Back at the library, they're sitting and reading or writing in their notebooks. They all look up when she comes in.

"Priestly. You're next."

Priestly shoves up out of the chair and shuffles out without answering, but he's waiting for her a moment later when she walks back into the hallway.

"What did he ask you?"

"He beat me with a rubber hose until I confessed. What do you think he asked? 'Where were you on the night of the murder?'"

"Was it rough?"

"Of course it wasn't rough. He's a dumbass small-town cop."

He forces a laugh, then shuffles down the hall, head down, shoulders hunched. She lights a cigarette as soon as she's outside and walks rapidly to her car.

(23)

Doug is already at the same computer he used the day before when Mo gets to the lab. Two of the others from the research methods class, Beth Trebeck and Robert Thyme, occupy stations one and two along the wall behind them. Alanna Taylor waves to them from her post at the central computer.

"Back for more, huh?"

"Can't stay away," Mo says, returning her smile.

She slides in at the computer on Doug's right.

"Hey, handsome. Is this station taken?"

"I've been saving it for you, cute stuff. How come you're late?"

"I was getting interrogated."

"My buddy Sergeant Lafferty, no doubt."

"The same. Are you OK? It must have been awful."

Doug glances around at Beth Trebeck and Robert Thyme. "We're even," he says quietly. "Now we've each discovered a dead boy. What did Lafferty want?"

"He's talking to everybody in the mystery class."

"You're all suspects?"

"They're casting a pretty wide net. They don't seem to have a lot to go on."

"God, Mo. Another one."

"It doesn't have anything to do with my being here."

"I know, but still—"

She squeezes her hands together in her lap so hard, her knuckles ache. She forces herself to unclench. "You always see a pattern," she says, keeping her voice calm.

"It's human nature. We look at the stars and see constellations."

"Didn't Mrs. Wilkerson tell you that there had been other murders around here?"

"She didn't say they were murders."

"Deaths, then."

"Yeah. A rodeo rider and a country western singer."

"If there's a pattern, it's with this place, not my being here."

"I apologize, honey. I don't think you're a Judas."

"Jonah. Judas was the betrayer."

"Right. And Jonah was the guy who took a ride in a whale's belly."

He puts his hand on top of hers in her lap. The tense moment passes.

"What are you working on?" She nods toward his screen. "Baseball stats?"

"Not really."

"Checking the market?"

"No. I'm letting the market take care of itself today."

"What, then." She cranes to get a better look at his screen. "What's this?"

"I was just getting a little background on the late Fletcher Downs."

"Douglas Stennett, are you going Hardy Boys on me?"

"No!" He actually blushes.

"You're not looking for motives for murder?"

"Maybe a little. I feel kind of involved, you know."

"Oh, I know. Believe me."

He smiles ruefully. "I guess I understand a little better how you got so tied up in those other murders."

"Hard to just turn away and pretend it didn't happen."

"I'll make you a deal," he says after a pause.

"What's that?"

"No Nancy Drew for you, and no Hardy Boys for me. We'll let the experts take care of this."

"Deal. Sealed with a kiss." She leans over and brushes his lips with hers.

Her computer screen jumps to life when she touches the mouse. She logs on to the research class website, finds her folder, and opens her quiz. She frowns at the questions she's left unanswered, then closes the folder and logs onto the Internet instead.

While she waits for the connection, she glances at Doug's screen and sees that he's got one of his baseball sites up. She guesses at a website address for the local paper, types in www.shepherdstown-dailydispatch.com, and gets the hateful "Site Not Found" message. She tries other combinations, also without success.

"Doug? Will you be OK here if I run downtown for a little bit?"

"Of course. Honey, I'm fine. Really."

"I just need to do some more legwork. I should be back in an hour or so."

"Want me to come with you?"

"That's OK. You look happy right where you are."

"Yeah. It does kind of take my mind off—"

He doesn't need to finish. She kisses his forehead, and he cups the back of her head and kisses her lips.

"Hurry back," he says. "And be very careful."

"I might be an hour and a half. I thought I'd see if I could interview the editor at the paper. What's her name? Hafner?"

"Yeah. Mo." He puts a hand on her arm. "That's all you're going to investigate, right? Your class assignments?"

"Yes! We've got a deal, remember?"

She feels the tension in her neck and shoulders as she walks out to the car in the brilliant sunshine of the late afternoon. The fact that there has been another death, possibly a murder, has unnerved her more than she wants to admit. And despite his assurances to the contrary, Doug has to have been deeply shaken by discovering the body. She knows that special horror all too well.

She finds a parking space in front of Philips Street Books and—remembering to feed the meter—walks the two blocks to Allen's Alley, a short block of old two-story houses converted to commercial use. She finds art galleries, crafts shops, a movie house not yet open for the night, a bakery now closed for the day, and a leather shop with a display of hats in the window. The street dead-ends at the fork of Buck's River that meanders through town.

Glancing in the window at Allen's Alley Art Mart, she sees a middle-aged woman in a crisp print frock standing behind the counter and decides to go in. She spends a few moments walking along the wall to her right, looking at watercolors and oils of local landscapes, wildlife, and a few portraits, all by local artists, none especially noteworthy to her eye.

"If I can help, just let me know," the woman says from behind her.

"I do have a question, actually." Mo walks over to the counter, where the woman has been working the Sudoku puzzle in the local paper.

"Fire away, but I warn you, I'm just babysitting the store for the owner. I really don't know much about art."

"This isn't an art question. I was wondering why they call this street 'Allen's Alley.' Was there a famous artist named Allen from the area?"

She smiles. "There was a famous Allen, all right, Allen Lehman, and he grew up in this very house."

"Lehman. I'm afraid I haven't heard of him."

"You would have if you were a Badger football fan. Allen Lehman is the only Heisman Trophy winner the university in Madison has ever had."

"The football award?"

"Right. For the best college football player in the country each year. Allen Lehman won it in 1940. Led the nation in rushing yardage and points scored. He even did the punting and kicked extra points."

"Did he play professionally?"

"Enlisted after Pearl Harbor. He was reported missing in action in 1943. The family waited over four months before the Navy finally told them he was dead. His picture's over there." She nods toward the wall behind her.

Mo walks over and studies a small portrait of a handsome young man in drab brown football uniform, grinning out from under a leather helmet that doesn't look as if it provided much protection.

"Folks started calling this 'Allen's Alley,' like the old radio show, when he won the Heisman. The name stuck."

Mo takes her notepad out of her purse and writes "Allen Lehman. Football star. Killed in WWII."

"Are you writing a book or something?"

Mo walks back to the counter. "It's for my research class."

"I just knew you were a writer. I'm Fran Neudecker. Welcome to Shepherdstown."

"Monona Quinn. It's a beautiful area."

"We like it."

"Are you a native?"

"Third generation. Granddaddy was a logger."

"Maybe you could answer another question for me."

"I'll sure try."

"The question's kind of strange. 'What's wrong with Philips Street?'"

"What's *wrong* with it?"

"I don't know what it means. She doesn't give any clues."

"Beats me. Sorry."

"Not at all. You cracked one of the tough ones for me. Was Philips Street named after somebody famous, too?"

"Sure. Phillip Shepherd, the one who owned the railroad. I think they named the town after him to convince him to run the line through here. They used his first name for the main street. I don't guess that helps with your question, though."

"You never know." Mo stuffs her notepad back in her purse. "Thanks again."

"Don't mention it. Enjoy the rest of your stay."

Instead of Allen's Alley continuing straight across Philips Street, it forks into two streets, Fairgrounds Drive and Water Street. The Triangle Market stands in the "v" formed by the two streets, a pie-shaped two-story building with second-story dormer windows on both sides.

That's easy enough, Mo thinks. They call it "The Triangle Market" because it's shaped like a triangle. But the journalist in her demands that she verify her guess.

The elderly man clerking in the tiny store, Edwin Noyes, is in fact the owner, as was his father before him. He tells Mo that the store got its name not from its shape but because they used to feed the loggers there, announcing that dinner was served by beating on a huge triangle that hung outside the door.

A trick question, Mo thinks as she walks back down Philips Street. And that's when it hits her. She takes out her notebook and writes herself a note to check the spelling of a name.

The clock in the bell tower of the Lutheran Church at the corner indicates almost five. The newspaper office is half a block farther on, and Mo figures the editor might have a moment to chat, with the day's edition finished and deadlines for the next one still hours away.

"Hi. Help you?"

A woman who doesn't look to be much older than seventeen looks up from her computer as Mo walks in.

"Hi. Sorry to bother you. I'm looking for the editor."

"That's me. Or 'It is I' if you're a grammarian." She gets up and comes out from behind the desk. "Becky Hafner," she says, reaching out to shake hands.

"Monona Quinn. I'd like to interview you, if you're willing. Is this a good time?"

Becky Hafner's eyes get huge—making her look even younger. "You're her!" she exclaims. "She!"

"Excuse me?"

"You catch killers and get your stories picked up by the Associated Press, and you want to interview me? I feel like asking you for your autograph."

"My reputation is greatly inflated," Mo says. "The interview is for a class assignment, but I'd also love to learn more about a colleague."

"Wow. Colleague. I love that. C'mon. We can sit over here. Would you like coffee? I'm afraid it's been sitting all day."

"No, thanks. I'm good."

Becky Hafner leads her to a large circular table covered with newspapers and computer printouts. Mo takes one of the three chairs and gets out her notepad while Becky arranges herself as if sitting for a portrait in the chair across from her.

Mo begins with easy questions and draws out the young editor's background.

She's a local, always loved reading, discovered Jane Austen and the Brontes early, wrote poetry and kept a journal as a kid. She edited the high school newspaper, went to the University at Eau Claire and majored in journalism, came back and landed a job at the hometown paper. Within two years she was the editor. She has one part time reporter and must rely on local press releases and wire copy to help fill the slender news hole every weekday afternoon and Sunday morning.

"Isn't this town kind of small to support a daily newspaper?" Mo asks.

"It's part of a chain of locals. The owners apparently have big plans. Meanwhile, it's a real hassle getting the paper out every day."

"I'll bet. I have all I can do to get out a weekly. What's the toughest story you've had to cover?"

"That guy who got hit by the train two summers ago," she says immediately, "right after I became editor."

"I heard about that. It must have been awful."

"It was. Thank heavens it wasn't anybody from around here. Oh—that sounds terrible."

"No, no. I understand. I've had to cover two—well, you know."

Becky nods eagerly. "You didn't just cover them! I hope you'll let me interview you when we're finished."

Mo brushes it aside. "Is that the only death you've had to cover?"

She shakes her head. "We had another one last summer, a country western singer who drowned in the river. That was pretty rough, too."

Mo takes a big breath. It's time to hand her sister scribe a third story about death—and a chance to scoop the big city papers and get a story picked up by the Associated Press.

"I'm afraid you've got another tough one to cover," she says, watching the young editor's eyes get huge again. "And this one might not be an accident."

24

He checks his watch as Mo turns in at the circular drive: 6:11. Finally. Over an hour late. Totally unreliable about time.

He goes back to his book. The car pulls up. The door slams. Her feet make soft shushing noises on the pine needles.

"Please don't be mad. I'm sorry."

"I had a bad book to keep me company." He tosses the thick hardcover on the table, where it lands with a solid thud. "Maybe I shouldn't say 'bad.' I'm no expert, and lots of folks eat this stuff up. Besides, it isn't nice to speak ill of the dead."

"Doug, I—"

"Ms. Taylor offered to let me stay in the lab while she went to dinner, but I told her to go ahead and lock up, and I'd wait for you out here. Shaping up to be a beautiful evening, isn't it?"

The sun is still well above the trees beyond the building. A gentle breeze stirs the air. Tomorrow could be a great morning for running—if he's able to run.

"The interview took a lot longer than I thought."

She's still standing, notepad in hand. He flexes his right leg, and pain shoots up from his heel.

"Oh, Doug—I figured out the answer to the question. About Philips Street. Let's go get some dinner. I'll tell you on the way."

"Tell me now."

"You are angry, aren't you?"

"I'm not angry. You did say you'd be back at five."

"Around five. I said around five."

"Six-eleven is not 'around five.' Even on 'Mo time.'"

"I said I was sorry."

He fights down the anger. What is the matter with him? He certainly should be used to her chronic lateness, and there's no real harm done. Must be the damn pain.

"Tell me the secret of Philips Street."

"OK. I was going through some back stories in the *Dispatch*—she's got the last three years on computer, since the chain bought the paper—and I ran across a story about Phillip Shepherd."

He feels his anger slipping away in the face of her enthusiasm. "The guy the town's named after?"

"Yes. The railroad guy. A lady at the Art Mart told me that they'd named Philips Street after him. And there it was right in front of me."

"There what was?"

"His name. 'P-H-I-L-L-I-P.' Two 'L's. They spell the street with one 'L.' They spelled it wrong."

"That's it? That's what's wrong with Philips Street?"

"I can't imagine what else it could be."

"Seems like a lot of fuss to make over not much."

"I really am sorry I'm late. I know you hate it when I keep you waiting. But I—"

"I don't hate it. It just shows lack of respect when you're chronically late."

"I'm not—"

She bites back whatever else she was going to say. He swings his legs off the bench and hops up, forgetting.

"Ow! Damn it!"

"What's the matter? Is it your heel?"

"It's nothing. I had a little trouble with it this morning." He dusts off his trousers and tugs on the legs to straighten the creases.

"Did you go out running?"

"I always run."

"I know, but—"

"Mo, it's nothing, really. It will work itself out."

"I know. You'll 'run it off,' like that horrible coach in high school told you to 'run off' a broken nose."

He laughs. "Wild Bill Lavelette! What a piece of work that guy was. His solution to everything was 'run it off.' C'mon. Let's get some dinner."

"Don't forget your book."

"Right. Library book. Don't want to lose that."

"You're really limping!"

"It's nothing."

"Maybe you should rest it for a few days. It wouldn't kill you—"

"Where do you want to eat?"

"I don't care. There aren't a whole lot of choices. We could try that other restaurant downtown."

They both start around the car to the driver's side.

"I'll drive," Doug says. "You don't really like to drive this car anyway."

"I don't mind. Doesn't driving hurt your heel?"

"I told you—"

"I know. It's nothing. You drive." She tosses him the keys.

"Let's just go home," he says when they're both strapped in. "I don't really feel like eating at a restaurant tonight."

"There's nothing to eat at the cabin."

"We can pick something up. We pass a KFC."

"You never eat fast food!"

"Tonight I'll eat fast food."

He tries to fight down the anger and frustration, no doubt born of pain, her being late, and the shock of finding a corpse in the woods. She's got something more she wants to tell him, something she's pretty sure he won't like, and she'll tell it when she's ready and not before. He's learned not to try to rush her.

"It's going to be another beautiful sunset," she notes as they drive around the oval and out onto the county road.

"Two minutes earlier than yesterday. You don't even notice it yet, but the days are already getting shorter."

"Don't remind me."

"It happens, whether we mark it or not."

"We can use the drive-thru if you want," she suggests as they approach the KFC, fourth in the lineup of eight franchise eateries blighting the landscape at the edge of town.

"I'm not in a hurry. And I hate the drive-thru window." He wrenches the wheel too sharply, and the tires squeal as he turns in at the lot. Air pressure must be low. He'll check the next time he finds a station that has an air hose.

Inside, he studies the menu board while they wait in line behind a woman, a man old enough to be her father, and two kids, a boy, probably eight, and big sister, maybe ten or eleven. Big menu, little choice, just recombinations of the same few greasy items.

"Do you want to get the eight-piece bucket?" Mo suggests. "We can have a picnic with the leftovers."

"I'm just going to have a sandwich."

"Oh. OK."

The girl wants chicken strips. The boy wants drumsticks. The woman thinks they should get the twelve-piece bucket and wonders if they can get different kinds of chicken with that. The man, who turns out to be her father-in-law, just wants his grandchildren to shut up and to get out of there for under thirty bucks.

It's a long, tense negotiation, made more difficult by the fact that the young lady taking the order seems not to speak English—or any other language. She is quite proficient at grunting and shrugging to indicate her complete lack of caring one way or the other.

The family feud finally resolved—the kids get exactly what they want, while the spineless grandfather digs a little deeper into his pocket—Doug steps to up to the counter.

"Here or to go?"

"Here."

"I thought—" Mo begins.

"Let's just eat it here." And then, to the clerk, "I'll have the chicken breast sandwich. I don't suppose I could get that baked."

She grunts, shrugs, shakes her head.

"OK. Chicken sandwich. Nothing on the bun, please."

She gives him a perfectly blank stare.

"No butter or mayo."

"I don't know if we can do that."

"Don't the buns come out of the package without butter and mayo?"

"Yeah. But then they put butter and mayo on."

"Never mind. Chicken sandwich. No fries."

"Potato wedge."

"How's that?"

"We don't have fries. We have potato wedges."

"I don't want potato wedges, either. Just the sandwich. And a glass for water."

"Number four, extra crispy," Mo tells the woman.

"Sides?"

"Wedges and beans."

"Biscuit or corn bread."

"Biscuit."

Miss Congeniality punches in the order, collects his money, counts out the change the register indicates. "Number seven three nine," she says, handing him the register slip.

They wait for their order by the counter and then sit in two molded plastic pods by the window. He hands her the plastic tray with her dinner and arranges his wrapped sandwich on a napkin in front of him.

"They sure waste a lot of paper wrapping all this stuff up, so we can transport it the ten feet to the table and then throw it all away. It's criminal."

She chews on a potato wedge and looks out the window. He unwraps his sandwich—the bun is soggy with butter and mayo—and refolds the wrapper into fourths. He scrapes off as much of the glop as he can from his sandwich.

"Did you and the editor talk shop?" he asks, hoping to break through the gloom he has undoubtedly helped create with all his carping.

She finishes chewing before speaking. "The *Dispatch* is part of a chain of about twenty little newspapers across northern Wisconsin and the U.P." She plucks another potato wedge from its cardboard envelope and dips it in the lump of ketchup on her tray. "The same ads run in five or six papers in an area, and she's supposed to sell local ads. They tell her how much space to fill, she sends stories and photos, and the papers come back. She doesn't know what the paper will look like until she sees it."

"That sounds easy enough."

"It sounds awful!"

He peels the skin off the chicken before reassembling his sandwich.

"You like the set up you've got with Pierpont better?"

"Yes! He actually lets me edit. I'm lucky."

He'll just have to wait her out. She'll tell him what's on her mind when she's ready. He finishes his sandwich and waits for her to spoon up the last of the beans. He buses their table, stuffing all the packaging in the trash and setting the tray on the shelf.

The sun balances on the tip of a pine tree as they walk to their car.

They drive in silence. At the sign for Heavenly Acres, it's another three tenths of a mile to their turn. If he runs from their cabin out to the Heavenly Acres riding stables and back, it's 7.4 miles. If he turns the other way at the highway and runs out past the Buck's Lake Trailer Park and back, it's 5.8 miles.

He slows as they enter the Merrynook grounds. The nightly bonfire is already blazing, the parents absorbed with their talk and beer drinking while their kids run wild. The lights are off in the Wilkerson's house.

"Shall we have a fire?" he asks when they get inside their cabin. Her silence has become unnerving. "It's really cooling off nicely tonight."

"A fire would be nice."

There's no nice in her voice.

He gets the fire going and pours the wine, and they settle in on the couch, with space between them. He forgets and puts his feet up on the table, and pain shoots up from his right heel. He slowly brings his feet down.

"I found out something pretty interesting from nosing through those back issues of the *Dispatch* this afternoon," she says.

Here it comes. Finally.

"What's that?" He hopes he sounds interested, but not *too*. He figures he's lucky she didn't wait until he was going to sleep to tell him.

"Do you remember those other two deaths that happened in this area?"

"The rodeo cowboy and the singer?"

"Right. I looked up the stories. The country western singer was Kenny Laine."

"Never heard of him."

"He had a couple of hits maybe ten years ago. They found his body in the river. He'd been drinking. The police report said he appeared to have slipped while trying to wade and hit his head on a rock. They ruled it accidental death."

"Sounds reasonable."

"Two summers ago, it was the rodeo rider, Tommy Preston. From Lodi, actually. About twenty miles from Madison."

"How'd he die?"

"Got hit by a train walking across a train trestle at night."

"He must have really been blitzed."

"They decided he must have thought he could beat the train across. Another accident."

"And then there's our buddy Fletcher Downs. They say trouble comes in threes."

"All three were from out of town, and all three were famous."

"Fletcher Downs was famous. But a rodeo rider and a second-tier country western singer? Isn't that stretching it a bit?"

"They were all performers, anyway."

"Still not outside the realm of coincidence. At least for rational thinkers who don't buy the Intelligent Design theory of the universe."

"Just a minute. I want to show you something."

Obsessed with dead folks again, he thinks as she goes to get her book bag. But at least she's talking to him.

"Here." She settles in next to him on the couch and hands him two photocopies.

RODEO STAR KILLED BY TRAIN

ON FAIRGROUNDS DRIVE TRESTLE

By Becky Hafner, Dispatch editor

"Not a bad story," he says, handing the page back. "Just the facts. No histrionics."

"Read the other one."

TOMMY PRESTON, CW STAR,

FOUND DROWNED IN RIVER

By Becky Hafner, Dispatch editor

Another straight-forward, solidly reported story. He tries to hand her the clip, but instead, she thrusts the first one back at him.

"Look at the dates."

"They're both dated July twenty-ninth. Both died on the twenty-eighth. Another coincidence."

"Fletcher Downs died on July twenty-eighth. Pretty big coincidence, isn't it?"

"Yeah," he admits. "It's a damn big coincidence. But in real life, coincidences happen all the time. It's only in novels that everything has to have an explanation."

"Or maybe it isn't a coincidence at all."

"And you're always accusing me of seeing patterns in everything."

"It's possible, though. Isn't it?"

"Sure," he says. "I suppose it's possible. But it's also possible that all three were accidents that just happened to occur on the same day, a year apart.

"And for both our sakes," he adds, getting up to add wood to the fire, "I certainly hope that's the case. I don't like the idea of either one of us getting cozy with another murderer."

25

The fire dies down, and they sit in the darkness, talking and watching the lights shimmering on the lake, until the chill drives them into bed and under the covers. Then they talk some more. Doug finally admits that the three deaths on the same date seem more than coincidental. He also admits that, if foul play were involved, it's unlikely that the local police would be up to the task of tracking down a potential serial killer.

"Handing out parking tickets seems to be more their speed," he notes.

But he remains adamant—to the point of raising his voice, which he almost never does—that she will have nothing to do with any murder investigation.

Mo agrees, of course. She will still drive down to Madison Friday night, as originally planned, and spend Saturday catching up at the paper and giving Jackie a little TLC after a week in the house with only Naomi to look in on him and feed him. She'll go to Mass Sunday morning and drive back in time for them to have dinner together. When they'd first discussed it, he'd complained about being "dumped" for the weekend, but she knows he loves to be alone and only protests to avoid hurting her feelings.

In light of recent revelations, however, there is one big change in the plans. In the morning, Mo calls LaShandra Cooper, the Dane County Sheriff's Department detective who helped track down

Father O'Bannon's killer, and briefly explains the events of the last three summers. Since one of the victims was from Dane County, Mo suggests that the detective might be able to get her boss, Sheriff Roger Repoz, to let her drive up north and investigate personally. Detective Cooper agrees to ask.

Again, Doug stresses that she is to have nothing to do with any investigation.

Fair enough, she thinks as she drives to campus for her Friday morning classes. But that doesn't stop her from thinking about it. How could she not think about it? She has no problem positing all sorts of reasons why someone might want to harm Fletcher Downs—jilted lover? insulted student? betrayed wife?—but those motives won't stretch to explain the murders of a rodeo cowboy and a country western singer on the same date.

Perhaps there's really no connection after all. Doug insists that it still might be three unrelated deaths, and he's the expert on statistics and probability.

At least she feels confident about the quiz due in research methods. Unless her answer to the "what's wrong with Philips Street" conundrum turns out to be wrong, she's pretty sure she's gotten nine out of nine. She's come up with a tenth question that would probably stump the rest of the class and even the teacher, since it seems to have escaped everyone's notice, including the local police: What happened on July twenty-eighth in Shepherdstown the last three years in a row?

But she's decided not to ask it. Making the connection public, even in such a small way, might alert the killer—if there actually is a killer—that someone has figured out his pattern. Mo will let LaShandra Cooper make that sort of decision. And if the detective decided not to investigate—or wasn't allowed to—Mo will simply hand the photocopies over to Sergeant Lafferty and try to put the whole mess out of her mind.

Fat chance of being able to do that.

She's still trying to come up with an acceptable tenth question when she parks a block from the entrance to the grounds and tromps in past all the cars.

June, the obese historical novelist from Dubuque, and local train buff Jim are the only ones beside Mo to get all nine questions right. The others have fallen for the obvious—and wrong—answer for the Triangle Market, and Bobbie Barnes is the only other one to get the Philips Street question right.

Alanna Taylor rewards the three perfect scores with chocolate coins wrapped in gold foil. Then they go around the room reading their tenth questions and seeing if anyone can answer them.

Mousy Joanna poses one that only Jim knows: "What's unique about the Buck's Creek School?" which still stands on what are now the grounds of the Shepherdstown Logging Museum. It was the last functioning one-room schoolhouse in the state, he informs them.

Bobbie Barnes is able to fool them all by asking them to name the strangest court case in Shepherdstown history. "Strangest" could certainly have been disputed—and indeed Jim does dispute it—but even he has to admit that the case is strange. In 1896, Arland Phillips (with two L's, Barnes notes with a wink) brought suit in Circuit Court to force a neighbor, Frederick Franck, to take custody of and assume responsibility for Mrs. Phillips who, her husband alleged, was giving Mr. Franck all of the advantages of the marital state without any of the attendant obligations.

The suit was denied, Barnes adds with a laugh.

Mo has been casting about for a question while listening to the others. She can think of seemingly no end of great questions—but she doesn't know the answers. When her turn comes, she blurts out the first plausible thing that comes to mind. "What was Herman Chandler's first starring role in a play?"

She knows because she slipped into interviewer mode when she met him and mined a great deal of information about his career in local theater.

"Geez Louise," Jim yelps. "That's not local history!"

"Of course it is," Alanna Taylor says. "Mr. Chandler has directed the Writing Without Walls School in Shepherdstown for twenty-five years. He's a local institution.

"You appear to have stumped the experts," she adds to Mo when nobody can answer.

"He played George in *Who's Afraid of Virginia Woolf?* in Madison."

"Yeah," Robert says. "I can see that."

Alanna ends the class by passing out another quiz sheet, this one on Wisconsin authors, to be completed for the final class session in one week.

From class, Mo goes directly to the noon forum, today composed of a series of three-minute "one-act plays" from the screenwriter's class. Robert appears in two of the skits and to Mo's eye seems much more poised and polished.

At the end of the last skit, Herman Chandler calls all the actors back for a curtain call, but as the applause dies and the players depart, he casts a serious eye out over the audience. The presence of Sergeant Lafferty on campus yesterday afternoon to interview members of the fiction writing class has of course hit the school grapevine, and news of the death of Fletcher Downs has circulated all morning.

"I just wanted to take a moment, on behalf of the teachers and staff, to express our shock and sorrow at the death of Fletcher Downs," he says. "Although Mr. Downs was new to our community this year, he had already made many friends among us. Local authorities are investigating the circumstances of his death."

Chandler continues, raising his voice over the buzz of the audience. "Irene Crowley, a veteran fiction instructor here at the school, has graciously taken over the mystery writing class." He looks down at the notecard in his hand. "If any of you have any information that might be helpful in the ongoing investigation, you're urged to call Detective Sergeant Lafferty."

He gives the phone number, repeats it twice, and then, instead of his usual plug for WWW merchandise on sale in the cafeteria and his cheery admonition to "write-on!" he simply turns and walks off the stage.

Dozens of conversations erupt as Mo slips out a side door. She's taken only a few steps down the hall when Myrna Gillory steps out from the shadows.

"You startled me!" Mo says, fighting the urge to step back.

"Can we talk for a minute?"

"Of course."

Mo follows her out into the bright sunlight.

"Over there?" Gillory nods toward the nearby grove of fir trees and birches. When they reach the trees a hundred or so yards from the building, she takes a candy bar out of her jeans pocket, tears off the wrapper, and has it almost to her mouth when her eye catches Mo's.

"You want some?"

"No, thank you."

The entire candy bar disappears into her mouth. She's a minute chewing before she tries to talk. "It's about that cop, Lafferty, and our little interrogation yesterday."

Mo nods noncommittally.

"Mind if I smoke?" She already has the cigarette out and in her mouth.

"Go ahead."

Matching plumes of smoke stream from Myrna Gillory's nostrils. She frowns and takes another long drag on the cigarette. "I lied," she says, words and smoke coiling out together. "He asked me when I last saw the, uh, deceased. I suppose he asked everyone."

Mo waits.

"I told him I'd last seen him in class Monday, like everybody else. Oh. Sorry."

She has blown smoke directly at Mo, who waves it away.

"You saw him after that?" Mo asks.

"I spent the night with him. When I woke up in the morning, he was gone."

She drops the cigarette and grinds it into the dirt with her heel. She takes out another candy bar and unpeels it. The sun has gone behind some clouds, and the wind has picked up from the west.

"Do you think the cops will find out?" Gillory asks after she has chewed and swallowed the candy.

"Yes. I think they'll find out."

"That won't look so good, huh?"

"Lying about it looks worse."

"I didn't kill him!"

Mo looks down at the hand gripping her forearm, and Gillory releases her.

"I should tell Lafferty, shouldn't I?"

"Yes," Mo says. "Right away."

Gillory nods. "I knew that. I knew that." She turns pleading eyes on Mo.

"They'll understand, won't they? Why I lied?"

"I don't know."

"They'll think I killed him!"

"You'll be a suspect. If you didn't kill him, you—"

"I didn't!"

Again the tight grip on the forearm. Mo looks down at the hand.

"Sorry." The hand drops to her side.

"It will be a lot better if they hear it from you."

"I'll go down there right now."

She walks swiftly away, lighting a cigarette before she disappears around the side of the building. The first fat, warm raindrop hits Mo's cheek, startling her. Having given this scant warning, the skies open, and hard rains drench her instantly.

Already as wet as she's going to get, Mo walks slowly out to her car. She has decided to skip the fiction class and get on the road. She'll have a lot of time to think on the long drive to Mitchell. Among the topics she'll ponder, she's sure, is just how much, if at all, she believes Myrna Gillory's assertion that she didn't kill Fletcher Downs.

26

Lafferty puts his beefy hands on his knees and leans forward, the chair creaking beneath him. The kid, Elzie, leans back, as if needing to keep a certain space between them. He's the kind of kid who still thinks the world's a joke only he gets.

"So, you followed Lloyd out into the parking lot. Then what happened?"

"I wasn't following him. I was just leaving."

"You left your gear in the break room."

"Yeah. Forgot it." Elzie picks at something on his left palm.

Lafferty leans in again, thrusting his face into the kid's space. "You and Lloyd got into it in the parking lot. What was that all about?"

"Whattaya think? He'd just gotten me canned."

"It was his fault you got fired."

"I shouldn'ta let him get me pissed. I know that."

Lafferty fishes his coffee mug off the table. The coffee, which started out bad, is now cold and bad. He catches Elzie's eyes on him. The kid stares him down. Tough guy.

"I guess he must piss you off a lot, huh?"

"You have no idea."

The kid watches the coffee mug move to Lafferty's mouth and back to the table. He's got that ratty cloth cap of his twisted up in his lap.

"You know Lloyd was out there when Mr. Stennett found the body."

"I heard."

"We think maybe somebody killed him. You wouldn't know anything about that, would you?"

"No!"

"You weren't anywhere near there?"

"No. I was home."

"Anybody see you there?"

Elzie starts picking at the callus again. He mumbles something.

"What's that?"

"No."

"You didn't have any visitors?"

"No."

The girl taps on the door.

"Yeah!"

She sticks her head in. "That reporter is on the phone again."

"Which one?"

"The one from the Associated Press." She flinches, as if she thinks he's going to throw something at her.

"Tell him I died."

"I told him that before. He didn't believe me. Maybe you should tell him."

"Tell him again!" He forces his voice down. "Be more convincing."

The door snaps shut.

"Hey!"

The door reopens a cautious inch.

"Get me more coffee, willya?"

The door closes. Lafferty turns his attention back to the kid, Elzie. "Did you go see your friend Roberta in the trailer park that night?" he asks.

"She's not my friend."

"Did you go see her?"

"No!"

"She says you two are close. Real close."

"She's nuts."

"You don't have a lot of friends, do you?"

"You gonna arrest me for not having friends?"

"Should I?"

"Because if you aren't, I don't have to stay, right?"

"What's 'Elzie' short for? Elizabeth's the only thing I can think of. Your mama didn't name you Elizabeth, did she?"

"It isn't short for anything. It's just a name."

The tapping at the door again.

"Yeah! Bring it in!"

She opens the door barely wide enough to slide in sideways, holding the coffee at arm's length, as if she's trying to feed it to a crocodile and is afraid of losing a hand.

"Another reporter's on the phone. He says—"

"Tell him he can read all about it in the *Shepherdstown Daily Dispatch*. I got anything, I'll give it to Becky, same as always."

"There's also a woman here who says she needs to talk to you."

"Tell her—"

"She's not a reporter."

"What is she?"

"She says she was a student in that man's class. Her name is Myna something."

"Myrna? Myrna Gillory?"

She nods in relief. "Yeah! That's it."

"Tell her I'll be with her in a minute. See if she wants coffee."

The door shuts. The kid stares at it. Lafferty leans back and gives his belly a good scratch. He could throw the kid in a cell for twenty-four hours, maybe scare him a little, but what good would it do?

"Get out of here," he says. "But don't go far. I might need to talk to you again."

The kid can't leave fast enough, closing the door harder than he needs to but keeping it just this side of a slam.

One, two, three, four, fi—the tapping.

"Give me two minutes," he says.

He sips his coffee. Further aging has not improved it. He decides he'd better take a leak before seeing what Myrna Gillory has on her mind. These days he never passes up an opportunity. He doesn't have cancer, after all, just a prostate infection. That and what the doctor calls a "generous prostate." He's getting to the age when everything he's got is either drying up or leaking.

He empties his bladder in the tiny half bathroom off the utility closet.

"OK!" he hollers after he settles back in his chair. "Send her in."

She has the look of a woman who used to be fat and has lost a lot of weight. It's like the fat's still there but invisible.

"Have a seat, Miss Gillory."

She manages to get across the room and into the chair without looking at him. He picks up his notepad, pulls the pencil out from the twist of wire holding the pages together, and flips the notepad open.

"What's on your mind?"

"I lied."

He makes a sloppy tic-tac-toe grid on the pad. "What about?"

"The other day. When you asked me when I'd last seen Fletcher. Mr. Downs."

She has a small smear of something by her mouth. Chocolate, maybe.

"Why'd you go and do a thing like that?"

"I was scared you'd get the wrong idea."

"What's the right idea?"

"I spent the night with him."

"At Heavenly Acres."

"Yes."

"Monday night."

"Yes. When I got up in the morning, he wasn't there. He didn't leave a note or anything. I thought he must just be out to get cigarettes or something. I went back to my motel to get ready for school."

Lafferty sketches a crow on his notepad. He doesn't like the way it turns out.

"When's the last time you actually saw him?"

"He woke me up once when he got up to use the bathroom."

"What time was that?"

"I don't know."

"About?"

"I didn't look at the clock."

He draws a large question mark on the pad, sketches a little noose on the end of it.

"Are you going to arrest me?"

"What for?"

"For lying to you."

"No, Ms. Gillory. I'm not going to arrest you. That night, while you two were discussing the fine points of literature—" He smiles at her "—or whatever it was you were discussing, did he mention any problems he might be having with anybody?"

"What kind of problems?"

He's got the beak too big. That's the problem. "A fan stalking him, maybe. You read about that kind of thing."

"No. Nothing like that."

"Everything was fine at home? With his wife?"

She shows no reaction. "He didn't mention anything."

"You knew he was married."

"Yes."

"Right. Of course you did. You two didn't get into it, did you?"

"'Get into it?'"

"Have a disagreement?"

"No."

"Not even a little one?"

"No."

"Had you known him before the conference?"

"We'd corresponded. By e-mail."

He sketches a second crow. "How'd you wind up roommates?"

"He invited me to dinner."

"Uh huh."

"I'd asked him to read my manuscript. He suggested dinner."

"And had he? Read your manuscript?" The second crow looks like Myrna Gillory.

"Yes."

"What was the verdict?"

"He said it showed great promise. He said I had a natural flair for storytelling."

"But—?"

"But the manuscript needed a thorough revision."

"How'd you feel about that?"

"What do you mean?"

"Were you disappointed? Angry, maybe?"

"I was flattered."

"Flattered."

"That he liked it. That he'd even read it."

"Did you pay him for this evaluation?"

"No. I—No."

"He must have been a real nice fella."

He prints the word "novel" on the pad, draws a circle around it, puts a line through it. He catches her trying to read what he's written. He smiles. "So, you sent him this manuscript before the conference started, right? If he'd already read it."

"Yes."

"Did you send anything else along with it?"

"Like what?"

"Like your picture, maybe? I mean, you knew what he looked like, from all those pictures on the covers of the books, right? But you two had never met face to face before the conference. Isn't that what you said?"

"Yes."

"So, maybe you sent him a picture, so he'd know what you looked like?"

"Yes. I think I did send a picture."

She starts when the girl taps on the door.

"Someone from the FBI is on the phone."

"The F—" He groans and slashes another tic-tac-toe board on his pad. "Tell him I'll call back in fifteen minutes."

"It's a she. She sounded pretty urgent."

"A she. Well, well." He taps the eraser end of his pencil on the pad. The pencil slips from his fingers, bounces straight up off the pad, and he catches it, as if he'd planned the whole thing. "Tell her I'll call her back in fifteen minutes," he says.

The door closes.

F—B—I. Shit on a hockey puck. He starts to sketch another Myrna crow, this one with its leg caught in a trap.

"Can you think of anybody who'd want to kill him?"

"No. No one."

"And you didn't see him again after he got up in the night to use the facility?"

"That's right."

The third crow definitely has Myrna Gillory's face.

"You're planning to stay for the rest of the conference?"

"Yes."

"I can reach you at Coach's Inn?"

"Yes."

"One more question. Why did you come in and tell the truth now?"

"It—seemed like the right thing to do."

"But lying felt like the right thing to do when I talked to you before?"

"Like I said, I was afraid you'd get the wrong idea. I felt bad about lying. I knew it was wrong as soon as I did it."

Maybe you were afraid I'd get the wrong idea before, he thinks after he ushers her out. But I don't think that's what you're afraid of now. I think you're afraid I'll get the right idea.

He tosses his notepad on the desk. F—B—freaking—I. If that isn't the icing on the dog turd. With a groan, he gets up and goes to get the phone number from the girl.

27

LaShandra Cooper had been quite open about her lack of interest in going to Shepherdstown to investigate the two-year-old death of some obscure rodeo cowboy from Lodi that maybe, just maybe, might be a homicide. Hadn't been, that is, until Mo showed her the three same dates for the three deaths.

That seemed to persuade the sheriff, too. He gave Cooper the OK to go north, but for no more than a day, two tops, to take a look around.

With Cooper planning to drive up the next day in her own car, Mo heads north alone Sunday afternoon with the growing conviction that they might in fact be dealing with a serial killer. The key, she figures on the long drive back, is obviously the significance of the date. If all three deaths were in fact murder, and if the same person were responsible for all three, then the motive must have something to do with the date.

She'd searched the databases from the *Doings* office during a break from her Saturday workathon for any sort of historical tie-in with July twenty-eighth. She'd unearthed any number of fascinating nuggets. On July 28, 1945, for example, a United States Army bomber had crashed into the seventy-ninth floor of the Empire State Building, killing fourteen people, a chilling precursor of September 11, 2001. Mo rather doubted the more recent deaths could somehow be related to that. Nor could she really imagine them being retribution for the death of Thomas Cromwell, executed on that date in 1540. A massive earthquake devastated northern China in 1976, killing at least 242,000. It hardly balanced the scales, but on July 28, 2002, nine coal miners were rescued from a flooded mine in Somerset, Pennsylvania.

July twenty-eighth birthdays included Jim Davis, creator of "Garfield," and Sally Struthers, who played Archie Bunker's daughter, Gloria.

She'd checked July twenty-ninth as well, reasoning that the day the deaths were reported might be the significant factor. She discovered that Jack Paar hosted his first Tonight Show on July 29, 1957 and that Charles and Lady Di staged their royal wedding on that date in 1981. The actress Clara Bow, "King of Torts" attorney Melvin Belli, and Homer of the old bluegrass team of Homer and Jethro had all been July twenty-ninth babies, as had Peter Jennings, the network news anchor.Helpful in Trivial Pursuit, maybe, but none of that seemed to indicate a good—or even a lousy—motive for murder. If the dates had any significance, it was likely to be a private one, known only to the murderer.

She'd also tried to find some connection among the three victims—if indeed they were "victims" of anything more than bad luck and bizarre coincidence. All were performers, as Doug had noted. Kenny Laine was thirty-seven when he died, born and raised in West Covina, California. He'd once opened for Kenny Rogers at the Sahara Tahoe and had a couple of successful singles, but he was no Randy Travis.

Tommy Preston, the local boy from Lodi, Wisconsin, was only twenty-three when he died. He was raised on the farm, 4-H and FFA, won ribbons for his calves at the State Fair, played football for the Lodi High School Blue Devils. An All-American boy, trying to make a go of it in what surely must be one of the toughest sports in the world.

And, of course, Fletcher Downs, internationally known novelist and man of the world, sixty-one when he died. He hailed from York, Pennsylvania and, if publishers' bios were to be believed, had dropped out of high school, worked construction, hitchhiked across the country, and been arrested in Bakersfield for vagrancy before getting his GED and enlisting in the Navy.

All the while he was also apparently spending time in public libraries, reading tons of fiction, good and bad. He scribbled stories in cheap notebooks, filling them with the characters he'd met in flophouses and in line at soup kitchens. He'd gotten his big break while a student at the state college in Bakersfield when his creative writing instructor, impressed by his stuff, had sent it to her agent.

The rest was publishing history.

Word was that the man couldn't spell, seldom wrote a complete sentence, and was famous among copy editors for his howler dangling modifiers. But underpaid, overworked editors cleaned up his stuff and turned it into marketable prose.

Second-level country singer from southern California. Rodeo cowboy from rural Wisconsin. Best-selling author from rough-and-tumble. The common thread? Maybe LaShandra Cooper could find one.

Waves of fatigue hit Mo just north of Wausau, where the Interstate dwindles into a two-lane highway, and she finds herself crawling behind a battered old pickup truck going ten miles below the posted speed limit. She cranks up the air conditioning—a definite benefit to driving the CR-V, she must admit—and turns the radio up high, hoping the driving beat of the country western music will keep her awake.

It doesn't. Still fifteen miles south of Shepherdstown, she nods off for a second, the motion of her head falling forward and the sound of gravel pinging the underside of the car waking her as she drifts onto the shoulder.

Adrenaline rouses her momentarily, but she still pulls off at a convenience store in the tiny town of Gleason, buys a twenty-ounce Diet Coke, and walks down to the fairgrounds and back before trusting herself behind the wheel again.

She has promised Doug to be back in time for dinner, and she reaches Shepherdstown a little after six. To her surprise, the downtown streets are jammed with traffic, the sidewalks crowded with pedestrians. She spots two television mobile units parked on side streets. Becky Hafner might have had her scoop for a day, but now the big-city media have pounced on the story. The death of Fletcher Downs under suspicious circumstances is, after all, big news.

Should she stop for take-out? No. Doug will probably have prepared a welcome home dinner, somehow finding a way to whip up a fine meal in their primitive little kitchen. She imagines dining by candlelight on the deck—even if the candle would have to be the smelly kind that repels mosquitoes. Her two days away from Doug have made her keenly anticipate whatever homecoming he has planned for her.

Which makes the scene at the cabin all the more shocking.

The door stands ajar. Doug's jogging clothes drape the back of the couch in the living room. His shoes, streaked with dried mud, huddle on the kitchen floor. A half-drunk bottle of raspberry ice tea sits uncovered on the counter. An open bottle of Advil lies on its side, five capsules spilled on the counter.

For another man, the scene might be normal, the clutter of a bachelor weekend. For Doug, it's as if a tornado has struck.

"Doug!"

"In here." A weak moan.

She charges through the living room to the bedroom door. Doug lies on top of the unmade bed, propped up with pillows, his right leg resting on a cushion from the sofa in the living room. He's wearing only his briefs. His right foot is wrapped in a towel with a freezer bag full of ice. Stubble darkens his chin. His tangled hair is damp and matted.

"Doug! What happened?"

"I'm OK."

"You don't look OK. What's wrong?"

"It's the damn heel spur. It must have inflamed a tendon or something."

She kneels next to the bed and takes his hand in both of hers. His skin is clammy and sticky with sweat.

"Have you seen a doctor?"

"Up here?"

"So that's a self-diagnosis."

"Yeah. I could take antibiotics for the inflammation, but there's not much else to do until it settles down."

"Have you eaten anything?"

He thinks about that. His eyes seem cloudy with pain and fatigue. "A banana. Cold cereal. That's about it. What time is it?"

"Quarter to seven. Tell me what happened."

She puts his hand gently back on the coverlet, stands, pulls a chair over to the bedside, sits and takes his hand in hers again. He doesn't seem to mind, and she needs to be attached to him. Her legs are shaky, her stomach roiling. She has never seen him like this.

"When I went out for my run this morning, the heel was hurting a little worse than before."

"You didn't consider not running?" She tries to keep the anger out of her voice.

"These things generally work themselves out."

"And you didn't want to break your streak."

"No." He closes his eyes, and his head sinks back on the pillow. "I didn't want to break my streak. I guess it'll get broken now, though." His voice breaks, and she senses the enormity of his struggle and the strength of his inner demons.

"The pain kept getting worse. I had to stop and walk. Again. That happened to me when I found the body, too. It really hurt a lot."

She squeezes his hand gently. An admission of pain from Douglas Stennett could only come at great cost.

"Something really strange happened. Not this morning. The other time. It almost seems now as if I imagined or dreamed it. It doesn't seem real."

"What doesn't?"

"That strange little man. Lloyd. He just kind of appeared. I guess I didn't hear him with all the rain. All of a sudden, he was just there. It actually scared me."

"What did he do?"

"He didn't do anything. He was just there. He had this grin on his face. I—I started to run. But then I came back. That's when I found the body."

He heaves a sigh, his breath snagging on something, perhaps pain.

"Did you tell the police?"

"I don't know. I'm not sure. I think so. A man found me this morning. Colas. Juan Colas. He runs the stables for the resort. He gave me a ride back in his pickup. He asked me if I wanted to go to the ER in Wausau. A real good Samaritan, huh?"

The effort to tell the story seems to have exhausted him. "Could you put some fresh ice in the baggie? It seems to help."

"Of course!"

"And maybe get me a couple of Advil. And something to take them with."

"Would you like something to eat?"

"Maybe in a little bit. Mo? I'm real glad to see you."

A groan escapes her. She brushes his hair back and kisses his forehead. He smells of stale sweat.

"I'm going to get a cold cloth for your forehead. I think that would feel good."

"Thanks."

She hurries to the kitchen, dumps the warm juice, finds a cold, unopened bottle of lemonade in the fridge. The ice is only half reformed in the two tiny ice trays. She empties the trays into the sink, refills them and slides them back into the freezer compartment. She packs the baggie with what little ice she has, then gets two more baggies, fills them with water, and puts them in the freezer. She brings ice, Advil, and lemonade into the bedroom, where darkness has gathered.

"Do you want the light?"

"No. Thanks."

He takes the Advil, then the lemonade. He stiffens when she lifts his leg to slide the ice bag under the heel.

"I'm sorry!"

"That's OK. Thanks. That feels good."

"Would you like something? Scrambled eggs, maybe?"

"Yeah. That sounds good. You eat, too."

"I will. You want the radio on?"

"If you can find a game or some classical music."

She can't, and they decide nothing she can get on the little bedside radio improves on the silence. She goes into the kitchen and starts hustling up some food. Her hands are shaking, and she has to sit down and breathe slowly and deeply for a few minutes.

She prays, then, for strength and courage for them both, and in thanksgiving, for in all things, God has blessed them. Lightness and calm fill in the jagged core of panic she experienced at the sight of her husband lying vulnerable and in pain on the bed, and she understands, on a level deeper than words, that, for the first time in their marriage, he truly needs her.

28

"Deadline what?"

"Deadline *America*! With Gayle Majors! You mean you don't watch it?"

"I've never heard of it."

The girl seems genuinely shocked. "It's huge!" she assures him. "Everybody watches it. Except you, I guess."

On his way in, Detective Sergeant Lafferty had spotted the mobile van with the satellite dish parked on the side street and the platinum blonde in her spray-painted red suit, surrounded by her entourage, out front. He parked in back and slipped in the back door, but there's no escaping wide-eyed, star-struck Adele.

"What's she want?"

"She wants to interview you! For national television!"

"Oh, for the lovea—"

Herman Chandler looks beyond uncomfortable perched on the edge of a chair in the area Adele insists on calling "reception." He offers Lafferty a weak smile.

"I'll be right with you, Mr. Chandler," Lafferty tells him. "Listen, now," he hisses, turning back to the girl. "You keep this Gayle Majors away from me. You hear? Anything I got, I'll give to the *Shepherdstown Daily*, same as always."

"What should I tell her?"

"Tell her I'm busy tending to my own business and hope she'll do the same. Tell her to interview you!"

"Oh, my God!" Adele's hand flies to her hair and begins frantically patting and pushing. "Do you really think she would?"

"Why not? You know what's going on around here better than I do."

"Is it all right? I mean—"

"Knock yourself out."

"But I'm not—I don't—"

Lafferty turns to his other problem. "Thanks for coming in so early, Mr. Chandler. I really appreciate it."

"Sergeant Lafferty?"

Reluctantly, Lafferty turns back.

"Someone from the IRA called. He wants you to call back."

"The Irish Republican Army called me?"

The girl frowns. "He didn't sound Irish."

"Perhaps she means the IRS," Chandler offers from his perch.

"That's it! IRS!"

"What's he want?"

"He didn't say. He just said to call right away."

"Perhaps I should come back later," Chandler says, fussing his hands in his lap.

"Let's get 'er done. This shouldn't take long."

Chandler stands, still looking uncertain.

"Coffee?"

"No, thank you."

"I should give the stuff up. Makes me jumpy. Adele, bring me some coffee."

He maneuvers Chandler into his office and deposits him in the chair across the desk from his. He sits down with a satisfied grunt, leans back in the chair, and smiles. He leans forward, smiling, and clasps his big hands in front of him on the desk.

"We're all simply devastated," Chandler says. "I had a long talk with Mrs. Downs on the phone last night. She's having the body flown back to Connecticut as soon as they release it."

Lafferty is still smiling. "I know how busy you are, Mr. Chandler, so I'll get right to 'er, and you can be on your way."

"Thank you. I wasn't sure why you wanted to talk to me again. I told you—"

The tapping at the door makes Chandler start.

"Yeah! Bring it in! You sure you don't want anything?" This last to Chandler.

"It's still brewing," the girl says, sticking her head in at the door.

"Bring me a mouthful of grounds to chew on, then."

"It's Gayle Majors."

"Deadbeat America."

"Dead*line* America."

"Deadline America. Do you watch it, Mr. Chandler? Adele here seems to think I'm the only person on the planet who doesn't."

"No. I—"

"See there!" Lafferty beams in triumph. "Mr. Chandler doesn't watch it either."

"Actually, I don't own—"

"What about Gayle Majors? Didn't you tell her to interview you?"

"She doesn't want to interview me. She says she needs to talk to you. She's says she doesn't have to tape it. She says you can be an ananomous source if you want."

"I can be a what?"

"I think she means 'anonymous,'" Chandler offers.

Lafferty shakes his head. "Not ananomous. Not unanimous. Not anonymous. Not even amorous." He winks at Chandler.

The girl looks crushed.

"Adele?"

"Yes?" All the world's misery packed into a single syllable.

"Maybe the coffee's ready? If not, just bring a dirty mug, and I'll suck on it."

"OK."

"When you're talking to that gal," Lafferty tells Chandler after she leaves, "you have to snow for quite awhile before she gets the drift."

Chandler is giving his hands another workout. Lafferty leans forward, clasping his hands in front of him on the desk again. "Say, would you like one of those diet colas? I can't stand them, myself, but the girl guzzles them by the gallon. I can have her—"

"No, thank you. I'm fine, really. I wonder if we could—"

"Right. To business. You've got all those writers to tend to."

He smiles. Chandler fidgets.

"I heard you and Mr. Downs had an argument. What was that all about?"

Chandler seems to notice his hands doing their gymnastics and quells them. "An argument?" he says.

"Voices were raised, I'm told."

"Who told you that?"

"Did you and Mr. Downs have an argument, Mr. Chandler?"

"Not an argument, really."

"What, then?"

"We did discuss the financial arrangements. He had signed a contract, which spelled out all the terms for his appearance at the school, but he—"

"Wanted more money?"

"Yes."

"Isn't that something? A contract doesn't mean doodly squat anymore. Same with marriage vows. 'Till death do us part' or until I get bored. It's just a question of which hand basket now, don't you think, Mr. Chandler?"

Chandler risks a smile but doesn't try for a chuckle. "People don't seem to take commitments very seriously these days, I'm afraid."

"That's it right there! That's what's missing. Commitment." Lafferty picks up his pencil by the point and begins drumming it on his notepad. "What did you tell him when he asked for more money?"

"I told him I didn't have the authority to change the terms of the agreement like that, even if I wanted to. And besides, the school—"

"And why should you? A deal's a deal, right? He knew the terms when he signed on. Isn't that right?"

"Yes, that's—"

"Absolutely!" The pencil bounces off the pad. Lafferty swipes at it, but instead of catching it, he bats it onto the floor. Chandler bends to retrieve it.

"Oh, just leave it," Lafferty says. "I'll get it in a minute."

Chandler already has the pencil and now doesn't know what to do with it.

"How'd he react? When you took the hard line with him."

"I wouldn't call it a hard line, exactly."

"Don't sell yourself short, Mr. Chandler. A lot of people would have caved. If Mr. Superstar walks out on you, a lot of people want their money back, right?"

"Oh, I don't – "

"In fact, I'll bet you've got folks demanding their money back now, don't you?"

"People are certainly disappointed. I think Mrs. Beringer may have mentioned a few students who—"

"Mrs. Beringer?"

"Genevieve Beringer. She functions as my on-site coordinator when school is in session."

Lafferty fishes a sheet of paper from under his notepad and frowns at it. "I don't see a Beringer listed on the staff," he says.

"Oh, she isn't paid. She volunteers. This is her sixteenth—No, I believe actually it's her seventeenth year helping out."

"Is that a fact? Could I see that pencil a minute?"

"Surely."

"B-E-R-R ..."

"One 'R.'" Chandler spells the name for him.

"Thanks. I'll be sure to talk to her." He puts his hands on his thighs and shoves to his feet. "I'll let you get back to school, Mr. Chandler. I certainly appreciate you taking time out of your busy schedule like this."

"Not at all. I want to cooperate in any way I can. Are we—?"

"All done. See, hardly hurt a bit, huh?"

"Hardly." Another feeble chuckle.

Lafferty walks him out. The girl is pouring his coffee, and he takes the mug from her as they walk by. When they reach the front door, Chandler reaches for the knob, but Lafferty's thick hand grasps it first.

"When Mr. Downs didn't show up Tuesday, did you think maybe he had just walked out on you? Because of the money?"

"That thought did cross my mind."

"What do you do in a case like that? I mean, would you sue him, or what?"

"That would be a matter for the board of directors to decide. It would certainly constitute a breech of contract."

"Absolutely! A hell of a breech, I'd say."

Again the little man reaches for the doorknob, and again, Lafferty gets to it first.

"See that woman out there?" He nods at the window. "The one in the red suit?"

"Yes."

"Her name's Gayle Majors. I don't know who the rest of those folks are, but if you walk out that door, they'll be all over you like flies on stink. You might want to consider leaving by the back door."

"Yes. I believe I will. Thank you."

Lafferty steers him back across the room. "They say any publicity is good publicity," he says, "but I guess having your star attraction get killed isn't the sort of thing the school wants to brag about, huh?"

"Certainly not."

"Well, thanks again, Mr. Chandler."

"I do hope you get to the bottom of this."

"We're give it our very best shot."

"You don't think whoever did this might try to hurt somebody else at the school, do you?"

"Interesting question." Lafferty taps his teeth with his pencil eraser. "Since we don't know the motive for Downs getting killed, it's really impossible to say."

Chandler looks stricken. "Yes," he says. "Of course."

Lafferty watches through the window as Chandler creeps along the back of the building, glancing around the corner before disappearing. Reluctantly, he turns back to the office. He's got himself a murder to try to solve—if Gayle Majors, the FBI, the IRS and God knows who else will let him alone long enough to do it.

29

Doug refuses to let her drive him back home and take him to a doctor in Madison, insisting that he'll be fine while she's at school and promising that he will not, under any circumstances, do anything more strenuous than going to the bathroom. He even agrees to keep Mo's cell phone next to him by the couch so she can call him between classes from the pay phone at the school.

He lets her tell Ethel Wilkerson that he's laid up, and she immediately pledges to bring him "a good, hot lunch, and Juney for company."

He makes one further concession, letting Mo drive him to a clinic in Shepherdstown early Monday morning, where he gets a cortisone shot in his heel to relieve the pain. That's his first doctor's visit since they moved to Mitchell.

"Doctors," he has told her on several occasions, "are for sick people," and Doug never gets sick.

He insists that Mo finish out the second week of school and promises to find a doctor in Madison if the heel isn't better by then.

"I really feel much better already," he assures her as she gets him set up on the couch with his novel, his Sudoku puzzles, water, Advil, ice bag, and television remote. "That cortisone is great stuff. I could use a shot of that in my head once in awhile."

Mo wants to believe him. But she knows how difficult it is, under any circumstances, for Doug to sit still. And he seems quite distressed to have to break his silly record.

She calls from campus after her research methods class. Assured that he's fine, she gets a sandwich from the canteen and takes it to the noon forum, where several poetry students read their work. Most read in that breathy, halting way poets adopt, and most of the poems seem precious, obscure, or sappy. But one older man shares some funny doggerel about the woes of a married man. Doug would love it! The thought makes her fight off the urge to call him again.

Irene Crowley again takes over the mystery writing class. She teaches them, Mo suspects, the same material she's using in her other classes. That's fine with Mo, since it's all new to her, but some of the other students pepper her with questions she can't answer about mystery writers, and the class degenerates into a free-for-all, with the poor sub trying to keep up as best she can.

After class Mo waits while another student—she looks to be in her early twenties and is very pretty—uses the pay phone. Mo backs off a discreet distance to wait while the young woman wrestles with a dispute with her dinner date for that night. When the phone is finally free, her cell phone rings four times before he picks up.

"I hope I didn't wake you."

"Nope. I was out on the porch, trying to finish *Blood Brothers*."

"Slow going?"

"I guess it's just not my style."

"You don't have to finish a book just because you started it, you know."

But she knows better. Doug does have to finish a book, or anything else he starts.

"I only have about fifty pages to go. I guess I'll see it through."

"I'm on my way home. What can I bring you? I bought a bunch of paperbacks at the used book sale here."

"Don't hurry. I'm doing fine."

"I could use a little time in the computer lab, if you're sure it's all right."

"It's fine! If I need any help, believe me, Mrs. Wilkerson will be all over it."

"How was lunch?"

Doug laughs. "She brought a picnic, and we ate out on the porch. Tuna melts, on some kind of wonderful bread from the bakery in town. Juney stands on her hind legs and puts a paw on your arm to tell you she wants some."

They talk for a few more minutes. Doug again assures her that he's fine, and Mo promises to bring home something healthy for dinner.

She works for an hour and a half on her Wisconsin author quiz, then stops at the Subway downtown for sandwiches. She intends to head straight home, not all that sure she trusts Doug not to get up and try to do too much. But when she reaches the turnoff for Heavenly Acres, she follows a strong urge to turn onto the narrow dirt road.

What could you possibly expect to find, she asks herself. She's already looked around, the police have no doubt examined the whole area with a microscope, and she, reputation aside, doesn't really know the first thing about investigating a crime scene.

Still, poking around is her nature, and she's learned to follow her instincts. She finds a parking place near the back of the lot and walks slowly back down the road she has just driven, coming upon an area off road that, although no longer cordoned off with yellow crime scene tape, has clearly been combed over thoroughly. For the fourth time since moving from Chicago, Mo finds herself at a site where someone has recently been murdered.

Jays squawk, squirrels chatter, and an afternoon breeze flutters the leaves. Whatever has happened here, nature pays it no heed. The herd has been culled by one; life goes on.

She stuffs her hands in the pockets of her tan shorts and walks back up the road, the breeze at her back cooling the fine film of sweat on the back of her neck. A pickup rattles by in the other direction. The driver raises her hand in acknowledgment, and Mo waves.

A group of middle-aged men are playing volleyball in the field next to the resort; the game mostly involves someone walking to retrieve the ball while the others stand bent over, hands on knees, sucking wind. She watches until one of the men notices her and waves.

She walks around the building on the field side, away from the lake, and looks in at the fish-cleaning shed, which is immaculate but smells of fish guts. Three children are playing on the jungle gym in the sand by the lake. A woman pushes a small child in a swing. Two women sit on a bench, talking softly.

The breeze off the lake smells fishy and vaguely foul. Perhaps some dead thing has washed up in the nearby reeds. She hears a soft hissing and sees movement from the corner of her eye. She turns toward the building and sees a woman standing in the back doorway. The woman motions Mo to come closer.

As she approaches, Mo recognizes the woman—the maid who was cleaning Fletcher Downs' room. What was her name? Maria something.

"Señora," the woman hisses as Mo approaches.

"*Buenas tardes*, Señora Morejon," Mo says, surprised to be saying the name and hoping it's the right one. "*Como está?*"

"*Bien, bien*. I have something to show you. Come here a moment, can you?"

Clearly agitated, Maria Morejon disappears inside. When Mo follows her through the door, she sees the short, stocky woman walking rapidly down the hall, glancing back over her shoulder to make sure Mo is coming. She unlocks a door and steps inside. By the time Mo reaches the door, the maid is pushing her cleaning cart out into the hallway and closing the door behind her.

"Here!" Glancing up and down the hall to make sure no one is looking, she thrusts a handful of papers at Mo.

"What's this?"

"I found these in the room of Señor Downs, in the waste, when I was cleaning Tuesday morning. I thought there might be something here to help you."

The pages have been torn from a notebook and covered with large, looping handwriting in dark red ink.

"Why didn't you give these to the police?"

"You were his friend. You take."

A man and woman in swimming suits, towels over their shoulders, turn the corner and start down the hall toward them.

"You take," Maria Morejon says again, pushing the papers at Mo.

The couple, still wet from the pool, glance at Mo before resuming their conversation as they walk past. Maria pushes the cart down the hall away from her.

"*Gracias*," Mo calls softly, but the maid gives no indication of having heard.

Mo hurries outside, finds a plastic chair away from the others on the beach, and sits facing the lake, the dead man's pages in her lap. When she finishes reading a few minutes later, she knows she will have to take them to the police.

30

The voice on the telephone is full of southern, but Lafferty isn't in the mood for charm.

"Detective Sergeant Lafferty?"

"Yes, ma'am."

"My name is LaShandra Cooper. I'm with the Dane County Sheriff's Department."

Lafferty gets an ear full of static. Damn cell phones. There oughta be a law.

"I just passed the Shepherdstown Pioneer Museum, and I'm headed your way."

"Hold on, now." Lafferty shifts so he can pull a notepad and pencil toward him. "You say you're coming here?"

"That's correct. I just wanted to be sure you'd be in. I won't take up much of your time. I'm sure you're very busy, what with that author being killed and all."

Lafferty prints "COOPER" in block letters on the pad and starts sketching a face that's supposed to be Gary Cooper in *High Noon* but looks more like Gregory Peck in *To Kill a Mockingbird*.

"And you're calling in connection with the Downs murder investigation?"

"No, sir. I'm investigating a possible homicide that took place in Sherpherdstown two years ago."

"Well, now, Ms. Cooper." He puts an "X" through the sketch and starts on a buzzard wearing a bow tie. "I surely do appreciate all the extra help I've been getting around here. But just why would you be doing a thing like that?"

"We've received info—from Dane County—reason to believe—"

"You're breaking up, Ms. Cooper. Maybe you should just wait until—hello?"

He glares at the dead receiver before tossing it back on the desk, where it plows a path through some papers and bumps up against the desk lamp.

"Cell phones. Scourge of humanity."

The tapping draws his glare to the door.

"I heard you talking," Adele says, eyebrow raised.

"That's fine work, Adele. Maybe we ought to promote you to detective."

Adele hangs in the doorway.

"Something I can do for you?"

"That newspaper lady is here to see you again."

"Becky Hafner's here?"

"No. The one from out of town. The one who catches killers."

The one who catches killers. He loves that.

"Grand. This should make the day complete." He heaves a sigh. He no doubt has this killer-catcher to thank for Dane County's sudden interest in his jurisdiction. "Well, why don't you ask her to come in?"

"OK."

Adele slinks away, leaving the door cracked, and a moment later, the one who catches killers enters.

"Ms. Quinn. Always a pleasure."

Lafferty grunts as he stands—he sounds more like his father every day—and offers a handshake. She shifts some papers from right hand to left to accept.

"Please sit down. Coffee?"

"These came from Fletcher Downs' room. I think you'd better have a look."

"Sit down, Ms. Quinn. Let's see what we've got here."

He eases himself into his chair. The other chair makes a tiny squeak when she sits. Adele is talking to someone on the phone in the outer office. He scans the first sheet.

What is this stuff?"

"Notes Fletcher Downs made about a manuscript from one of the students."

Lafferty skims the notes, reading a few phrases aloud. "'Self-indulgent.' 'Overwrought and overwritten.'" He looks up, folds the sheets lengthwise and tosses them on his desk. "I'm no expert on literary criticism," he says. "But off hand, I'd say he didn't much care for it."

"Apparently not."

"How'd you come to be in possession of these notes?"

"Someone who works at Heavenly Acres thought I should see them. I don't want to get her in trouble."

"Why would she think you should have them?" He picks up the pages again, leafs through them.

"She thinks I was a friend of Fletcher Downs."

He worries the crease he has put in the pages. "Do you have any idea who he did write this for?"

"Yes. One of the other students in the class, Myrna Gillory."

"Ms. Gillory." He picks up his notepad, thumbs back until he comes on a sketch of a crow. Ah, yes. Ms. Gillory. The one who has taken two shots at it so far and still hasn't gotten her story straight.

"According to these notes, the woman in the novel kills her husband. Do writers do that a lot, kill off husbands in their novels?"

"I've never written a novel, but I did read somewhere that Anne Lamott said revenge is a wonderful motive for writing fiction."

"This Lamott killed her husband, did she?"

"No. But she does write novels."

"I suppose there's some would say that's just as bad."

"Do you think this might have been enough of a motive for murder?"

"Well, now, Ms. Quinn, I have heard that some writers have a pretty tough time accepting criticism. I don't guess we can rule it out, can we?"

"Do you think it ties in at all with the two other deaths occurring on consecutive July twenty-eighths?"

"I don't see how, but there again—"

Adele taps on the door and peeks in.

"There's a woman here to see you. A LaShawna Cooper?"

"Show her in."

"Yes, sir. Sir?" Adele glances at Quinn, then back at Lafferty. "She's *colored*!"

Lafferty fights the temptation to ask which color. "Well, now, that's OK, Adele. I've heard folks are doing that now."

Adele ducks back out.

"I take it you know this Cooper," Lafferty says to Quinn.

"Yes. She worked on the investigation of the murder of Father O'Bannon, the priest from Mitchell."

"Helped you solve it, did she?"

"The other way around. I was able to help her a little."

"Ms. Cooper? Come on in."

Lafferty stands as a short, solid but not fat young colored gal enters. She's wearing a cream skirt and coat over a light blue blouse that fits her just right snug. She's what Mrs. Lafferty might call "stylish" or even "tailored." She carries a white shoulder bag. She's got her hair up in those whatchajingies, "corn dogs" or "corn cobs." Rows. Corn rows.

"Detective Sergeant Lafferty? It's very good of you to see me on such short notice." She gives his hand a firm shake from across the desk. Her skin feels rough. She smells strongly of soap.

Didn't think I had much choice, he thinks but says instead, "Pleasure. I take it you two have met."

The two women don't seem to know exactly how to greet each another and settle for a handshake and head nods.

"Have a seat, Detective Cooper."

Cooper takes the only other chair in the room, a mismatch to Quinn's on her left. She sits up straight, her back not touching the chair, her knees together. Her skin is the kind of dark, rich black that almost looks blue.

"You're here about the fella who died two years ago. Is that right?"

"Yes." Cooper takes a notepad from the shoulder bag and finds the page she wants. "Tommy Preston. He rode with the rodeo."

"Right. Young fella. And he's from your county?"

"That's right."

"As I remember, Ms. Cooper, he got himself hit by a train while trying to cross the trestle over the river out by the paper mill. We figured he'd tried to beat the train across and miscalculated."

"You ruled it accidental and closed the case."

"Yep."

"Did it strike you as strange that he wouldn't have jumped off the trestle before the train hit him? Take his chances with the river. You see what I'm sayin'?"

"Oh, yes, ma'am. I do. I believe we gave that some thought. 'Course, we didn't have the help of the Dane County Sheriff's Department at the time."

He smiles at Quinn, who looks noncommittal as she takes notes, and then at Cooper, who smiles back.

"Is that why you're here, Ms. Cooper? To find out why Tommy Preston didn't jump off that trestle?"

"I understand that last year another gentleman, a singer, also died under mysterious circumstances. I believe his name was Kenny Laine."

"Right. Country western singer. Turned up drowned in the river. He'd been drinking. We also ruled that one an accident." He bounces his pencil by the eraser end on the desk. "As I recall, he was from back east someplace. Not from anywhere near Dane County."

"That's correct. He wasn't from Dane County."

"But you figure the two deaths might be connected?"

"Yes."

"Because they happened on the same date."

"That does seem rather suspicious, wouldn't you say?"

"To tell you the gospel truth, I hadn't made the connection until the lady sitting next to you there pointed it out to me."

He nods toward Quinn, who glances at Cooper, who glances back. Nobody does any smiling to speak of.

"And then, of course, there's this other matter." Lafferty bounces the pencil off the desk, catches it with a swipe of his hand, and leans back. "The one that's brought all this fame and glory to our quiet little town."

"The third consecutive July twenty-eighth that someone has died here," Cooper says.

"Yep. So Ms. Quinn, here, noted."

"What do you suppose the odds are of that being a coincidence, Detective Sergeant Lafferty?"

"I have no idea, Detective Cooper. Maybe Ms. Quinn's husband could help us with that one. I understand he's real good with numbers."

Cooper puts her pad and pencil back into her shoulder bag and stands, hand extended across the desk. "I wanted to let you to know I was here. I'll be poking around for a day or two."

"If there's anything we can do to help—"

"Actually, I was wondering if you'd mind getting the files together from those other two deaths so I could review them. Maybe I could see them tomorrow morning?"

"I can have the gal get them for you right now, if you'd like to wait."

"No, that's all right. I need to find myself a place to stay. I saw a lot of no vacancies on the way in."

"That could be a problem, all right. We're pretty booked up, with all these writers in town. And now, what with the media and all—"

"I'll give you my cell phone number," Quinn says, flipping a page in her notepad. "We're staying in a cabin at a place called 'Merrynook.' We've got a couch you're more than welcome to."

Quinn tears the sheet from the pad and hands it to Cooper

"Thank you. It's good to have a backup plan."

"Always good to have Plan B," Lafferty agrees, coming out from behind the desk to walk Detective Cooper to the door.

"Ms. Quinn. If you could stay for just another minute?"

"Of course."

With Detective Cooper gone, he resettles in his chair. Quinn remains standing. "I don't know if this is important or not," he says, fiddling with the cover of his notepad, "but there were two students from the writing class who were absent a couple of days, Lester Brady and Elsworth Priestly. Those names ring a bell?"

"Yes."

"Who could forget a name like 'Elsworth Priestly,' huh? I was just wondering if this Brady character had shown up again."

"No. You don't think he might be involved in this, do you?"

"Well, now, Ms. Quinn, like I always say, you don't want to rule anything out. Murderers can turn up in the strangest places. I guess I don't have to tell you that. Well." He puts his hands on his knees and shoves out of the chair with a grunt. "I won't take any more of your time, then."

"I can find my way out."

After she leaves, he sits back, his notepad in his lap, and works on the sketch until he gets it to look like the Marshal in *High Noon*. What was that fella's name? Lucas McCain? No. That was the sheriff in the *Rifleman*, starring Chuck Conners. Paul Fix was the Sheriff. Mica something? Fine character actor.

Damn. Now the name of the Marshal in *High Noon* will be bugging him all night.

Maybe Marjorie would know. She's seen that picture at least a dozen times.

With that, he decides to call it a day and head home.

31

The light's still on in Room 154. Someone has left a drink cup from the Dairy Queen on one of the desks. Herman Chandler corrals the cup and deposits it in the metal receptacle, where it makes a satisfying thunk.

Herman pauses in the doorway, his hand on the light switch, and takes in the circle of chairs, the words "Protagonist," "narrator," "catalyst," and "hook" in precise script on the chalkboard, the lingering aura of warmth and smell from the bodies that have recently occupied the room. He clicks off the light, and the glade of trees becomes visible in the twilight outside the window. He shuts the door, jiggles the knob, and moves down the hall.

Paul is waiting for him in the main hall. "You're just like the old town sheriff," he says, "making his rounds to make sure everything's quiet in his town."

"I'd more likely be cast as the deputy," he says, smiling. "A fat Barney Fife to somebody's Sheriff Taylor."

"You are *much* too good looking to be Barney Fife."

"I'm no romantic lead, and you know it."

"You should be very proud of the roles you've played—and your ability to lose yourself in them. Remember how stunned James Rowan was when you told him you'd played the social worker in *A Thousand Clowns*? He'd seen the show and didn't even recognize you."

They reach the office, where Gen Beringer looks up, frowning, from the pile of computer printouts on her desk.

"I've still got Sarah Marty registered in two classes at the same time," she says, "and I have no idea when Mr. Curry intends to turn in his revised rosters."

"That's our Mr. Curry. Wildly creative and rather disorganized," Herman says.

That prompts a snort. "Why don't you two go on home? I can lock the front door as well as you can."

"I still have to check with the office in Wausau to see about getting the air conditioning turned down and to see if they can get the roofers to work somewhere else for the next few days."

She glances at the wall clock. "Won't be anybody there now," she tells him. "You might's well wait until morning. Not that they'll do anything about it then, either." She picks up a hefty file folder and hands it across the desk. "Here's the paperwork the district wants filled out, and the forms from the business office, and—"

"I can do those," Paul says, taking the file and holding it out of Herman's reach. "Gen, dear, did that detective talk to you today?"

"I have a note here someplace to call him," she says. "Mary took the message. Guess I'd better get my alibi straight, huh?"

"You haven't spoken with him yet, then?"

"Nope. Been up to my armpits in agitators all day."

"I wonder why he wants to talk to you," Herman says. "I already talked with him this morning before I came out to school. He asked me to come in."

"Maybe we ought to compare notes," Paul says. "To make sure we're on the same page about who was where when."

"Get our stories straight, you mean?"

"I certainly wouldn't phrase it that way, Gen, dear."

"How would you phrase it?"

"More like a rehearsal, perhaps," Herman says. "Is that what you meant, Paul?"

Gen glares up at Paul over her half-glasses. "You two go on home," she says. "Take a nice long walk or something. Put all this out of your minds."

"Easier said then done," Herman says. "It's dreadful."

"Yes," she says, straightening the pile of papers on the desk. "It is dreadful. And it will still be dreadful tomorrow, and we'll all be another day older. Go on, get!"

She stands and comes out from behind the desk, and for a moment Herman thinks she intends to take him by the elbow and guide him out.

"Don't worry about me," she says, looking at Paul. "I won't say the wrong thing to the sheriff. You ought to know by now that I'm pretty good at keeping secrets."

32

Going back into town to give the notes to Sheriff Lafferty has made her late, and Mo worries about Doug, alone and hobbled all day, as she speeds back to their cabin. She hopes he's at least taken Advil; the man would refuse a blindfold for a firing squad.

Since she's in a hurry, of course she gets wedged behind a driver who seems to be stuck in first gear, and the two-lane highway is too narrow and curvy for passing. She hates to see her prejudices reinforced, but the driver of the almost-new Cadillac in front of her is obviously quite old—she catches a glimpse of bluish hair—and barely tall enough to see over the dashboard.

That'll be you one day, she reminds herself, God willing. Except that she can't imagine herself driving a barge like that. Doug's boxy CR-V is too big as it is. Ah, but never say never, she decides. Perspectives change.

She should use the time to pray, but when she prays for the soul of Fletcher Downs and for all who have been hurt by his death, her mind wanders to Myrna Gillory. If it weren't for the July twenty-eighth connection, the abrasive Ms. Gillory would have to be the leading suspect, at least of the ones Mo is aware of. She spent the night before his death with Downs—and lied about it—and he gave her a scathing critique of her novel. The woman didn't strike Mo as a murderer—crass and self-absorbed, yes, but not homicidal—but Mo has learned first hand that murderers don't wear nametags. And hell hath no fury like a novelist scorned. Maybe that's motive enough for murder.

"Pull up the anchor, lady," Mo mutters as the forest slowly rolls by outside the car window. She pulls out on a short straight stretch of highway, but immediately a car appears coming in the other direction, and she noses back in behind Grandma Molasses.

Take a breath, Quinn, she tells herself. She eases her mind back to praying, a slow, careful Our Father, taking time to dwell on each phrase. She has repeated that simple prayer thousands of times, often without thinking about the words, but sometimes, like today, it seems new and newly meaningful. The power of the Word.

The Cadillac slows even more as they approach Mo's turn, and she's afraid she'll have to follow it all the way to her cabin door. But the old woman doesn't turn, and Mo gratefully guns the CR-V into the turn, making the tires squeal before reining herself in. She's nervous about what she might find at the cabin, after the shock of seeing Doug in pain and living in what for him qualified as squalor.

But to her amazement, she walks into an immaculate cabin, complete with a roaring fire and good smells coming from the kitchenette.

"You must be feeling better," she says as Doug emerges from the bedroom, dressed in clean shorts and polo shirt but still walking gingerly on the bad heel.

"That cortisone is great stuff!" he says, grinning.

His lips are warm and soft, his kiss more than casual.

"Definitely feeling better," she says. "Everything looks great, but I hope you haven't been overdoing."

"Actually, dear Mrs. Wilkerson insisted on tidying, and the mister brought in firewood and got the fire going. I just threw a few things together for dinner and got a good, hot shower."

"You're supposed to be staying off that heel."

"I am."

"You're always saying you wish you had more time to read."

"No. *You're* always saying you wish you had more time to read. I'm always agreeing with you. Actually, I started six of the paperbacks Ethel Wilkerson left, but nothing grabbed me. What I really need is an Internet connection out here!"

"Let me serve dinner. You sit down and get your foot up."

"I'm fine, really!"

"Go be fine out on the porch. The lake looks so beautiful. Do you want wine?"

"Better not. I'm taking pain pills."

"Doug, you're taking Advil!"

"Those are pain pills. Have we got any of that diet cranberry juice left?"

She reaches up and runs her hand through his thick, wavy black hair. "I'll go look," she says. "If not, I'll go back into town after dinner and get some, and anything else you need to keep from getting too restless."

"You're all I need to keep from getting restless."

They eat on the porch. The heat of the day has leached out of the air as the sun slipped behind the trees. Kids play down on the beach, their cries and splashing making a kind of music. Mo and Doug sit next to each other on the bench looking out at the lake.

"LaShandra Cooper arrived. She and Lafferty had a *tête-à-tête*," she tells him.

"Irresistible force meets immovable object, huh?

"That's for sure. I gave LaShandra my cell number and said she was welcome to sleep on our couch if she can't find anything else. I hope that's OK. I should have asked you first."

"That's fine. We've got room." He leans over and nibbles her neck, his breath tickling her. "As long as she doesn't mind lots of smooching going on in the next room."

"Are you sure all you've had is Advil?"

When she gets up to carry the dishes in to the kitchenette, he hobbles in after her.

"I'll wash. You dry," he says.

"I'll wash. I'll dry. You sit."

"Mo, come on. I'm going out of my mind just sitting around."

"I'll wash. You dry. Sitting down."

"Aye, aye, Captain."

She really needs to do some homework. But Doug seems so jumpy sitting in the chair by the fireplace trying to get through one of Ethel Wilkerson's paperbacks. She suggests a game of hearts, and he eagerly accepts. From hearts they move on to gin, Tennessee rotgut and poker, playing for long kitchen matches from the jar on the mantel.

Soon the lake is quiet, the fire is embers, and an owl lets them know that the nocturnal creatures are taking over.

"Time for the patient to get back into bed," she announces, gathering up the cards.

"Only if the nurse puts him there."

"Doug, you are—"

"Irresistible? Is that the word you're going for?"

"Actually, I was going for 'incorrigible.'"

He kisses her. "You can have first dibs on the bathroom. But don't be long."

He has just crawled into bed next to her when the cell phone rings from the other room.

"Oh, for—"

"I'd better get it, Doug. It's probably LaShandra."

"Right."

By the dim light of the floor lamp in the living room, she has trouble finding the cell. But the caller is persistent.

"Yes?"

"Monona? I am *so* sorry. I don't think there's a place to stay within a hundred miles of here. I've been calling around, but it's no go."

"Not a problem."

"Are you sure? I can sleep in the car. I've done it before."

"You will *not* sleep in the car. It'll make up the couch for you."

"I really do appreciate it. Are you hard to find?"

"Where are you?"

Mo hears the throaty rumble of a truck on the highway. "Something called 'LottaSav,'" LaShandra says.

"You're not far."

Mo carries the phone into the bedroom as she talks. Doug has turned the table lamp on beside the bed.

"I'll let Doug give you directions."

Doug looks at the phone in her outstretched hand as if it might bite him but takes it.

"Detective Cooper? No, no bother. Get back on old Highway 8 heading east. Yes. Away from town. From the signal at the LottaSav it's two point six miles to our turnoff. You'll pass a sign for Heavenly Acres just before our turn. Yes. Take a left. Then another half a mile. We're the next turnoff. Merrynook Resort. You can only turn right."

"Tell her I'll walk out to the end of the drive to meet her," Mo says.

"Have you got all that? It can be tricky in the dark. Mo says she'll walk out to the road to meet you."

He hands the phone to her.

"You don't have to do that," LaShandra is saying.

"It's easier than trying to tell you how to find the cabin," Mo says.

"Thanks, girl. I owe you big time. I'll be there in a few minutes."

"Right. See you."

Girl! She doesn't recall them having reached that level of intimacy when they were trying to figure out who killed Father O'Bannon.

Drat! She should have asked her to pick up some of Doug's diet cranberry juice.

"We've got a boarder, huh?" Doug says, pulling back the covers.

"Yep. We'll have to be sure to tell the Wilkersons. There might be an extra charge."

"Are you kidding? Fred will probably want to build an addition onto the place for us. And charge less because of the noise." Doug eases his leg out from under the covers.

"What are you doing?"

"We said we'd meet her at the road."

"I said *I'd* meet her at the road. You stay put."

"I'm going with you."

"You'll do no such thing."

"Watch me." He stands. "Ta-da. He walks. He talks."

"Doug, you shouldn't be—"

"Honey, it's night, and there was a murder near here a week ago. I'm going with you."

"OK. We'll walk very slowly."

They put on the clothes they just changed out of. She keeps her arm around his waist, trying to encourage him to lean on her, as they walk up the hill and past the Wilkersons' house. A flickering blue light shows in the window, the television in the living room overlooking the lake. She supposes she'd get used to the view, would actually turn away to look at something on television. But it's hard to imagine.

The adults ring the communal bonfire where the drive turns up toward the road, and one of the women cradles a sleeping baby. Close by, an owl announces its presence. Mo squints into the darkness, knowing she'll never spot it. Another owl answers from the woods.

They stand in silence, his arm around her shoulders, hers around his waist, at the head of the dirt drive. A half moon illuminates the thick trunk of a dead tree across the road. Lightning must have struck it, for the trunk is split starting about ten feet off the ground, and the wood still bears charring. In the moonlight, the bare trunk looks as white as bleached bones.

The bonfire cracks and pops, punctuating the low night murmuring of voices. The owls alternate their five-beat call: hoot HOOT! Hoot hoot hooooo. For a moment all is silent. She squeezes him, and he squeezes back. The low grinding of a car moving slowly up the road reaches them.

"That was quick," Mo says.

"Too quick. I was enjoying this."

"Me, too."

Twin lights appear between the trees and then disappear as the car turns with the winding road. The lights reappear on the straightaway fifty feet down the road. Mo waves, and the lights flick, up-down-up-down. The car pulls even with them, and Doug opens the passenger side door and holds it for Mo.

"You found us."

"Your husband's directions were right on, to the tenth of a mile."

"He's very precise."

"Scootch on over," LaShandra says, patting the seat next to her. "We can ride three up front, cheek to cheek. "Good to see you, Mr. Stennett," she adds as Doug gets in.

"And you, detective. Turn in here."

"Good thing you met me here. I mighta missed it."

She makes the turn, and they creep up the gentle incline, the car bucking with the ruts in the road.

"So, you feel up to catching a killer?" Doug asks, sounding almost jovial.

"Oh, I figure your wife will do that, like last time. I'm just here to slap on the cuffs and take the credit."

"Follow the road to the right here," Doug says.

"Glad this is the county's car. This road's hell on the suspension. Whoa. Somebody has a campfire! Look at that row of beer bottles on the porch railing. They've been having themselves a party!"

"Up on the left, that's the Wilkersons' house," Mo says. "They own the resort."

"We're just a little farther down the road," Doug notes. "It's pretty steep."

"There's the cabin," Mo says a moment later. "You can park next to us."

Doug gets out and holds the door for Mo, but he doesn't make eye contact. Great. He's upset again because of the reference to her part in catching the man who killed Father O'Bannon. She'll just have to reassure him, make sure he understands. There's no way she'll get anywhere near another killer.

Unless, of course, the killer is already nearby.

33

"Knock, knock!"

Marjorie sticks her head in at the door.

"Hello, beautiful," Detective Sergeant Lafferty says, getting to his feet and lumbering out from around the desk.

"What made you change your mind about coming home?"

They brush lips. She smells of that spray starch she uses when she irons. The seductive aroma of her chicken stew seeps out from the covered pot in her hands.

"Did you make biscuits?"

"I did."

"You are an angel!"

"I've been telling you that for years. Why didn't you come home?"

He snatches up wadded napkins, coffee-stained Styrofoam cups, balled-up pieces of notepaper off the desk, stuffing everything into an already overfull wastebasket.

"We can use the conference room if you like," he says.

"This is fine." She sets their places on top of a layer of file folders. "I figured if I didn't bring you dinner, you'd do without."

"I would have eaten something."

"Those disgusting Twinkies. Or sugar cereal right out of the box."

"Vitamin enriched. Says so right on the label."

He spoons up the first mouthful of stew, looks across the desk at her, his cheeks bulging, and crosses his eyes. She laughs.

"God almighty, but that's good stew!"

"Thank you, dear. It's a well-established truth that the way to a man's heart is through his stomach. Are you going to tell me what happened to keep you heree?"

"Someone's coming in."

"This late?"

"She finally returned my call a little while ago."

"She?"

"Myrna Gillory. The wannabe novelist."

Marjorie wrinkles her nose. He laughs. "You can stay and chaperone."

"Maybe I should. The little tramp."

"Oh, now."

"Well, what do you call it? Sleeping with her teacher just so he can help her get her silly book published."

"We don't know that for certain."

"She might have even killed him!"

"You never know. Murderers turn up—"

"I know. 'In the strangest places.'"

He works on his stew. Every time he looks up, she's watching him eat.

"You're not doing it justice." He nods toward her bowl.

"I tasted while I was making it."

"Can I have another biscuit?"

"Surely. So, what are you—?"

She stops as the scanner in the other room crackles.

"Deputy Faye. What is your location? Over."

The night dispatcher, Shirley Knopf, works from home, so she can take care of her husband, the former sheriff, who's bedridden with the end stages of liver cancer. Marjorie's the day dispatcher, has been since Lafferty joined the department twenty-eight years ago.

"Deputy Faye. Please report."

"Yeah, yeah. I was out of the car for a second. Sorry. I'm at the LottaSav."

"Anything going on out there?"

"They got a sale on Crest toothpaste. Want me to pick you up a couple of tubes?"

"No, thank you, Deputy Faye. Deputy Patterson. What is your location? Over."

Lafferty turns his attention back to his stew, sopping up the dregs with his third biscuit.

"I wish you could come home now. It's almost time for *C.S.I.*"

"You go on home. I'll be along shortly."

"I guess I will, then. I left the kitchen a mess."

Her notion of a "mess" is leaving a dirty spoon in the sink.

"Don't you want to stick around and see what the little tramp looks like?"

"I do not! I'm sure she's voluptuous."

The way she says "voluptuous" makes him laugh. "A regular bavishing rudy," he says.

He walks her to the front door, then walks slowly back to his office, missing her. Funny how, at home, they can go for hours without talking. But he always knows she's there, and the house doesn't feel right when she's away visiting her sister or "down the hill," as she calls it, shopping in Wausau.

Been married so damn long, they don't even finish each other's sentences any more. Don't even need to start them.

He sees Myrna Gillory pass in front of the window and goes to meet her at the door.

"Ms. Gillory. Thank you for coming in."

He can't decide if she's really annoyed or scared and trying to cover it by looking annoyed.

"I thought you were finished with me."

Scared and trying to cover, he decides. Is she scared because she doesn't know what he wants, or scared because she does?

"I've got a couple of loose ends I was hoping you could help me tie up. We can sit in my office. Coffee? I guess it's pretty late for coffee."

"Yes, actually, if you've got it. I'll be up late. I write at night."

She takes the seat Marjorie has just vacated, and he gets a coffee from the break room. He brings back a fist full of packets of sugar substitute and those little plastic thingees of non-dairy creamer with the coffee and puts them all on the desk in front of her. He sinks into his chair, reaches down, slides open the bottom left drawer, and pulls out the pages Monona Quinn gave him. If she recognizes them, it doesn't show on her face.

"These were in Fletcher Downs' room the morning he was killed."

He puts the sheets on the desk, turned toward her. She glances at them.

"What is it?"

"You haven't seen these?"

"I don't think so. What is it?"

He waits for it, and she doesn't disappoint, rubbing her nose with the back of her hand.

"Apparently it's some notes he wrote about a novel he read."

He picks up the top sheet and tosses it toward her. She doesn't look at it.

"Recognize it?"

"Yes. Now I do. It's Fletcher's critique of my novel."

"He was pretty rough on you."

"Constructive criticism is very helpful."

"'Presumptuous, preposterous, and pretentious.' He had a thing for p-words."

"He said I showed great promise. He was willing to read a revision." She folds her arms across her chest and looks away.

"Do you believe in the old saying about the third time being the charm?"

"What do you mean?"

"We've had two cracks at this thing, and I don't believe we've got it right yet. I'm hoping we'll get 'er done this time."

He opens his notebook and leafs to the page he wants. "You said you spent the night with Downs in his room at Heavenly Acres Monday night. Is that right?"

"Yes."

"You were still there the morning he was killed."

"Yes. But I told you—"

"And you woke up once in the night, when Downs got up to answer the call of nature."

"Yes. I don't know what time it was. There was no light on in the room."

"You also said you didn't wake up again until late morning, and he was already gone. Isn't that what you told me, Ms. Gillory?"

"Yes. I—I think I might have woke up one other time."

"When would that have been?"

"It must have been near dawn. It was starting to get light outside."

"And Mr. Downs was already gone?"

"No. He was out of the bed. Putting his clothes on."

"Did you say anything to him?"

"No."

"Why not?"

"I guess I didn't have anything to say."

"So you pretended to be asleep."

"It wasn't like that. I didn't pretend. I just didn't say anything."

"What was it like?"

"I was groggy, half asleep. I figured he was going out to smoke. I thought he was coming right back."

"So what did you do?"

"I didn't do anything. I went back to sleep."

"You didn't get up?"

"No! Why would I?"

"You didn't follow him?"

"No! I told you, I was barely even awake."

"Why didn't you tell me this before?"

"I don't know." She picks up her coffee cup, puts it back on the desk without drinking. She folds her arms again, as if hugging herself.

"Sure you do," Lafferty says.

"Shirley? You copy? Over."

The voice makes her start. Robbie Faye on the scanner.

"I copy. Over."

"Just checking in."

"Where are you?"

"Parked out on the old highway behind the trailer park."

Lafferty gets up, walks past Myrna Gillory to the office door, and gently pushes it shut. Her coffee looks the color meat turns when it starts to rot.

"I thought it would look bad," she says.

He looks at her. She looks away.

"I didn't get up. I swear it. I went back to sleep."

"And when you woke up again, it was, what, nine? Ten?"

"Later than that."

"You're a late sleeper. Didn't you wonder where he was?"

"I figured he must have come back while I was asleep, took what he needed, and went to the school."

"Did he have a morning class?"

"No. He just taught the one seminar." She looks up, brightening. "He was supposed to speak at the noon forum that day. He would have needed to get there early for that."

"Have you been to this school before, Ms. Gillory? Other summers?"

"You probably checked the school records."

"You're right. According to those records, you were here the previous two summers."

"That's right."

"Last two weeks of July, right? Just like this year."

"So what?"

Lafferty lets that sit between them for a minute.

"Is there anything else you've forgotten to tell me, Ms. Gillory?" He pauses just slightly before the "forgotten."

She shakes her head.

"You're sure?"

She shakes her head again but says, "Yes."

He tosses his notepad on the desk, where it plops on a pile of papers. "Thanks so much for coming in," he says.

He walks her to the door in silence, watches after her as she walks down the street. He roams around the office, turning off the coffeemaker and the lights. He pauses at the chief's office door, staring at the blue and white spirals on his computer screen. He ought to go home, get under the covers with Marjorie, and go to sleep. But he's too restless to sleep. He decides to get the last cruiser from the lot out back and drive around for awhile.

Even with the tourists and writers and all the extra cops and media folks in town, the downtown is quiet now. He creeps slowly down Philips, glancing at the storefronts, making sure everything's buttoned up. He thinks of Marshal Matt Dillon, walking his rounds in old Dodge City, his town, late at night.

"The first man they look for," he says softly, hearing the old radio voice, "and the last they want to meet." He smiles. William Conrad. Great voice. But too fat for TV. They wanted Duke Wayne, but he turned it down, told 'em they should hire a buddy of his, James Arness. That seemed to work out OK.

Damn it! What *was* Gary Cooper's name in *High Noon*? Usually after he's left something alone for awhile, the answer is waiting for him the next time he thinks about it, but now he keeps thinking of Orson Welles in *Citizen Kane*. Based on the life of William Randolph Hearst, although Welles, the *enfant terrible* of Hollywood, insisted it wasn't. Kane was alone when he died. So who heard him say "Rosebud"?

"It's a chancy job," he says softly, hearing William Conrad. "And it makes a man watchful. And a little lonely."

Accompanied by the loping rhythm of the old *Gunsmoke* theme, he drives out to the paper mill, where the train trestle crosses the river.

He's still there fifteen minutes later when he gets the call.

34

They sit in front of the rekindled fire, sipping hot chocolate and talking. Actually, LaShandra does most of the talking, telling them about the still-unsolved drive-by shooting in South Madison she's been investigating and about a suspected arson in the Allied Drive neighborhood she believes is connected to drug dealing.

Doug has been nodding. His head falls forward, and he jerks awake.

"I think Doug and I better call it a night," Mo says, getting up, taking his mug from Doug, and carrying it out to the kitchenette to rinse in the sink.

"I'm sorry! Just listen to me chatter away! I'm such a night owl. I forget other folks want to sleep."

"You're welcome to stay up and read, listen to the radio, watch television. There's just the one bathroom, so—"

"Why don't I take a little walk while you two get ready for bed? I can lock the door behind me and take the key."

"Oh, you don't have to do that."

"I can use the exercise. Besides, I'd like to get the lay of the land."

After the detective leaves, Mo helps Doug get ready for bed as much as he'll let her and crawls gratefully under the covers with him, leaving the light on in the living room. She's still awake when

LaShandra comes back perhaps half an hour later. She hears the gentle swishing of turning pages from the living room. When she wakes up, the cabin is dark and silent. She senses that Doug is awake next to her. She reaches out to rub his shoulder under the covers, and he puts his hand on top of hers and squeezes.

When she wakes again the air is thick with darkness and silence. She lies still, straining to hear. But when the noise comes again, it's loud and close, a deep, animal rumbling. Her first thought is that a bear has somehow gotten into their cabin.

The low rumbling comes again, and Mo almost laughs out loud. Dane County Sheriff's Detective LaShandra Cooper is snoring! And not just a little.

"Some concert, huh?" Doug's whisper comes from very near.

"Did she wake you up?"

"I've been awake for awhile. That's some big noise for such a little lady, huh?"

"Is the pain bad? Why don't you take some more Advil?"

"It's OK."

"You should try to stay on top of the pain. I'll get some Advil for you."

She starts to shove out from under the covers but feels his hand on her arm.

"I took some awhile ago."

"What's the matter?"

He is silent so long, she wonders if he intends to answer. Even as her eyes adjust to the darkness, she can't make out his face a few inches from her.

"Doug?"

"I'm not sure I can put it into words."

There's something in his voice she's never heard before, something she can't name.

"It's like fire ants."

"Fire ants?"

"Yeah. Under my skin. It's like fire ants crawling under my skin."

"Are you feverish?" She gropes to feel his forehead, which is cool and clammy.

"Cabin fever, maybe."

"You're used to being so active. This must be hard for you."

LaShandra snorts loudly. Mo waits until the snoring starts again.

"Why don't I go get you something to help you sleep?"

"Now?"

"The LottaSav is open."

"I don't want you running around this time of night."

"If I got you something to help you sleep, would you take it?"

"Like what?"

"Just one of those over-the-counter meds you're not supposed to take before operating heavy machinery."

"I hate that stuff."

"I know you do. But you need to get some sleep."

"I hate to make you do that."

"You're not making me. I'm volunteering."

"I'll go with you."

"You will not go with me."

The air is cold on her bare legs. She pulls on her jeans, shrugs off her nightgown, and wiggles into her sweatshirt. She won't be the first person to shop the LottaSav braless.

As she drives the twisting road out of the woods to the county highway, she replays the conversation she has just had with Doug. Fire ants! The poor man! She heard a new quality in his voice—vulnerability, uncertainty, even bewilderment. He so likes to be in control of things, including his own feelings, and now he has to deal with something he can't control or even put a name to.

No stars show in the sky, no moon. No lights shine from the forest. She doesn't encounter another car on the drive into town, and the parking lot at the LottaSav is empty. Only the florescent lights assure her that the store is open and that she might not, in fact, be the only person on earth up at this hour.

Relief floods her as the pneumatic door hisses open. The title of a Hemingway short story comes to her—"A Clean, Well-Lighted Place."

The girl sitting on the counter by the only open cash register turns at the sound of the door's whoosh.

"Hi, Roberta! You've got the graveyard shift, huh?"

"Yeah. Lucky me."

"I'm looking for something to help my husband sleep."

"Aisle fifteen. We've got about a thousand different kinds."

"Thanks."

Mo finds the aisle, which also has pain relievers, decongestants, and cough suppressants. She does indeed confront a bewildering array of sleeping compounds. She reads a few labels, realizes that she doesn't understand what she's reading, and buys the most expensive kind, one she has seen advertised on television, hoping that high price might somehow equate with safety and effectiveness.

"I'm surprised you remembered my name," Roberta says when Mo gets to the register.

"You must be memorable."

Roberta blushes slightly. "I'm terrible with names," she admits.

"Mine's Monona. Mo."

She scans the package. The register makes a high-pitched bleep.

"I was here with my husband when your friend got fired."

"He's not my friend exactly."

"How's he doing? Have you heard from him?"

She shakes her head. Mo hands her a ten dollar bill and waits for her change.

"I went by his house a couple of times. He wasn't there. Or else he just didn't come to the door."

She drops the coins into Mo's upturned palm and slips the package into a plastic bag before Mo can tell her not to bother. Mo takes the bag but doesn't move away.

"I'm worried about him," Roberta admits.

"Because he got fired?"

"Not just that."

The door hisses, and they both turn as that strange, fat little man steps in.

"Hi, Lloyd."

"Hi, Bert. You got candy for sale?"

"The Butterfingers are only a nickel."

"My favorite!"

He grabs up five candy bars from the box by the register and dumps them on the counter. He looks up at Mo, smiling, as he digs his hand into his pocket, dragging his short pants down and straining his suspenders. His fist emerges, and he dumps coins, along with shards of tissue and candy bar wrapper, on the counter.

"OK. Here's a dime." Roberta slides the coin toward her with her index finger. "That's ten cents. How much more do you need?"

Lloyd frowns in concentration.

"You've got five candy bars, and they're five cents each. So, five times five is—"

"Fifty five!"

"Not that much. Count by fives."

"Five. Ten. Fifty."

"Fifteen."

"Fifteen. Fifty."

"Fifteen. Twenty."

"Twenty-five! Twenty-five cents!"

"Right. And I've already got ten cents. So you owe me another dime—" She slides the second dime over. "—and this ugly, dirty old nickel!"

He claps his hands in triumph, snatches up a candy bar, and tears off the wrapper.

"Eat them over there," Roberta tells him. "At the tables."

"OK."

"How's Elzie doing?"

Lloyd shrugs. "OK," he says, looking at the candy bar in his hand.

"You go ahead and enjoy your candy."

Lloyd shuffles over to one of the plastic tables and plops down in the chair facing the window, his back to them.

Roberta lifts a purse onto the counter, rummages around for a dollar bill and two quarters, and puts them in the till along with Lloyd's twenty-five cents.

"He lives with Elzie. The one who got fired. It's hard for him, Elzie, especially this time of year."

"Why's that?"

"I probably shouldn't say."

"You don't have to if you don't want."

"His father abandoned him and his mother when he was eleven."

"That must have been rough."

"Three years ago, she ran off with one of the musicians from the country western show. She'd known him for all of three nights. Nobody's seen or heard from her since, that I know of. Elzie and Lloyd have been on their own ever since."

"That's awful."

"I don't know how she could do it, do you? Just abandon her family that way?"

"No, I really don't," Mo says. Her mind races back over everything she has learned during her ten days in Shepherdstown, waiting for the pieces to snap together.

"So, how do you do it?" Roberta asks.

"Do what?"

"Remember people's names."

"I taught myself when I was in journalism school. The trick is to make sure you hear the name the first time. Most of the time when we meet somebody, we're nervous and thinking about what we're going to say, and we don't catch the name. After that, we're supposed to know it, so we're too embarrassed to ask."

"Yeah. I do that."

"I make sure I say the name at least once right away, and if I can, I connect it to some prominent physical characteristic or make a word play out of it to help me remember."

"What characteristic did you use to remember my name?"

"For you, I didn't have to use anything. Roberta is a beautiful name, and it just seemed to fit you perfectly."

The fat, homely young woman blushes deeply.

Mo waits until she's out of sight of the store to pull over onto the gravel shoulder of the road. She fishes the police detective's card out of her purse and punches the number in on her cell phone.

Nothing.

"Damn!"

She turns the phone off, swings the car around, and drives back toward town. Reception is lousy throughout the area, but she seems to be able to get a strong enough signal out by the school, so she heads that way, stopping on a rise in the road a few hundred yards from the entrance. She leaves the motor running and the headlights on.

This time she gets a tone.

"Shepherdstown Police."

"Detective Sergeant Lafferty, please. This is Monona Quinn."

"This is night dispatch. He's off duty. Can I put you through to someone else?"

"I really need to talk to Sergeant Lafferty."

"What about?"

"It concerns a case he's working on."

"Hang on."

Mo waits, praying the signal doesn't cut out. A deer pokes its head out from the trees fifty yards ahead of her. Deciding it's safe, the deer ambles out onto the road, followed closely by another, and then a third. Mo sits transfixed as the first two cross the road and disappear into the trees on the other side. The third waits by the side of the road.

"This is Lafferty. You OK, Ms. Quinn?"

The deer decides to risk it, seeming to float across the road before bounding into the dense thicket on the other side.

"Ms. Quinn?"

She takes a deep breath. "It's about the three people who died. I think I know who killed them. I think I know who killed all three of them."

(35)

Elzie Odoms lies on the couch, his head resting on a wad of dirty clothes, his feet hanging over the edge, eating fistfuls of Cheerios dry from the box and playing a video game on the television screen.

He's been playing the game for several hours, blasting enemies to bloody bits. Occasionally his mind wanders, and his character gets blasted to bloody bits. It doesn't much seem to matter. He stops only to light a new cigarette, to get another glass of grape Kool-Aid, and to visit the bathroom.

He got the cigarettes, a carton of generics, from the LottaSav, along with the Cheerios, a loaf of white bread, two packages of baloney, several boxes of Kool-Aid packets, a jar of Skippy creamy peanut butter, and four tins of Chicken of the Sea chunk albacore tuna, packed in water. When he slipped in through the door on the loading dock in back, these were the closest items to him, and they fit in the cloth bags he had brought. He would have liked to get some cola, too, but it was too much to carry.

Another couple of days, he figures, and he'll get another job. Then he can get his cable reconnected. Maybe Gruden at the video store will take him back. If there's one thing Elzie knows, it's flicks. Martial arts, horror, sci-fi/fantasy, he knows them all, and he's always been able to talk folks into renting an extra movie and buying some of the crap from the sale bin by the register.

The heavy pounding on the door makes him choke on a swallow of Kool-Aid, and some spills on his bare chest. He hops up and bounds over to the window, peeking out through the corner of the curtain. Lloyd stands in the shadows, staring at the door.

Elzie creeps over to the door and waits for Lloyd to pound again. When he does, Elzie yanks the door open suddenly, and Lloyd stumbles into the room, flailing his arms to try to catch his balance. He falls in a heap on the bare floor.

"Ow. I hurt my elbow."

"You don't have to knock, stupid!"

Elzie suppresses the urge to kick the little man, who rolls onto his stomach and awkwardly shoves to his feet.

"I'm not stupid." The flickering image from the video game catches his attention. "What are you doing?"

"Harpooning sharks in a toilet bowl. What does it look like I'm doing?"

"Playing video games."

"Way to go, loco!"

"I amn't loco."

"There's no such word as 'amn't.' I'll bet you don't even know what 'loco' means, do you?"

Lloyd hasn't taken his eyes from the television screen. When he doesn't answer, Elzie waves a hand in front of his face. Lloyd blinks.

"Where'd you get the cool ache?"

"I boosted it from the LottaSav."

"You shouldn't steal. Can I have some?"

"It's in the fridge. Where have you been?" Elzie taps out a cigarette from the half-empty pack and lights it. He blows the smoke at Lloyd.

Lloyd frowns, dragging his attention away from the screen. "You shouldn't smoke," he says.

"Don't remember, do you?"

"Do so."

"So, tell me. Where have you been?"

Lloyd looks around the room, his gaze pausing on the screen. "She told!" he says. "About Mama."

"What are you talking about?"

"Berta. She told that woman about Mama."

"*What* woman?"

"You know. The one that was at the store when you—"

"When I what?"

"When you got, you know."

"When that prick Soggins fired me?"

"You shouldn't swear."

"What did Roberta tell her?"

"About Mama!"

"What about her? Ow! Shit!"

The cigarette has burned down and singed his fingers. He throws it on the floor and grounds it out with his heel.

"You know. How she left. With that man."

"Shut up!"

Lloyd watches the movement on the screen.

"What did the lady do? After Roberta told her?"

"She paid for her pills."

"What did she do then?"

"She got in her car and drove away. Then she stopped. I saw her. I ran after her.

"Why did she stop?"

Lloyd puts his hand to the side of his head, thumb and pinky finger extended.

"She talked on the phone?"

"Yeah, yeah. Then she drove away. Can I play the game now?"

Elzie puts a hand on Lloyd's shoulder. "Thanks for telling me, OK? That was really good that you told me."

Lloyd smiles and nods. "Can I have some cool ache?"

"Sure. All you want. And you can play the game, too."

"Yeah!"

"I have to go someplace."

"Where are you going? Can I come?"

"Not this time. I won't be gone too long." Elzie hands the remote to Lloyd. "You can play the game all you want."

"Can I watch television?"

Elzie takes Lloyd by the arm, more roughly than he intends, and sits him down on the couch. He aims the remote at the television and punches a button, and the game disappears, replaced by loud static and snow. He punches another button, and a picture appears, some stupid *Home Improvement* rerun. Without cable, there's never anything on.

"You watch TV until I get back. OK?"

"OK. Can I have a candy bar?"

"I don't have any candy bars. You can eat whatever's in the kitchen."

"I want a candy bar."

"Will you please just watch the television? Here. Have some Cheerios." He picks the box up off the floor and hands it to Lloyd.

"Thanks!"

Elzie runs into the kitchen and scoops up a fresh pack of smokes. He checks his jeans pockets. A few wadded up bills and change. Keys. Wallet. A nail.

Matches. How the hell did a nail get there? He puts it all back in his pockets.

He pours a Kool-Aid for Lloyd and carries it back into the living room. Lloyd doesn't take his eyes from the screen. A commercial for erectile dysfunction medication, the one where the guy is trying to throw the football through the tire swing, flickers on the screen.

"I'm going to lock the door when I leave."

"Can I come with you?"

"You're going to stay here and watch television, remember?"

"Yeah."

"Do you remember how to turn the television on and off?"

The erectile dysfunction ad has been replaced by an ad for pickup trucks.

"Lloyd? Do you?"

"Yeah. I know how."

"Turn it off and on for me."

"I know how to do it!"

Elzie reaches for the remote, but Lloyd clutches it to his chest and hunches down over it. "Where are you going?"

"I need to talk to the woman Roberta talked to."

"How come?"

"Because she could cause trouble for us, and then we wouldn't be able to live together anymore."

Lloyds face clouds, and for a moment, Elzie's afraid he's going to pitch one of his fits. "It's OK," he says quickly. "I'll straighten everything out."

"I'll bet you don't know where she lives."

"I'll find her."

"I know where she lives!"

"You do?"

"Yeah, yeah."

Lloyd points the remote at the screen and pushes a button. The screen goes black with a pop of light. He pushes the button again, and the picture reforms. The Tool Man has a power saw, which means he's about to do something really stupid.

"I told you I knew how."

"Good. Tell me where she lives."

"Who?"

Elzie fights down another surge of anger. "The woman who was talking to Roberta."

Lloyd frowns at the screen.

"Well?"

"What?"

"Are you going to tell me?"

Lloyd scratches his mop of hair. "It's near where 'Berta lives."

"In the trailer park?"

"No. Another place."

"What other place?"

"The one with the dog."

"Merrynook?"

"I guess so."

"OK. Thanks."

"I'll show you."

"That's OK. I can find it."

"I want to come too."

"No!" Elzie again fights down his rage. "Listen, pal," he says, getting down on one knee by the couch. "I really need you to stick around here and keep an eye on things until I get back. OK? Can you do that for me?"

Lloyd watches the screen. It's a commercial for a bathroom sanitizer that releases little puffs of good smells.

"I'll let you wear my cap."

"OK!"

"Shake on it."

They shake hands. Elzie takes his filthy cloth cap off and plops it on Lloyd's head, tugging at the cloth brim to pull the cap down over Lloyd's eyes.

"No!" Lloyd says, laughing. "Not that way!"

Elzie gets the cap positioned the way Lloyd likes it.

"OK?"

"OK."

"You'll stay here until I get back."

"OK."

Lloyd follows Elzie to the door and stands in the open doorway, watching Elzie walk slowly out to the road. When he gets near the road, he squats by a tree. You should always look both ways when you cross the street. Nobody's coming now. It's late at night. Even so, you should always look both ways.

Elzie jumps up and runs across the pavement. When he reaches the other side, he jumps, and for a moment, it's like he's hanging in the air. He disappears into the thick brush on the other side of the road.

Lloyd stands in the open doorway, staring at the place where Elzie disappeared. The television is on behind him. Elzie is gone. He doesn't recognize the people on the screen. The old one is laughing, and the young one is angry.

Lloyd aims the clicker at the television, and the screen goes black.

36

She's waiting for him, parked parallel to the curb with the engine off and the window open. Lafferty pulls the cruiser up next to her, head to head, and opens his window. He leaves the engine running. The air conditioning hisses.

"Roberta didn't know the exact date when his mother left," she says, "but she said it was right around this time of year."

"It was July twenty-eighth. I checked. The kid called it in and tried to get us to arrest the guy she ran away with. I don't know why in hell I didn't make the connection."

"I don't see how you could have."

"I'm terrible with dates. The only reason I remember my wedding anniversary is because we got married the same day Denny McLain won his thirtieth game for the Tigers in 1968. September fourteen. We'll be married—Geez. It'll be thirty-nine years."

"Congratulations."

"Baseball trivia I remember. Who played Amos McCoy on television and what movie he was in with Ricky Nelson and Dean Martin? That I know. Anything real? Forget it."

She squeezes out a little laugh to be polite.

"I'll head out to Elzie's place."

"I want to come along."

"No can do. No telling what the kid'll do if he thinks he's cornered."

"Do you really think he might have done these murders?"

Lafferty shakes his head. "I sure as hell hope not, Ms. Quinn. I've known those two all their lives. They've had a real raw deal. I'd hate to see it end like this."

He pushes the button to raise the window, but something in her face makes him stop it halfway up. "And don't follow me out there. I don't want to have to be worrying about you. Go on home."

She nods, but she doesn't like it.

He waits, watching through the rearview, until she disappears around the corner, headed east out of town. Now he's got the theme song for *The Real McCoys* going through his head. He remembers every damn word.

But what *was* that guy's name in *High Noon*? It's going to drive him crazy. He snatches up the phone and speed dials the night dispatcher.

"What's up, Harry?"

"What was the name of the character Gary Cooper played in *High Noon*?"

"What?"

"Never mind. What's the address for the Odoms kid?"

"1313 Blue Jay Lane."

"You're kidding? Double thirteen?"

"You're not superstitious, are you?"

"Hell no. Besides, wouldn't two of them cancel each other out? That's a left off Highland, right?"

"Right."

"'Right' it's left, or 'right' it's right?"

"'Right,' it's left. That's the only way you can turn. Blue Jay tees at Highland."

"I want backup. Who's closest?"

"Freddie's out by the fairgrounds."

"Anybody closer?"

"Nope."

"OK. Send him out there. Oh, hey?"

"I'm still here."

"No lights, no sirens."

"I'll tell him, but I can't promise anything."

Lafferty hangs up and starts down Philips. He ought to limit Freddie Ferdeen to one bullet and make him keep it in his pocket, like Barney Fife. He's gone through the entire cast of *The Andy Griffith Show* and whistled the theme twice by the time he turns onto Blue Jay Lane. Howard McNair and Parley Baer were in that, two of the all-time great character actors. Both were on the old *Gunsmoke* radio show. Everything ties together. Zero degrees of separation.

He waits at the end of the street, lights off, whistling the Andy Griffith theme soundlessly through his teeth, until Ferdeen draws up next to him. He gestures for the officer to roll down his passenger side window.

"Get out. We'll walk from here."

"Roger."

Ferdeen eases his cruiser forward and parks at the curb. He's unsnapping his holster as he gets out of the car.

"Keep it in the corral, partner," Lafferty says.

Ferdeen frowns. A lifer, like Lafferty, short, fat, nearly bald.

"We're just going to ask the Odoms kid a few questions," Lafferty says. He realizes that he's whispering, even though 1313 is in the middle of the next block.

"What for? Did he beat Lloyd up again?"

"Oh, probably."

Ferdeen's got his hand on his holster flap again. Lafferty looks at the hand until Ferdeen lets it drop.

The neighborhood is quiet, no lights showing in any of the houses. A small animal bolts down a driveway toward the end of the first block and runs to where Blue Jay Lane ends in forest. The animal stops and looks back at them, ears up. Coyote. Them and the cockroaches will outlast them all.

"You go around to the back," he hisses as they approach the house.

"Roger."

The driveway is unpaved, two dirt ruts, axle-width apart, separated by tufts of weeds. The house and yard are untended. One of the front shutters is gone. The other hangs loose from the top hinge. Lafferty waits until Ferdeen clears the driveway and disappears around the back of the house.

Chances are Lloyd won't be there, and that would help. Probably out wandering around in the forest.

Lafferty takes the two concrete steps of the front stoop. The bottom step is crumbling to rubble. Lafferty balls his fist and pounds on the door twice. The house feels empty. Lafferty pounds the door again, five times fast.

"Elzie. This is Sergeant Lafferty. I need to talk to you."

Nothing. He imagines Ferdeen hiding in the backyard, gun drawn, knees quaking. He hears no noise from inside the house. Does he need a warrant? Does he have probable cause to enter the dwelling?

He tries the knob, and the flimsy door swings open. Lafferty steps inside. The front room is dark, but a faint blue glow comes from under a closed door to the right. He sees a television, a ratty couch, litter. The floor creaks when he takes a step. He freezes, straining to hear. Two more careful steps bring him to the door.

"Elzie? I need to talk with you, son. It's Lafferty."

Under the oppressive silence, he thinks he hears a faint popping noise coming from behind the door.

"I'm coming in!"

He plunges through the door, turning rapidly to check the four corners of the room. On a desk by the wall opposite the door, a computer cycles through its screensaver, gladiators hacking at each other with swords. The screen makes the soft popping noise. He looks around the room, cast in eerie blue glow from the computer. A ton of dirty laundry, take out food bags, and God knows what else.

Lafferty checks the bathroom and kitchen. He looks out the kitchen window. A stand-alone garage slants about fifteen degrees off of plumb.

"Get in here!" he yells out the back door. "It's clear."

Ferdeen slides out of the shadows of the garage. "I had you covered," he says.

"Come on. He ain't here. Neither's Lloyd."

"Where'd they go?"

Lafferty waits until Ferdeen reaches the back steps. "Now, if I knew that," he says slowly, "we wouldn't be out looking for him, would we?"

"I guess we'd better look for him, then."

"Put your damn gun back in the holster."

Lafferty walks back through the house and out into the night, not really caring if Ferdeen is following him or not.

(37)

Elzie hears the car coming from a long way off. He scuttles down the embankment, stumbling on the loose rock and sliding the final few feet on his knees. He scrambles into the woods and crouches behind a tree to watch. The headlights get bigger, and the car passes, driving too fast for the narrow road, seeming to swallow its own funnel of light down the straight stretch of road.

Blood trickles down his right leg from his knee. It has taken him most of the night to make his way out the old highway. He can talk to her when she gets up, before she has a chance to talk to anyone else.

Twice he's sure he's being followed, but both times he wais, crouching in the brush to the side of the road, and sees no one. Formless furies, his mother used to call it, coming to get you in the night. More like the DTs in her case, probably.

He scrambles up the embankment, both knees stinging, and jogs along the dirt shoulder on the left side of the road, in the direction the car has gone. The road slopes gently down as he bears left onto the access road.

Got to think clearly, he tells himself.

At the dirt drive, he has to stop and fight for breath, hands on knees, head down. *Damn* cigarettes. His breathing eases. An owl hoots from nearby. He turns in a slow circle. A bare tree, twisted and split by lightning, glows white as bone in the light from the quarter moon directly overhead.

He crosses the road. No reason to hurry. Rounding a turn, he looks down a gentle grade at a large cabin and a fire pit. He creeps around the back of the cabin and comes upon three cars parked on the packed dirt between the large cabin and a smaller one, which is dark. Her blue Honda isn't among the cars.

Sticking to the fringe of the woods behind the cabins, he moves parallel to the road toward a long one-story house, the word "office" carved and painted red on a white board by the door. The road continues around the house to the right. Another small cabin sits on a rise to the right of the road. It, too, is dark, and there are no cars parked nearby.

He creeps down the slope, still paralleling the road, stopping suddenly when he realizes he's almost upon another cabin, tucked into the side of the hill. Farther down, moonlight shimmers on the lake. Water laps the shore.

The blue Honda sits next to a dark four-door sedan on a dirt slab carved out of the hillside. He creeps forward. The other car is a black four-door Ford sedan, last year's model. He circles it from behind, keeping the car between himself and the cabin. He reads the insignia on the car door: "Dane County Sheriff's Department."

What in the holy hell is a Dane County sheriff doing here? He detects no noise and no movement from the dark cabin. He crouches between the Ford and the Honda, trying to figure out what to do.

His knees throb, and his right calf is cramping. He rises into a half crouch and steals out from between the cars and up the embankment. He finds a flat spot among the trees and squats, looking down at the cars, the cabin, the lake. He lets himself fall back on his butt and sits, legs stretched out in front of him, back against a tree. The bark sticks him, but he wants the pain to keep him alert.

He needs a cigarette so bad he can taste it, has been tasting it for some time, but he doesn't dare light a match. His pants are torn at both knees, and blood has caked and started to dry on his right knee. His right sneaker is torn on the side. He doesn't remember when that happened. The laces have each broken and been tied, and there's barely enough lace to tie a tiny, one-loop bow in each one. He's not wearing socks, and his ankles itch where he's brushed against nettles.

His calf starts cramping again. He gathers his legs under him and rises slowly, putting weight on the cramping leg, but it doesn't help. He hobbles a few steps to one side and back, then walks in a tight little circle until the cramp loosens its grip. He sits down carefully, keeping the bad leg as straight as he can, and resumes his watch.

He feels himself falling from a tree and jerks himself awake. There's still no sign of false dawn in the eastern sky, and the cold, hard stars glitter like glass eyes. He's had to take a piss for a long time, and he can't ignore it any longer. He gets up stiffly, pulling his pant leg loose from the wound on his right knee. The pain makes him sick to his stomach, and he waits for the nausea to pass. Shielded from the cabin by a tree, he unzips and directs his stream down the hill. His piss splatters on the dirt. He zips up, wipes his hands in the dirt, and goes back to his tree.

Perhaps he sleeps again. When he opens his eyes, the sky is light in the east, although the sun isn't yet up. He has a headache. His neck is stiff and sore. His back hurts. His left leg is cramping. He feels nothing in the right leg.

He hears movement from down the slope—somebody inside the cabin. Whooshing. A toilet flushing. He has to piss again.

He tries to get his legs under him to stand and almost falls over. His right leg is asleep. He rubs it hard with both hands, and the leg tingles painfully. He hears a whimpering and freezes, holding his breath. He bites his tongue hard, tasting salt.

He bends his left leg and rolls to the left, pushing off with both hands and struggling to his feet. The cabin door opens, and he flattens himself against the tree. The door closes with a soft click. Then nothing.

He peeks out from behind the tree. Someone stands on the porch, back to him, facing the lake, raises both arms and stretches on tiptoes. A woman! A soft grunt escapes her. The woman turns, revealing her profile. She's black!

He hears a skittering behind him and whirls, pain knifing up his right leg into his groin. A squirrel stares at him at eye level from the trunk of a tree a few feet away. A flurry of skittering, and another squirrel pops out two feet lower on the trunk, and the two chase each other up the trunk and out onto a branch. The lead squirrel leaps, the branch bowing and arcing, and grabs the branch of an adjacent tree, dangling upside down for an instant before righting itself and bolting up the branch, the second squirrel close behind.

He turns back to the porch, and for a moment he can't find the black woman. Then he sees her, standing beside the sheriff's car. She's looking down at the lake, her back to him. As he watches, she turns and begins walking up the dirt road toward him.

38

Mo opens her eyes to darkness. The little bedroom feels close, familiar, home for now. Doug makes sputtering noises when he breathes through his mouth. The first faint light of false dawn is spreading outside, still so feeble, it can barely penetrate even the thin curtain on the one small window.

Something else. A stirring. She remembers. LaShandra Cooper is spending the night on the couch in the other room. Soft footfalls on bare wood floor. A barely audible snap and a weak scrim of light from the lamp. Soft humming. "Swing Low, Sweet Chariot."

The springs of the couch squeak, and Mo imagines from the rustling that LaShandra is wrestling on her shoes. In confirmation, shoes click on the bare wood as LaShandra walks to the kitchenette, finds a glass from the cupboard, and runs water from the tap.

Mo breathes in deeply through her nose. The smell of the gunk Doug rubbed on his heel makes her eyes sting. She smells something else, mothballs, faint but unmistakable, from the thin blanket on their bed. She likes having him in bed with her when she wakes up, but she knows he will suffer for not taking his pre-dawn run. He has always gotten up early to run, rain or shine, summer or winter, whether he's gotten a good night's sleep or only a couple of hours. He never took a day off—not Christmas, not his birthday, not their anniversary.

She hears the cabin door click shut. LaShandra is outside on the porch. Mo follows her footsteps over to the railing and imagines her looking out at the lake. She should get up and make coffee, but the bed is warm and snug, the air will be cold, and she's pretty sure she has more sleeping to do.

The sleeping tablets have zonked Doug out completely, and he'll be in a fog when he finally wakes up. Medications hit him hard. But he'll still want to run. She knows the story well, has heard him tell it at parties when someone (usually a woman) comments on how thin he is and asks, "How do you do it?" Doug ran cross-country in college but allowed himself to get out of shape after he graduated and took a job with an investment firm in the city. (She has seen pictures; he was never anything but rail thin, but he insists he was in terrible shape.) At the urging of a colleague, he went out running with a group from work but found himself gasping for breath after only a few minutes and couldn't keep up with the others.

Humiliated, he went out jogging alone the next morning. Unable to run a full mile at first, he quickly built up to three miles a day, then began mixing in long days, running as much as twenty miles on a Saturday morning. He has kept a careful log of how far he has run each day, recording times, distances, and even information about the weather.

Mo hears a noise outside. A high-pitched, frantic yapping. Juney! From closer to the cabin, someone dislodges rocks and dirt on the hill. She thinks she hears sounds of scuffling. She freezes, all her energy directed at listening. Did she imagine it? Was it some sort of waking dream?

She hears a voice, LaShandra, uttering a single-word curse! She leaps up, grabs her bathrobe from the foot of the bed, and runs into the living room. She cinches the bathrobe tie and wriggles into her sneakers, not stopping to tie the laces.

The cold air startles her. Perhaps twenty-five yards up the road, LaShandra is grappling with a man—slight, narrow-shouldered. She sprints toward them. Juney is still barking from up the hill beyond them but doesn't seem to be coming any closer.

The man is slightly taller but not as heavy as LaShandra, but he fights with desperate ferocity. It's the kid from the store, the one who got fired—Elzie. She hasn't recognized him without his dirty cloth cap. He's facing her, his eyes wide with desperation, a cornered animal.

"Stay back!" LaShandra hisses at her.

He shakes loose, spinning and running up the hill. LaShandra slips to one knee, pressing her palm against her eye. Juney's desperate barking is coming closer now, and a second figure appears at the top of the hill, Lloyd, wearing Elzie's cloth cap. Juney literally nips at his heels, and the short, fat man screams.

"No, no!" Elzie shouts. "It's OK. Don't run!"

Lloyd veers, slips, and almost goes down before plunging into the thicket and up the embankment. He kicks Juney, and the little dog yelps and rolls down the hill into the road. Ethel Wilkerson appears at the top of the hill, screaming "Juney! Juney! Come back here this minute!" But the little dog charges back up the hill.

"Don't hurt him! Don't hurt him!" Elzie yells, turning back toward Mo, his chest heaving, a rock in his hand.

Footsteps close rapidly behind her, and Doug flashes past her. Elzie fires the rock, catching Doug full in the face. LaShandra charges. Elzie swings at her, but she ducks the blow, swipes her leg under his, and they both go down, LaShandra on top.

Doug is down on one knee, his hand to his face, blood flowing from between his fingers. Elzie throws LaShandra off, jumps on top of her, and hits her in the mouth with his fist. Mo jumps forward, grabbing his neck, but his elbow catches her on the side of the head, and she falls on her back in the dirt, pain mushrooming through her skull. Elzie takes a step toward her, but Doug steps between them.

Elzie whirls and scrambles up the embankment after Lloyd and Juney. LaShandra, is on her back, not moving. Mo tries to stand, but dizziness and nausea force her back down. Doug is on one knee, his head down, blood dripping into the dirt under him. She reaches up and touches his bloody cheek gently with the tip of her finger.

"Head wounds always look worse than they are," he says.

She grabs a fistful of her bathrobe and starts to dab at the blood, but he catches her wrist and gently holds it. Doug tries to stand but drops to both knees. LaShandra moans and rolls onto her side. Ethel stops halfway down the road, puts her hands on her hips, and screams up the embankment at Juney.

Mo staggers to her feet and runs to the embankment. About twenty feet up, Elzie is on his hands and knees, trying to cover Lloyd with his own body. Juney circles them, yapping and snarling. A car crests the hill, and Mo realizes she's been hearing a siren along with the barking and Lloyd's steady wailing. The car skids to a stop just short of Ethel, and Detective Sergeant Harry Lafferty bursts out the door, gun drawn.

"Up there," Mo manages, pointing.

Lafferty walks to the base of the embankment, the gun pointed at the ground.

Juney barks furiously, her mouth inches from Elzie's face.

"You folks all right?" Lafferty calls over without taking his eyes from the hill.

"I think so," Mo says.

"Son of a bitch," LaShandra says.

Lloyd wails, and Juney barks.

Murmuring "Oh, dear God!" and pressing her palms to her cheeks, Ethel reaches Lafferty's side at the base of the embankment.

"Looks like that killer dog of yours has the situation pretty well in hand," Lafferty says.

"Juney! You come here to mommy this instant!"

The little dog gives her cowering prey one more fierce yelp and bounds down the embankment, leaping the final four feet into Ethel's outstretched arms.

"Baby!" Ethel coos, cradling the little dog. "Are you all right? Did the mean men hurt you?"

His gun trained on Elzie and Lloyd, still cowering twenty feet up the embankment, Lafferty begins to laugh. He says something that Mo doesn't catch.

"What's that?"

"Will Kane! The name of the character Gary Cooper played in *High Noon*. No wonder I kept thinking about that Orson Welles movie."

39

"So, Elzie did kill him?"

Monona Quinn has had only a few hours of restless sleep. She and LaShandra Cooper have come in early to give their statements and try to piece together what actually happened. They are sitting in the two mismatched chairs across the desk from Detective Sergeant Harry Lafferty.

"Nope. Elzie didn't kill anybody, far's I know." Rafferty sits back in his chair, brings the Styrofoam cup of coffee to his mouth, but can't seem to bring himself to drink.

"Then who did?" LaShandra asks.

"And why on July twenty-eighth?" Mo adds.

The sergeant shakes his head. "The first two probably were accidents, and the date was just a bizarre coincidence, like your hubby said, Ms. Quinn."

"And the third?" LaShandra presses.

"I'm afraid I know," Mo says.

"Yeah. It was Lloyd. The poor guy. So far as I can figure—and everything he says comes out all jumbled up—he was out wandering the same time Downs was taking his constitutional Tuesday morning. Something—dog, coyote, who the hell knows?—apparently spooked him. He picked up a hunk of tree limb and started running and flaying, saw Downs and whupped him dead."

"How awful," Mo says.

"It's just a damn crying shame's what it is. After all those two kids have been through. You knew they were brothers, right?"

Mo just shakes her head.

"Elzie clonked his big brother with a metal swing when they were just tads, and poor Lloyd was never right after that. Several folks saw it and said it was an accident, but I think it's eaten on Elzie all these years.

"So—" He picks up his notepad and pencil and flips open to a blank page. "Before I get your statements, how's everybody doing after that melee?"

"Doug has a broken nose and needed two dozen stitches for cuts—oh, and a 'mild' concussion," Mo says. "'Mild' means a concussion that somebody else gets, I guess. The doctor kept him under observation for a couple of hours."

"That's standard," LaShandra assures her, "to make sure there's no evidence of severe brain trauma. Sorry," she adds quickly when Mo shudders. "That sounds pretty bad in cold medical terms."

"How about you, Detective Cooper? You got a bit staved in yourself out there."

"Two cracked ribs and some cuts. Nothing serious."

He turns his gaze on Mo. "According to the doctor," she says, "the medical term for my condition is 'getting your chimes rung.' He says I'll be fine."

"I guess we'll all live to fight another day, then. I am sorry about your hubby, though, Ms. Quinn. He really got brained."

"I don't understand what they were doing out by Mo's cabin in the first place," LaShandra says.

"I was wondering the same thing about you," Lafferty replies, nodding across the table at LaShandra.

She takes a sip of coffee, makes a face, and sets the cup on Lafferty's desk. "I was staying at Monona's cabin. I went for a walk, heard all the barking and fussing, and this Odoms character jumped me."

Lafferty nods and turns back to Mo. "Elzie ain't making much more sense than his brother at this point," he says. "But as near as I can figure, he was afraid you'd tell somebody about their living arrangement and get Lloyd taken away from him. He apparently didn't even know his brother had killed anybody."

"But how did you get out there?" Mo presses him. "The last I saw, you were heading out to Elzie's to question him about three murders."

"That's right. When I saw that both of them were gone, I headed over to Roberta's, because she's befriended both of them, and I figured they might head there. When I didn't find them, I started cruising this road and heard the barking."

"It's just so sad," Mo says. "What's going to happen to Lloyd?"

Rafferty tosses his notepad on the desk and leans forward with a groan. "Oh, he'll be institutionalized, all right, maybe in that place they got down in Madison for folks who are mentally ill who commit crimes."

"They'll turn him out in a year, and he'll end up homeless and panhandling on State Street," LaShandra says, shaking her head.

"It's hard to argue that Elzie should have custody of him," Rafferty notes, "given what happened."

"Do you think Roberta knew?" LaShandra asks. "About what Lloyd had done?"

"I dunno. I sure as hell ain't going to press the issue with her."

They fall into a thick silence born of fatigue and sorrow.

"Well." LaShandra gets up, wincing as her ribs remind her of their recent battering. "I'm going to head on back to Madison."

"Now?" Mo protests. "You must be exhausted."

"I got a couple of hours. I'll be fine."

"You should at least have something to eat first."

"I'll pick something up on the way."

"Are you sure?"

"Yep. The boss man gonna be all over me as it is for taking this little vacation."

"Some vacation!"

"Change of scenery, anyway." She winces as she bends to pick up her shoulder bag.

"Are you sure you're all right to drive?"

"Oh, hell yeah." She smiles. "You go on back and take care of your man."

"He usually doesn't need much taking care of."

"He does now."

Those words resonate in her mind as Mo returns to the cabin to find Doug lying on his back on the bed, eyes open, staring at the ceiling, his fists gripping the edges of the pillow. She goes to the side of the bed and drops to her knees. His body heaves with a suppressed sob. She touches his shoulder, gently grips it. He turns his face toward her. His hair is still sticky with blood, despite the nurse's best efforts to clean him up.

"I need help," he says.

"Should I take you back to the clinic?"

"Not that kind of help." He turns away. A low moan escapes him.

"Do you need more pain medication? The doctor said you could—"

"No!" The cry seems to have to fight up from his chest. "It's the inside."

"What's the inside?"

"My head." Wincing, he pulls himself into a sitting position. He lets his head rest against the wall, his eyes tightly closed. "I tried to run," he says, barely above a whisper.

"You what?"

"After you left this morning. I didn't think it would be too bad, and I felt so damn restless. I thought it would get better when the adrenaline started flowing."

She struggles to fight down her anger. "Doug, that's crazy," she says.

"Yeah," he says. "That's what it is. Crazy."

"I didn't mean it like that."

She takes his hand. He doesn't pull it away.

"I felt like I was going crazy," he says slowly, as if discovering the meaning of the words as he forces them out. "Or would, anyway, if I didn't run."

"I don't understand."

"I don't either, really. I knew nothing bad would happen if I didn't run. It was just—"

"Fire ants?"

"Yeah. Fire ants. Or like I was burning up under my skin. I knew it would stop if I ran. But I couldn't. I just couldn't."

"I'm so sorry," she says, still not understanding but imagining how much pain he must be in.

"I need help."

"We'll go back to the clinic. They can—"

"No." He reaches out and puts a hand on top of hers. "This is something else."

"Whatever it is, we'll deal with it."

"I looked it up online." His eyes again close.

"Looked what up?"

"Obsessive Compulsive Disorder. I googled it when we were out at the lab. I think I've got that. I think my father had it, too, although I don't think they even knew what it was then."

"Doug, you—"

"Just listen for a minute. Please. That's what turned Howard Hughes into such a nut job." His body spasms. His grip tightens on her hand. "Collecting his own urine. Letting his fingernails grow. I don't want to be like that."

"You won't be! You aren't!"

"I read the symptoms. Took a quiz online. I aced it, kiddo. I always was good at taking tests." He takes a deep breath. "I need a head doctor."

With her free hand, she pushes a sweat-matted curl off his forehead.

"I'm sure they've got plenty of good shrinks in Madison," he says. "Lord knows, they need them for all the nut jobs. Like me."

"You're not a nut job. If you've got some sort of mental— thing—if you do, it's not your fault."

His eyes stay closed. His breathing slows.

"We'll go home and get you whatever help you need."

"Yes," he says softly. "Please take me home."

He sleeps then, leaving Mo alone with her thoughts and the quiet Northwoods morning.

966 84/5

RECEIVED

BOOK
SALE
AUG - 5 2008

MOUNT PROSPECT
PUBLIC LIBRARY